THINGS AS THEY ARE?

BOOKS BY GUY VANDERHAEGHE

Short Stories

Man Descending 1982

The Trouble With Heroes 1983

Things As They Are? 1992

Novels

My Present Age 1984

Homesick 1989

Plays

I Had a Job I Liked. Once. 1992

THINGS AS THEY ARE?

SHORT STORIES

by

GUY VANDERHAEGHE

Canadian Cataloguing in Publication Data

Vanderhaeghe, Guy, 1951-
Things as they are?

ISBN 0-7710-8696-2

I. Title.

PS 8593.A53T45 1992 C813'.54 C92-094241-5
PR9199.3.V35T45 1992

Typesetting by M&S, Toronto
Printed and bound in Canada on acid-free paper

The events and characters in these stories are fictional. Any resemblance to actual persons or happenings is coincidental.

The publishers acknowledge the support of the Canada Council and the Ontario Arts Council for their publishing program.

McClelland & Stewart Inc.
The Canadian Publishers
481 University Avenue
Toronto, Ontario
M5G 2E9

To Morris Wolfe

with thanks for help and
encouragement from the beginning

Acknowledgments

Some of these stories have appeared previously: "Home Place" in *The London Review of Books, Best Short Stories 1988, The Minerva Book of Short Stories, Grain,* and *The Bridge City Anthology: Stories from Saskatoon,* and before first publication was broadcast on CBC Radio; "The Master of Disaster" in *Canadian Fiction Magazine*; and "New Houses" in *Border Crossings.*

In "Man on Horseback" certain sections have been typeset in italics to appear as direct quotation. They are not, with the exception of a fifteenth-century definition of a good horse taken from *Brewer's Dictionary of Phrase and Fable.* Nevertheless, I would like to acknowledge the following as sources of certain information used in this story: *The Horse in Blackfoot Indian Culture* by John C. Ewers, Smithsonian Institution Bureau of American Ethnology, Bulletin 159, Smithsonian Institution Press, City of Washington, 1955; *The Astonishing Adventures of General Boulanger* by James Harding, Charles Scribner's Sons, New York, 1971; *The Horse in West African History* by Robin Law, published for the International African Institute by Oxford University Press, Oxford, 1980; *Brewer's Dictionary of Phrase and Fable: Centenary Edition,* Cassel & Company Ltd., London, an affiliate of Macmillan Publishing Company Inc., New York, 1975.

I would like to acknowledge the financial assistance of the Saskatchewan Arts Board during the writing of these stories.

I would also like to thank my patient and thoughtful editor, Ellen Seligman.

Guy Vanderhaeghe
June 1992, Saskatoon

Contents

King Walsh

KING CALLED ME LONG DISTANCE from the city again last night. He said, "They're warning me to stay clear of Putt 'N' Fun Town, leave off playing the mini-golf."

"King," I said.

"I ain't going to do it," he said.

"Whatever you think is best, King," I said.

"Just so you know what's really going on here," he declared and hung up.

King is my brother. He's seven years older than me, turned seventy-eight last January. We were raised in Advance and both of us lived our whole lives here, until recent circumstances took King to the city.

Everybody in Advance knows King Walsh. For seventy years more heads were wagged in this town over King Walsh's mistakes than any other baker's dozen of ordinary men. But King got forgiven his little errors, people liked him all the better for making them, and it didn't hurt either that brother had a smile could light up a coal bin. However, the difference between an old man's mistakes and a young man's is that the ones the old man makes he's probably got to live with the rest of his life. King's learning that now, living his big mistake, the one that's trapped him in a basement suite in his son's house there in the city.

Albert Walker met up with King and me that day in the beer parlour and talked us into going along with him as moral support to The Senior Silver Jets' Wednesday afternoon Singles' Dance. So moral support sat on tin chairs watching a couple dozen old widows dancing the foxtrot with each other and throwing us boys the hopeful come hither looks. I been a bachelor all my life, and like it that way, so I kept my eyes mostly wherever theirs weren't.

Tell the truth she was a pretty lean stag line, consisting of just four old bucks – King, Albert Walker, me, and Rudy Schmidt, who was acting as master of ceremonies because he'd been a cattle auctioneer before he retired and so was accustomed to public speaking. Now Rudy is a professional when it comes to talking but even he can't hold a candle to Albert Walker. King was catching the brunt of it, that endless rambling on about this and that and a hundred per cent of nothing. But all of a sudden, out of the blue, Albert says something of interest. "King, remember that night you danced every dance on one leg at Kinbrae School?"

King said he sure as hell did.

The summer of 1935 was what they were talking about, the summer King broke his ankle, the summer I was fifteen and King had me drive his car out to Kinbrae School on a soft, starry night because he couldn't work the clutch with a cast on. My brother was twenty-two that summer, his hair red and full as a rooster's comb, and him a one-legged dancing fool. That night in Kinbrae he danced with every woman that didn't drive him off with a stick when he hopped up to her. Thirty-three answered the call – not many women ever refused King. His chums slung his arms over their shoulders and poured rye into him between tunes and the band agreed to play through the midnight lunch so King didn't cool down, go stiff, and bind up. Come two in the morning there were still more than twenty ladies, some old enough to have been his mother, lined up for a second go around. "Death before dishonour," King said and jolted through the entire mixed assortment. Last partner of the ball was Elsie Macintosh. The sun was standing in the window and her anxious father in the door when the band collapsed from exhaustion and the curtain came down on the spectacle. King married Elsie two years later. I wonder how many times she wished she could have took that final dance back.

"Those days are long gone now, aren't they, King? All the good times in the past," said Albert with a mournful last-day-of-summer sound to his voice.

If there's one thing that King never could stand, it was a pisser and a moaner. So naturally he contradicted him on principle. "I wouldn't say that."

"Well," said Albert, "your one-legged dancing days are a thing of the past. I know that much."

"Ha!" said King.

"You couldn't even *stand* on one leg," said Albert. "Remember, you're seventy-six years old."

Seventy-six or not, King got up and showed him. He wobbled some but he stood.

"Maybe you can stand," allowed Albert, "but you sure as hell can't dance."

Red flag to the bull. King scrambled to his feet, bellowing at auctioneer Rudy to get a goddamn polka on the goddamn turntable. Rudy said that wouldn't do, the ladies found the polka too energetic for their time of life. Pardon his English, but ladies be damned! roared my brother. King Walsh was going to dance all around the hall – and do it on one leg. For that, a polka was required.

Soon all the biddies had him surrounded and were clucking against rashness, but I could tell from the brightness of their eyes they truly hoped King would not be persuaded. He wasn't. Give credit where credit is due though. None of those women agreed to dance with him; they knew better than to risk life and limb in the arms of a madman. She was a sight for sore eyes, that horse's ass in the middle of the floor up on one leg like one of those pink flamingoes, his arms held out just as if they were cradling a woman.

Rudy dropped the needle on "The Beer Barrel Polka," King

took his first hop, and the sidelines erupted in wild applause. And kept it up. The harder those old girls clapped and hooted, the bigger the head of steam King built, jerking and jigging and bouncing along with his tongue hanging out like a three-legged dog. Halfway around the dance floor he negotiated his first fancy turn and the crowd went berserk. "Give 'er, King! Give 'er, you old son of a bitch!" Rudy shouted in his auctioneer's voice.

King gave her. Let me say he was never shy of being the centre of attention. His bearings were starting to smoke and he was leaking oil, but he cranked her up three more notches and gave a ki-yi every turn he twisted out. Around and around he went, the widows clapping, and the old bucks hooting and stamping their feet until the dust started to lift from between the floorboards. King was showing them one hell of a good time, just like he had his whole life long.

It was different with me. There, right in the midst of the hullabaloo, something peculiar happened. I never felt the like, before or since. Those fifty-five years that lay between a summer night in Kinbrae School and where I stood now, all that time folded in on me. Yesterday, today, even tomorrow, all of it went crooked and confused in my mind, I couldn't separate one from the other. That woman King had tucked in his arms – that invisible woman – was Elsie the way she was that night many long years ago, slim and fair. Or maybe as she would have been if she hadn't died in 1967 – old and tired like King and me. It was a lovely and terrible feeling both, the ends of life drawing in on you like that without warning.

Then King's hip bone snapped like a piece of chalk and down he dropped in a heap.

The doctor ambulanced him to the city to have the hip replacement, they can't do nothing that complicated in our hospital here in Advance. To cut a long story short, they operate, King catches pneumonia, almost dies, and then, soon as he can lift his head from the pillow, he starts agitating for release. They manage to hold him there for a time but in the end he gets an early discharge, on condition he promises not to live alone while he heals. This means moving in with his only child Sonny and precious daughter-in-law Myra.

Myra is Sonny's second wife and has a tight little mouth that looks like a cigarette burn on a plastic car seat cover. Lucy, the wife King liked, divorced Sonny about eight years ago. King's never forgot the day she drove herself out from the city to tell him she was going to ditch his boy and brought along a bottle of Crown Royal to do it with. As soon as King saw the whisky he started in speculating what could be behind it. It came into his head maybe Lucy was in the family way. That's the only news King could think of that went with a bottle of quality whisky. But, no, after she poured out a couple of shots at the kitchen table Lucy delivered her announcement. "King," she said, "I'm here to tell you I'm leaving Sonny."

Now this was a bigger blow than you might think it was, because King was struck on Lucy. By this I don't mean to say that he was cutting Sonny's grass or even eager to – although with King and women a person can never be certain of anything. What I mean is that I think King may have loved his daughter-in-law the way he had loved his dead wife Elsie, for the things she was and he wasn't.

An even bigger surprise came when he asked her how Sonny was taking it and Lucy said, "I haven't told Sonny. I left this morning with the car packed. As far as Sonny's concerned, I'm tail-lights."

King asked her what the hell she was up to, treating Sonny so inconsiderate.

Lucy looked him straight in the eye and said, "If I thought anybody would understand, I believed it would be you, King. Admit it. You can't stand being more than an hour in the same room with Sonny."

King denied this, even though what Lucy said is true. He just kept repeating that this was one shit of a way for Lucy to behave.

"Don't get holier than thou with me," Lucy told him.

"From what Sonny says, you skipped out on him twice yourself."

"It wasn't Sonny I walked out on," King said. "It was his mother. And I'll tell you something else, Lucy. I never made two bigger mistakes in my life."

"Let me tell you something, King," Lucy said. "I never got much out of seven years of marriage to Sonny, but I did learn something from seven years of watching you."

King asked what that might be.

"To take a chance on any number of mistakes as long as you make them running after life. I always had a soft spot for you, King," she said. "So let's make this goodbye a friendly one. And let's drink to life."

You can be sure that King never refused a drink to life. Which is how it came about that he was the one who said goodbye to his son's wife and toasted his son's divorce before Sonny even heard about it.

King surely hated the hospital. Not for any normal reason, but mostly because the doctors and nurses insisted on calling him Mr. Walsh. He wouldn't shut his mouth on the topic. I heard about it every time I visited.

"I can't get them to call me King," he said. "Nothing but Mr. Walsh."

"Maybe it's a rule," I suggested, "calling patients mister." I didn't suggest maybe he'd turned them stubborn, bullying them to have his way.

"They ought to call a person by their name," he said.

"Well, come to that, King isn't your birth certificate name," I reminded him. "You aren't really King." It was our Auntie Vi that gave him the name when he was three years old and strutting around my mother's parlour bold as brass. She said, "Now look at that one. Don't he act like he thinks he's a future King of England." And King he's been for seventy-five years since. Nobody ever said it didn't suit him.

King's got mad at me a time or two in his life, but never as mad as he was the day I told him his name wasn't really King. "I've never been nothing but King and by the Jesus nobody's going to change that now! Why do you think they want to mister everybody? I'll tell you why! It's easier to stack you here and stack you there if everybody's the same size, size mister! Call me King!" he shouted out the door and down the hospital corridor. "Give me my name back, goddamn it!"

Once King escaped City Hospital I knew he was never going back. It had put the fear of the Almighty God into him. If he hadn't been scared, none of what Sonny said would have had any effect on him. King would have done what he originally intended – gone back to his house in Advance.

But Sonny kept picking away at him. "You want to land up in hospital again, Dad? What if you fall in that house with nobody to help you? Don't be silly. Come live with us, Dad."

Of course, nobody knew that Sonny was promoting this charitable idea because the bank was threatening to take the house he was inviting his father to come live in. This was a result of Sonny overselling his financial situation to Myra when they were dating. Naturally when they marry, Myra has expectations, so Sonny buys her a house big enough and expensive enough to match the lies he's been telling her. For a while he just manages to carry the mortgage and then the recession hits, his commissions go in the crapper, he misses a few payments, and the bank starts clearing its throat. Still, for shame, Sonny won't come clean with Myra. He'd rather go to work on King. "Come live with us, Dad. We got the suite in the basement standing empty, your own bathroom, fridge, stove. Sell the house in Advance."

The really important part of this pitch is the part about selling the house, because it's the only way Sonny can get a sizeable sum of cash into King's hands where it can be pried loose. Finally, King caves in and sells. No sooner is the cheque deposited than Sonny comes out with his sorry tale of woe. He's in temporary difficulties because of the economy, the GST.

The goddamn government is a vampire, it's drinking his blood. The bank is a vulture picking his bones clean. But if the money from the sale of the house in Advance was used as a lump payment to reduce his mortgage to a manageable size, he could breathe again. Don't misunderstand him, Sonny says. If he only had himself to think about, the bankers could take it, flinty-hearted cocksuckers. But Myra, it's her dream home, she loves it, the air-conditioning, central vacuum, Jenn-Air grill, the underground sprinkler system, the chandelier in the dining room – he can't imagine what the shock of losing it would do to her.

When King tells Sonny he'll think about it, Sonny starts to cry. He's King's fucking son, he says. Look what he's offering in return for a few measly bucks: a home rent-free for life, utilities paid, people willing to look out for him. The whole package, tied up with a ribbon of love.

This information comes to me via King's late-night, long-distance phone calls. They're coming fast and furious now that he's getting the heavy-duty pressure over Putt 'N' Fun.

Sure, he says, room and board with his son is probably not the smartest thing he's ever done. But imagine what it's like to sit and watch a forty-eight-year-old man, your own flesh and blood, bawling the way he did when he was in short pants. What else could he do but write the cheque, fifty-five thousand dollars? It's only money, after all.

So here's my brother, seventy-eight, no money, no house, nothing signed, no paper trail to prove what he did for Sonny. What makes it worse is that Myra has no idea about the fifty-five thousand because Sonny made King swear he'd never tell her. And he won't. King's always been a stickler when it comes to his word. That's why I get the phone calls. Sonny forgot to specify me in the promise.

Now spring's here and another season of mini-golf has started up, King and Sonny and Myra aren't exactly seeing eye to eye.

The other day Sonny told King that playing mini-golf is ridiculous and undignified for a man his age. Myra added, "And let's not forget the spot of trouble you got in last year. Next, we'll be facing accusations of you know what."

King wanted to know what "you know what" was.

"Dad, it looks bad an old man hanging around where kids congregate," Sonny says. "You watch the TV, you know what we're talking about. Myra doesn't think you should go there any more, and I agree."

King goes to great pains explaining to me over the telephone how nobody's going to mistake him for a child molester. Why, the facts all contradict it. For one thing, he only went to Putt 'N' Fun when the kids were supposed to be in school. Ask the owner, ask Lila, if that isn't the case. Last year's spot of trouble would never have happened if those delinquents hadn't been playing hookey ten o'clock of a Monday morning.

It's early morning that King prefers for Putt 'N' Fun, he likes the course deserted and all to himself. Nobody but him in the streets of Putt 'N' Fun Town, everything quiet and still, the sun shining on the gingerbread house, the little brown church in the vale, the old mill with the water wheel, Mother Hubbard's shoe, the red schoolhouse. King says you got to see the whole layout to appreciate it. A work of art. Lila's husband made the new buildings winters when Putt 'N' Fun Town closed down for the season. It took him years and years. According to Lila, her hubby was a perfectionist, and there's not many mini-golf courses of such detail, such high-class construction and calibre anywhere else in the world. Take the church in the vale. It even has a tiny bell in the steeple. The kids are always ringing it despite the big DO NOT RING THE BELL sign, and the noise plays on her nerves. Every time she hears the bell tolling it makes her think of her husband who'll be dead five years this coming January. She's thinking of having it removed and put in storage.

King says, "It's so nice there that sometimes I forget my game and just start roaming the streets. I leave my ball rest in a hole and wander. She sees this, Lila hollers from the booth, 'Penny for your thoughts! Penny for your thoughts!' But I don't take no pennies for no thoughts. I just give Lila a wave over the roofs."

King claims Lila was surprised to hear he was a barber for fifty years. "People think of a barber they think bow-tie, Hush Puppies maybe. They think neat and skinny," said King.

King did his level best to never look an ordinary barber. He wore cowboy boots to work and knocked off a hundred push-ups before he unlocked the door in the morning and another hundred before he locked the door at night. He built himself big arms to match a big swagger.

King was an unusual barber. He'd call kids from Social Assistance families in off the street and give them no-charge haircuts and tell them it was on the house because he needed the practice. Any old man he knew was hard-up, King never took a cent from. "Can't make change for that today. Next time. Next time," he'd say, waving payment off.

Some louts and layabouts got the wrong idea from this, they figured King for a soft touch. "Catch you next time, my good man," Harvey Ferguson would say, climbing out of the chair. Harvey had eighteen months of haircuts on tick when one day King threw a head-lock on him in the chair. He squealed like a stuck pig, but King buried the clippers to his scalp, yanked him out of the chair, and pitched him into the street with a furrow through his thatch like a line down black-top. Nobody knew what set it off. I asked King, in private.

"Because he farted," said King. "Here the son of a bitch owes me for a year and a half of haircuts and he can't make the little bit of extra effort to pinch one back when I'm working on him? No, Harvey just lets her drift free and easy, like he's a rose in the Rose Bowl Parade. Well, I *drifted* him, I showed him a *parade*."

You'd believe King's unpredictability would be held against

him but it wasn't. It was appreciated. Some smirking fool was always sidling up to me. "Hear what your brother done now?" he'd ask.

The most unpredictable thing King ever done was run after Ruby Diehl. Given all the girls he'd had, or could have had, who'd ever have thought he'd fall for a woman like her? And, strange to say, it pleased people that King Walsh could lose his head over a homely woman.

Ruby tried, after a fashion, to make herself attractive. Unfortunately, her home dye jobs came out the colour of one of those creosote-treated railroad ties, a streaky, oily, rusty-black. Painting her fingernails and toenails wasn't such a good idea either because it drew attention to the size of her feet and hands, which was considerable. Too much face powder in the summer only succeeded in making her eyes and nose look all the redder and runnier when she was suffering from hay fever.

Ruby operated the switchboard for the town telephone exchange out of her father's clapboard house, details which give some indication of how long ago all this happened. Ruby was not King's first fling since he'd heard wedding bells. Already there had been the sort of girl who make themselves available to men like King, but never anything serious. I knew about these women because King got in the habit of asking me to lend him the use of an unoccupied room in the hotel where I worked as desk clerk. I didn't like to oblige him, but I knew it was better he put himself in my hands rather than somebody else's who might talk. I wanted no hurt to come to Elsie.

Ruby Diehl wasn't cut on the pattern of those other girls though. The ladies in Advance might deplore the way she trowelled the paint on, but there had never been a word spoken against her reputation. All that make-up was just spinster silliness, a woman thirty-five trying to lose ten years with a compact, they said.

I must have been one of the first to spot them together, although I didn't think anything of it at the time. Out driving in the country one Sunday afternoon, inspecting the crops, I met King's Ford on the road. I had to look twice to be sure I saw what I saw – little Sonny (he must have been about two years old then), standing up on the front seat between King and Ruby. Now that's strange, I said to myself. I never knew Elsie and Ruby were friendly. Because Ruby and King was so impossible a connection I never made it. I just assumed Ruby was in charge of the baby to give Elsie a break since King couldn't be trusted to do a proper job – wiping up shit and snot being beneath him.

But then people began to question me about my brother and Ruby. From the doubtful tone of their voices I could tell they couldn't believe what the signs were pointing to, and figured I had an explanation for it. But I didn't. For the life of me, I didn't know why King and Ruby were taking Sunday drives in broad daylight, or why he had been seen slinking outside Diehl's house when dusk was coming on, walking slowly up and down the sidewalk with a desperate hunch to his shoulders.

I knew my brother, I knew if I asked him for the straight goods he wouldn't lie. He was relieved, glad to talk to somebody about it. King seemed bewildered by what had happened to him, the strange way it had started. You see, Ruby had asked him to come to her father's house to cut the old man's hair. Her father had begun to wander in his mind. She was worried that he might cause embarrassment in the barbershop. He said filthy words out loud.

So King had done as she asked because he could always be made to feel sorry for people. And when it came time to settle up, he didn't want to take any money for a neighbourly act, but Ruby kept insisting and insisting until finally he told her that all the payment he wanted for cutting the old man's hair was a kiss from his pretty daughter. Now King meant this as a joke and never expected poor Ruby to take him up on it, but she did. She kissed him and then she kept right on kissing him. According to King there was no stopping her.

All right, I said, you made a mistake but *this* has got to stop. There's talk already. Taking Sonny in the car with you when you go driving with Ruby Diehl won't protect her good name any more. She's a lonely woman and its wrong to lead her on. You have to break this off.

"Maybe I don't want to break this off," said King. "Maybe I can't."

It was true. From the look on his face I could see it was true. He had tried to stay away from her but found he couldn't. He'd swear off Ruby, then turn around the next minute and telephone her to make an appointment behind the lilacs. This was how they spoke of adultery, behind the lilacs. When it got dark, Ruby stole out of the house with a blanket and lay down behind the Diehls' lilac hedge to wait for King to come to her. The hedge stood flush against the sidewalk. Occasionally they heard footsteps and their passion would turn to stone, the two of them hardly breathing until the passersby rounded the corner. King said when they went absolutely still like that and waited, all the world stood brave and clear to him in a way he had never known before, he could feel the stars staring down, the heavy sweetness of the lilacs pressing in, the damp grass under his hands. He could feel the life in everything around him, the life in himself.

When a man talks in such a peculiar way, you know the thing is far from being over. By winter what they were up to was common knowledge in the town and neither one seemed to be making much effort to hide it. As her father grew sicker and feebler in his mind, Ruby had less to fear from him, and she began inviting King into the house. After a light snow, a man's footprints could be plainly seen on the walk to the Diehls' door.

Anybody else but King would have run the risk of being laughed at for taking up with a woman older than himself, and an unbecoming one to boot. But not King. To the beer-parlour crowd he was a hero.

"She was saving it all those years. You know how crazy they get saving it."

"Itching for it."

"And King owns the scratcher."

"If I know King, he's got more than scratching up his sleeve. Mark my word, boys, thar's gold in them thar hills. Old Diehl has deep pockets."

"Fucking King. He was born lucky."

"You got to make your luck. There she was sitting on that little toy all those years, but it was King who unwrapped it and taught her how much fun it was."

"That son of a bitch."

Shortly after old man Diehl died, King and Ruby ran off together for the first time. My brother left a letter for me at the hotel asking me to break the news to Elsie. All Elsie said was, "We'll see." In forty-eight hours, hardly enough time for anyone but a wife or brother to notice they had gone missing, the two of them were back in town. During this elopement King had only one topic of conversation, Elsie's goodness and kindness. Ruby told him if that's the way he felt, they'd better turn the car around and go back to their former lives.

But in a matter of weeks King had had his fill of goodness and kindness and was back carrying on with Ruby Diehl like there was no tomorrow. It went on like this for two years, Ruby pressing him to make a choice and King delaying. Meanwhile Ruby was changing, she stopped painting and powdering her face, polishing her nails, dying her hair. Bit by bit her experience with King was teaching her confidence.

This may seem a strange claim to make when you consider that the second time they ran away together the same thing happened as the first. King sang Elsie's praises in every hotel room they stopped at, which seems to me a sure way to destroy a woman's confidence. But obviously it didn't injure Ruby's. She hopped a train in Winnipeg, headed east. King came back to Elsie and me.

The other night when the phone rang I expected it to be King. It was Sonny.

"Dad's gone and done it again," he said. "We're losing our patience here, Myra and me."

"What's he done?"

"The police brought him home last night."

"What's he done, Sonny?" I demanded.

"They picked him up roaming around that mini-golf course in the dead of night. Way past midnight. Myra and me didn't even know he'd slipped out of the house. He climbed a fence to get into Putt 'N' Fun. It's only about three feet high but God knows how he got over it with that bum hip of his. The police saw somebody moving around in there and suspected vandals so they went in to check on it." Sonny paused. "He tried to run from them."

"Jesus."

"You ask me, he's losing his marbles," said Sonny. "He goes there every single morning, doesn't miss a day, and now he's climbing fences in the middle of the night."

"What was he doing in there?"

"Search me. The police say he was just walking around, they thought maybe they heard him talking to himself. He isn't talking now though. I can't get anything out of him. No way he'll confess what he was up to. Could be he doesn't know himself. I hate to say it about my own father, but I don't think he's too sound in the head anymore. We try to discuss the situation with him but we get nowhere."

"He was always stubborn," I said.

I could hear Sonny take a deep breath on the other end of the line. "This Putt 'N' Fun is no joke. I mean you just can't go making free with people's private property like that. And then look what happened last summer with that boy. He keeps hanging out there it's bound to happen again. As Myra says, 'It's only a matter of time.' He doesn't know how lucky he was last year. If that friend of his, that Lila woman, hadn't lied for him, God knows the hole we'd have had to dig him out of."

I hadn't moved on to consider any of that. All I could think of was King wandering up and down the little dark streets, talking to himself. It made me cold, frightened.

"You know," said Sonny, "Myra and me, we're coming to the conclusion that maybe the city isn't the place for him.

There's too many ways he can get into trouble here. Dad's not a city person. He doesn't belong here."

Sonny waited for me to take the bait. But what am I supposed to do with King? All the accommodation I've got is the single I rent in the hotel where I worked all my life. I got no room for him.

"You struck a bargain, Sonny," I told him. "Keep your end of it."

Sonny claimed he didn't know what I was talking about.

Most people in Advance took King for nothing but a gay dog. Elsie and I saw the other side of him, the hidden side which moves him to climb fences, slouch up and down empty streets in the dark, mutter to himself. What Sonny's first wife Lucy said about King, about him running after life, was true. But King's got no clear notion of what "life" is, except maybe that it's the opposite of unhappiness. King was determined not to be unhappy.

The mood would creep up on him like a shadow. He might smile, even laugh, but if you watched him careful you'd notice it was only the muscles of his face doing a job. Everything was rote – the way he cut and combed hair, even the way his flat, empty laughter joined with everybody else's. At our regular Friday-night poker game I gave him a nudge to remind him to crow if he won, or curse if he lost. He drank his whisky like water and it had no effect. At home he lay on the sofa with a newspaper spread over his face, or sat in front of the radio, switching from one station to the other without pause, hearing nothing. He lost his appetite for everything but black coffee. There were times his hands shook so bad he had to hide them in his pockets.

No, nothing's wrong, he used to say.

Needing King back we got frightened, Elsie and me.

Sonny must have been reminding him of last summer. Every time he does, King phones to explain himself.

"They kept running up my heels," he said. "I was too slow for them."

"I know, King. I heard all this before."

"They were sniggering at me, him and the girl."

"You got to learn to ignore them, King."

"I was trying to line up a four-foot putt on the Hansel and Gretel hole. But I couldn't do her, not with all that giggling going on behind me. A fellow can't concentrate, those circumstances."

"They find old people funny, King."

"A sixteen year old wears his shorts ten sizes too big, hanging down past his knees, that's funny. What's he expect – to grow into them? Make up your mind, I wanted to tell him, don't get caught in no man's land. And you should have seen what the girl has printed on her T-shirt, little whore. It said, 'If it swells, ride it.' Can you believe that? 'If it swells, ride it.' Jesus."

"Was a time you'd have been one hundred per cent in agreement with the sentiment, King."

"That's not the point. The point is, I'm nobody's joke. So I turns around and I says to him, 'If you want to laugh at me, don't do it behind my back. Be a man. Do it to my face.'"

"Which he did." I reminded him.

"'Chill out, dude,' the kid says. I says, 'Tie your goddamn shoe-laces.' He was slopping along in these untied sneakers, it got on my nerves. 'Don't tell him what to do,' says the girl. 'You're not his old man.'

"'And a goddamn lucky thing for him I'm not,' I said. 'Or he'd have been fed to the pigs when his bones were soft.'

"'Oh, like wow, what have we got here? Excellent rural humour? Reruns of Jed Clampett and "The Beverly Hillbillies?" That's seriously droll,' the kid says. 'Melissa, did you catch what Jed said?' And they start with the laughing again.

"I tell him the name's King, not Jed. He says, 'King? King of what? King Shit of Turd Island?'

"I warn him if he's looking for trouble he's come to the right place. 'When I finish with you, sunshine,' I says, 'you won't know if your ass's been punched or bored.' 'What's that,' he says, 'faggot talk?' I show him my fist. He thinks this is funny. For kids like him, old people are just somebody you knock over getting on and off buses. I never took shit from anybody my whole life. I'm going to start now?"

"So you popped him."

"Goddamn right I popped him."

"With the putter."

"No putter. I give him the knuckle sandwich."

"From what I heard, the kid and his girlfriend claim you hit him with the putter."

"Conflicting testimony. What's he going to say, he gets laid out by a seventy-eight year old with a hip replacement? Lila seen it. She told the cops I punched him."

"Lila also said he pushed you first. I didn't hear you say that."

"Lila's a good girl. The fucking law is all technicalities. There's no self-defence unless he pushes me first."

"So she lied."

"Lila saw what Lila saw."

"His father threatened to sue, didn't he? For chipping the kid's tooth?"

"Jesus, can you believe it? I'm supposed to pay for the milk he didn't buy the kid? I told the bastard if he bought the kid a little milk to drink, his teeth wouldn't chip so easy."

"You shouldn't have done it, King. It's a different world now."

"You're glad I done it. The story of my life. Guys like you waiting for me to do what you shit-eaters don't dare."

Those moods of King's that Elsie and I feared would never lift, when they did, they lifted like spring comes to this part of the world, in a rush, ice to water. Saturday was the day he picked for thawing, the day the farmers came to town. "All work and no play makes King a dull boy," he would say, signalling the change which was coming over him. When she heard that, Elsie would phone the hotel to let me know she believed her husband, my brother, was back. He wasn't going in to work that Saturday.

King was a most particular man about his appearance, especially strutting Saturdays. Polishing shoes, brushing a hat, ironing a suit, dress shirt, and tie, occupied the morning. Then his shining self, new-made, a page out of *Esquire,* set off with Sonny to bless the afternoon. First stop, The China Lily Cafe, to buy two dozen cigars.

Rumours of King in pin-stripes rustles up a mob of kids. They swarm all over the steps of The Lily, elbow their way to the windows, peer in, whisper excitedly. The door swings open and they part like the Red Sea did for Moses, watch him pass in a hush. Silent as ghosts, they close ranks at his heels and trot down the hot sidewalks after him, a pack of hunting dogs. King doesn't give them a glance.

He stops at a cluster of farmers braced against car fenders and hoods, riding their boots on bumpers. Cigars all around. King's head tosses back with a stogie clenched in strong teeth, eye on the sky, prophesying the weather. There's nothing the man isn't expert on, women, livestock, cards, baseball, the grain exchange. Thumb in the ribs, hand clapped on the shoulder, sly wink to the sweet young thing in the sun-dress. And behind him the farmers' kids shyly edge in. They've never seen anything like him before, these little ones that count themselves lucky if they get a suck on a Coke or a box of Lucky Elephant Popcorn once a week. Their daddies are nothing like this daddy, they squeeze a nickel until the beaver shits and pile chores on their skinny shoulders to make the point life isn't cake and ice cream, not entirely.

King tips his hat, nods and smiles, asks after the missus and the crops in this heat. *Life's a bitch! Have a cigar!* He's on the move, there's life in those legs now, he stretches them out and seems to drag everybody along with him. He bustles in and out of stores scattering money, buying articles of no earthly use, a cheap harmonica, a pen and pencil set, last Christmas's artificial mistletoe, a rubber gorilla mask, chocolates, a water pistol, all this crazy spending driving up the excitement in the children the same way heat drives up mercury in a thermometer. Down one side of Main Street and up the other, more handshakes, winks, smiles, whistles. More stores, more everything. Then all at once, instead of more, there's no more. No more room in Sonny's arms for one more parcel, the last cigar gone.

The kids stand staring at him, biting their lips. King looks back at them in amazement, as if he has never laid eyes on them before. Who are they? And he turns to Sonny and asks in a loud, surprised voice, "Why, Sonny, I never knew you were so popular. Who are all your friends?"

Sonny, who hardly knows any of them from Adam because most of them are country kids, shrugs and shifts from foot to foot, awkward and embarrassed. For the others, everything hangs in the balance, like when Peter was asked whether he knew this Christ fellow. They hold their breath and their eyes flit from son to father, father to son. King's got his wallet out and is studying its insides. He looks in the wallet and looks at them, looks at them and looks in the wallet. A slow smile creases his face and he says, "Ice cream floats on Sonny! Floats on Sonny Walsh, the farmers' friend!"

That's the signal for all hell to break loose. They go stampeding up the street yelping and whooping, pushing and shoving each other in the race to get to the Chinaman's first. Ambling along in the rear comes King, lord of the manor. In The Lily he buys five dollars' worth of floats and french fries, enough to keep them eating until they puke, and distributes some of that cheap treasure he collected on Main Street to his admirers. This gets the noise level somewhere close to where he requires it but not all the way to the top so he feeds a few quarters into the juke box and cuts the rug with the waitresses while Lee cooks him an order of rare steak and mushroom fried rice. The mushroom fried rice is stomach liner for what comes next. Because what comes next is one rip of a blind drunk.

It generally fell to me to escort him home after one of these twelve-hour-long escapades, toting whichever of his parcels he hadn't lost or given away, steering him up the darkened street to patient Elsie. I remember one night when I got him to his door and he wouldn't go in. King had something to say to me. "I make mistakes," he confessed in a thick mutter. "Sometimes I'm not sure who I am. I ain't smart and I ain't rich. But I am big. Wasn't I the biggest thing in the street today? Nobody's bigger than King Walsh. Am I right or am I wrong?"

I said he was right. It was one o'clock in the morning and I had a headache.

King called. Myra had parked the car outside Putt 'N' Fun Town the other day and spied him going in there. Sonny got hot to trot, laid down an ultimatum. "Act your age. Shape up or ship out," he told King. I think King's the shape he is and it's too late to change him. I don't know how this is going to end.

Nobody in the city knows King. He is not used to streets so long and wide. He's an old man and we old men grow smaller, not bigger, before we die. King prefers a street he can fill, a narrow little street where he can look out over the roofs into the distance to an admiring woman calling and waving to him. He's running after the life he had. So toll that bell in the steeple, King. Ring it, brother, make a big noise. We're all of us going to be quiet a long, long time.

Man on Horseback

FOLLOWING HIS FATHER'S DEATH, Joseph Kelsey discovered, in his bereavement, a passion for horses. Joseph's passion for horses was not of the same character as the old man's had been; Joseph's was searching, secretive, concerned with lore, confined to books. It was not love. When his wife asked him what he was doing, staying up so late night after night, he said he was working on an article. Joseph was a professor of history.

The article was a lie. He was reading about horses.

A good horse sholde have three propyrtees of a man, three of a woman, three of a foxe, three of a hare, and three of an asse.

Joseph was born in a poor, backward town to a couple reckoned to be one of the poorest and most backward. It was a world of outhouses, chicken coops in backyards, eyeglasses purchased from Woolworth's, bad teeth that never got fixed. On the afternoon of October 29, 1949, when his mother's water broke his father ran down the lane to get Pepper Carmichael to drive them to the hospital. Rupert Kelsey didn't own an automobile, not even a rusted collection of rattles like Pepper's.

What Rupert Kelsey owned was seven horses. Horses slipped and slid through his fingers like quicksilver. When he was flush he bought more, when funds ran low he sold off one or two. Horses came and horses went in a continual parade, bays and sorrels, blacks and greys, chestnuts and roans, pintos and piebalds. His wife was jealous of them.

There was trouble with Joseph's birth right from the start. The hospital, staffed mostly by nuns, was tiny and antiquated, as backward as the town. Rupert Kelsey sat in the waiting room for an hour, and then a sister came out and told him they had telephoned everywhere but the doctor couldn't be found. It was understood what that meant. The doctor was either drunk – not an uncommon occurrence – or was off playing poker somewhere without having left a number where he could be reached. Rupert nodded solemnly and the nun left, face as starchy as her wimple.

The duty nurse behind the reception desk, a gossip, watched him closely, intrigued to see how he would take the news. He could sense her curiosity clear across the room and he was careful not to give away anything he was feeling. He had a country boy's wilful, adamant sense of what was private, the conviction that people in towns had no notion of what was their business and what wasn't.

Because this was his wife's first baby he knew that labour would likely be prolonged and hard. For three hours he sat, alternately studying the scuffed toes of his boots and the clock on the wall, his face held gravely polite against the duty nurse's inspection. The nurse was working a double shift because the woman who was to relieve her had called in at the last minute sick. She was bored and Rupert Kelsey was the only item of even mild interest in what was going to be a very long night. To the nurse he looked thirty, but seemed much older. Maybe it was the old-fashioned haircut which made his ears stand out like jug handles, maybe it was the way he shyly hid his dirty hands and cracked nails underneath the cap lying in his lap, maybe it was the bleak rawness of a face shaved with a blade sharpened that morning in a water glass, maybe it was the sum of all of these things or maybe it was none of these things which lent him that air of steadfast dignity she associated with men her father's age. He appeared to have nothing to do with her generation.

No one came out from the ward to tell Rupert Kelsey how matters stood. The Kelseys were not the sort of people that those in authority felt it necessary to make reports and explanations to. When the hands of the clock swung around to eleven he found it impossible to sustain a pose of calm any longer. Rupert got abruptly to his feet and started for the entrance.

The young nurse behind the desk spoke sharply to him. "Mr. Kelsey, Mr. Kelsey, where are you going?" In her opinion this was not the way a father-to-be with a wife in the pangs of childbirth ought to behave.

"I'll be back," he said, shouldering through the door.

It was cold, unusually cold for the end of October. The little town was dark, only its main street boasted streetlamps. Scarcely a window showed a light at this hour; in the days before television arrived, people here retired early, to sleep or entertain themselves in bed.

The barn where Kelsey stabled his horses was on the other side of town, but the other side of town was less than a ten-minute walk away. Just stepping into the heavy, crowded warmth of jostling bodies and freshly dropped dung, the ammoniac reek of horse piss, the dusty smell of hay and oats, the tang of sweat-drenched leather, made him hate that lifeless, sinister waiting room all the more.

He saddled the mare, led her into the yard, swung up on her back, and trotted through the town. The dirt roads were dry and packed and thudded crisply under the iron shoes. Like strings of firecrackers, dogs began to go off, one after another, along the streets he and his horse travelled. The mare carried her head high, neck twisted to the dogs howling out of the blackness, answering them with startled, fearful snorts. Easy and straight as a chair on a front porch, Rupert Kelsey rode her through the uproar and beyond the town limits.

It was a clear night, the sky pitilessly high, strewn faintly with bright sugary stars. Where the curtain of sky brushed the line of the horizon, poplar bluffs bristled. Beneath this cold sky Rupert Kelsey released his horse, let her fear of dogs and night bear human fear wild down the empty road, reins slack along her neck, hands knotted in the mane, braced for the headlong crash, the capsize into darkness. Her belly groaned hollowly between his legs, her breath tore in her chest. For three miles she fled, a runaway panicked.

At the bridge, the sudden glide of water, the broken shimmer unexpectedly intersecting the road caused the mare to shy, and as she broke stride he fought to turn her, striking back ruthlessly on the left rein, dragging her around open-mouthed like a hooked fish, swinging her back in the direction from which she had come, his heels drumming her through the turn, urging her, stretching her out flat down the road, back to the hospital.

By the time they reached the town the mare galloped on her last legs. On the planked railway crossing she stumbled, plunged, but kept her feet. Rupert whipped her the last five hundred yards to the hospital, reining her back on her haunches before the glass doors through which he could see the nurse as he had left her, at the desk. The nurse looked at him from where she sat and he looked at her. The mare trembled with exhaustion, a faint steam rising from wet flanks and neck. The nurse, finally realizing he was not about to dismount, got to her feet, came to the door, and pushed out into the night.

"Anything yet?" he asked.

She shook her head.

"The doctor come?"

She shook her head again.

He wheeled the horse around and was gone. For several moments the nurse stood straining for a glimpse of him, pink sweater draped over her shoulders, arms wrapped around herself against the piercing cold. Everything was swallowed up in darkness but the tattoo of hooves. She turned and went inside.

Back at the barn Kelsey pulled the bridle, blanket, and saddle off the mare and flung them on a four-year-old gelding, leaving the winded horse where she stood. Once again unseen dogs gave tongue, their wavering voices lifting along the streets. He rode hard into the countryside, the taste of a cold dark wind in his mouth.

The story was a favourite of the nurse's for a long time. "Three times he rode up to the hospital and asked after his wife and then rode away again. Different horse every time. Looked drunker every time too. They usually are. Last time it was just after the sun came up, around eight in the morning that I told him she had finally delivered a boy. You know what he said? Said, 'Tell the wife I'll be up to see her as soon as I can. I got some horses to look after.' Imagine. And that woman came near dying too. It was a near thing if she'd lost any more blood."

Joseph's mother always said to him. "You, you little bastard, you wore out three horses and one woman getting born. It's got to be a record."

Wolf Calf of the Blackfoot first received horse medicine. It was given to him in a dream by a favourite horse which he had always treated respectfully and kindly. This horse appeared to him and said, "Father, I am grateful for your kindness to me. Now I give you the sacred dance of the horses which will be your secret. I give you the power to heal horses and to heal people. In times of trouble I will always be near you."

Horse Medicine Men could accomplish miracles. Not only could they cure sick horses and sick people, they could influence the outcome of races, causing horses to leave the course, buck, or refuse to run. Pursued by enemies, they would rub horse medicine on a quirt, point it at the pursuer and drop the quirt in the path of the foe's horse, causing the animal to falter.

All Horse Medicine Men recognized taboos. Rib bones and shin bones were not to be broken in the lodge of a Horse Medicine Man. No child should ride a wooden stick horse in a lodge in the presence of a Horse Medicine Man. If he did, misfortune and bad luck would befall that child.

Before a vet arrived in the district, if a horse was sick or badly injured, its owner summoned Rupert Kelsey. Usually his father took Joseph along on these visits, although the boy wished he wouldn't. When Joseph was four a stud bit him on the shoulder. His mother told him that he had screamed bloody blue murder, screamed like a stuck pig. The purple, apple-green bruise lasted for weeks and if he hadn't been wearing a heavy parka, which had blunted the horse's teeth, the damage could have been a lot more severe. Years later Joseph would suppose that the sudden crushing pain, the breath hot on his neck and face, the mad glare of the eyes must have been the root of what, in a son of his father's, was an unnatural, shameful fear of horses. But he couldn't be sure. He had no memory of the incident. Envying his father's courage, he did all he could to conceal and dissemble his cowardice.

Once, when Joseph was eleven, a woman telephoned his father with horse trouble. Her husband was away from home working on the rigs and his horse had hurt itself. The woman said she was afraid her husband would blame her for what had happened to the horse, accuse her of carelessness and neglect as he had a habit of doing whenever anything went wrong. This man was infamous for his hot, ungovernable temper. His wife had been seen in the grocery store, eyes blackened, looking like a racoon. Rupert agreed to come at once to see what he could do to help the horse and, by implication, her.

He and Joseph drove out to her place and found the horse pacing a corral, a long jagged gash on its chest dangling a piece of hide shaped like an envelope flap, an animal tormented, driven half-mad by pain and relentless clouds of flies. Joseph was ready to bet his father was going to get killed trying to catch this crazy horse. To start with, it tried to escape, clambered up six feet of fence rails, grunting and pawing, toppled over on its hind quarters, and collapsed in a whirl of slashing legs. Then it scrambled to its feet and came straight at his father, squealing, wriggling, kicking, teeth bared. His father broke the charge, made the horse veer away at the last possible second by flogging it across the face and eyes with the stock whip he carried. Joseph, clinging to the fence, begged and shouted at his father to come out of there, leave that horse be, but he wouldn't listen. Around and around the corral the two went, horse and man. The dust hung in the lowering evening light like a fine, golden powder. As it settled on his father's clothes and hair it turned from gold to grey, turning him into a ghost.

At last his father lassoed the horse and snubbed him down as tight as he could to a post. Next he fashioned himself a makeshift twitch out of a bit of rope and stick and performed the dangerous sleight of hand of slipping the loop on the horse's nose and cranking it up like a tourniquet. The horse braced itself on widely splayed legs, mad eyes rolling, strong yellow teeth bared, slobber slopping off its bottom lip. But now his father had the son of a bitch, had him good. When he called Joseph to come and take the twitch, the boy came with no more protest than if God Almighty himself had ordered him out from behind the fence of poplar poles to keep a jug-headed man-killer squeezed into submission with a twist of hemp and dry wood. He was safe because his father was near, patiently sponging Creolin into the raw mouth of the laceration, painstakingly picking slivers and dirt from the butcher-flesh. His father was there talking quietly and matter-of-factly to both horse and boy. "Now when I pull this splinter loose, look out. Get set. He's going to breathe fire. Aren't you going to breathe fire, you no-nuts son of a bitch?" Nothing could go amiss or awry with his father there, speaking so calmly.

The wound was clean, there was nothing left to do but stitch the cut. Fishing through shirt pockets his father began to swear. Somehow his needle and thread had gone missing and he would have to borrow what he needed from the woman. Joseph was to hold the horse until he got back. "He won't be going anywheres on you if you keep that twitch tight. Just keep the twitch tight," his father reiterated and was gone before the boy could manufacture an excuse why he shouldn't leave him.

Over his shoulder, Joseph watched his father amble to the house, knock, and disappear into the porch when the door was answered. He turned back to the horse. The wound was bleeding, dripping slow, fat drops of blood into the dust. It was like watching the second hand of a clock. He counted the drops, watched three hundred fall. Three hundred drops equalled five minutes. Five minutes ought to be enough time to scare up a needle and thread. He glanced nervously toward the house to see if his father was returning. There was no sign of him. The boy swayed with panic. What was keeping him? Where was his father? How long was he supposed to stand holding this horse? He imagined the sun setting, his father still missing and night falling, alone with this glassy-eyed, devil horse, both rooted to this spot of ground by a twitch. Joseph's palms were slick with sweat. He thought of the stick slipping in his hands, the sudden blur of unwinding. The unwinding and springing of the fear twisted up inside him and the fear twisted up on a stick.

He began to count the drops of blood again. He would count another three hundred before he permitted himself to look again to see if his father was coming. Five minutes more. There were flies gathering at the growing puddle of black blood thickening on the ground. There were flies on Joseph. He could feel them crawling in his ears and at the corners of his eyes. He didn't dare swat them, he might lose his grip on the stick. One slip and that crazy horse might get him.

"Hurry up," he said aloud and the horse laid back its ears at the sound of his voice, changing the shape of its head, giving it a snake's sleekness. "Hurry up, please," he said. He was still counting in his head, the numbers very loud. He got mixed up. Started counting flies, not tears of blood. He began over. Once again three hundred. He looked back at the dead calm of the yard soaked in evening light; everything motionless except for the swallows swooping and flitting above the peaked roof of the house. In the final flight of these birds before the coming darkness he experienced his own desertion. There was no logic to it, except the logic of association. Somehow he understood he would never be his father. It was that simple. He could never be a man like his father. The realization left him bereft, made him cry.

He was still crying when he heard the scrape of boots on the fence rails. His father wanted to know what had happened. Joseph couldn't explain. When his father came nearer and repeated the question, Joseph smelled the whisky on his breath. Now he felt entitled to his anger at his father's failure to understand.

"You been drinking!" he said. The shrillness of his voice was a clue, if not an explanation.

"She gave me a drink," his father said. "I had to have a drink for coming out. She wouldn't have it any other way." He couldn't figure what was behind this. "I was only gone fifteen minutes," he said. "Did he come at you? Take a jump? Scare you? Is that it? I told you to hold him tight."

"Tell me another one. Fifteen minutes," Joseph said sullenly, trying to rub the tears on his cheek into the shoulder of his shirt.

"Okay, twenty minutes," said his father. "At the outside." He threaded the needle and set about stitching the wound. The light was failing, he didn't have much time. Each time the needle penetrated the skin, the horse shivered, its hide rippled with a life of its own.

"You ought to think," said Joseph.

"Think about what?" said his father. "You tell me what to think about and I'll think about it."

"Just think." *Think about me,* he meant.

"Wait until you're my age," his father said. "Then you'll know what thinking is."

Think about what'd happen if I let go of this stick. Joseph watched the poised needle. *You'd be sorry then.*

His father tied the thread in a neat surgical knot. He had a book of knots at home, there wasn't one he didn't know.

"Turn him loose," he said to the boy. His father was getting angry. What was he supposed to apologize for? "And another thing," he added, "just so you know who calls the shots in this outfit – get yourself ready for another fifteen-minute wait because the lady asked me in for another drink and I'm going to have it."

Joseph refused to go into the house with his father.

"Pout if you want," his father said. "It's no skin off my ass."

Joseph prowled around the house, chucking handfuls of gravel up under the eaves to drive the swallows out of their nests and into bursts of edgy flight to test the truth of his earlier feeling. He continued doing this until his father came roaring and raving outside, shouting enough was enough, he'd had all he could stand of this carry-on. Show some respect for other people's property or he'd get the worst jeezly licking of his life.

Another taboo broken.

After France's defeat at the hands of the Prussians in 1870 and the annexation of Alsace-Lorraine, the humiliated nation

cried out for revenge, for a saviour. The eyes of Frenchmen turned to the handsome General Georges Boulanger, The Man on Horseback. No one knew that The Man on Horseback had only learned to ride, to cut such a captivating figure, by the most diligent application. Boulanger after all was an infantry man, not a cavalry officer full of careless dash and daring. His riding school was an abandoned chapel which stood beside his house. Each morning at six o'clock the General would spur his horse through the doorway of the chapel and commence bouncing about in the sacral, coloured morning light falling through the stained-glass windows. The General was not a stupid man. Although he frequently toppled off his horse and took many embarrassing tumbles, he was careful to see to it that there were no witnesses to his hilarious accidents. His mistakes were made in private.

General Boulanger had an infallible sense of publicity. Everyone remembers the names of the horses of truly great generals. Alexander the Great and Bucephalus, Napoleon and the white stallion Marengo, General Lee and Traveller, Stonewall Jackson and Little Sorrel. But no general owed as much to a horse as General Boulanger did to Tunis. The General did not choose his horse himself, he left the choice of his mount to an expert, someone who knew his business. The man who picked Tunis for the General chose well. Tunis was a beautiful black which gleamed in the sunshine. Despite being a considerable age, the horse looked strong and had a striking carriage. He moved and pranced elegantly, with great elan, with great presence. Perhaps most important for a general who had only recently become an equestrian, sitting on Tunis was as comfortable as sitting in his own armchair beside his own fire. The horse's disposition was tested by trumpeting bugles in his ear and discharging rifle volleys under his nose. The animal didn't turn a hair, didn't startle. There would be no unfortunate and mortifying surprises for The Man on Horseback.

On July 14, 1886, the anniversary of the Fall of the Bastille, General Boulanger introduced Tunis to the public in a military review at Longchamps. By three o'clock in the afternoon a crowd of one hundred thousand had gathered on the field to view the parade. Gunfire and military tunes announced the arrival of a squad of spahis followed by fifteen generals, hundreds of officers and the military attachés of all the embassies. When they had passed, a solitary figure made his entrance on a black horse; General Boulanger garbed in turquoise dolman with gold epaulettes, pink trousers and black boots.

The crowd went wild. Cries of Vive Boulanger! *drowned out the weak smattering of applause which greeted those dowdy, drab politicians, the Prime Minister and the President of France. While those two fussily took their seats in the presidential box, General Boulanger and Tunis capered about the field looking strenuously military, the eyes of the crowd fastened adoringly upon them.*

When the review began, many of the common soldiers broke protocol by saluting General Boulanger rather than the President of the Republic. Thousands of voices thundered "Vive Boulanger!" *again and again. As the last troops departed, the hysterical crowd burst through the police and onto the field, men shouting frantically, women weeping. Only with the greatest reluctance did the overwhelming mob permit their darling to canter off on his beautiful black horse. For hours, like jilted brides and forsaken bridegrooms, they wandered about Longchamps, disconsolate. That night every restaurant and café in Paris was full, the streets were jammed with people shouting for Boulanger.*

The striking figure he had cut on Tunis insured Boulanger's popularity and led to a ubiquitous celebrity. Over three hundred popular songs were composed in his honour. Photographs of his striking features sold out issues of eight hundred thousand. There were pottery statuettes of the General and cheap clay pipes with their bowls fashioned in the likeness of The Man on Horseback. You could scrub yourself with Boulanger soap and eat your dinner from a Boulanger plate. His office in the Ministry of War was flooded with letters from the women of France offering their bodies to him with fervent, erotic patriotism. France gave its heart to Boulanger, but Boulanger's was pledged to his mistress, the Vicomtesse Marguerite de Bonnemains, lover, advisor, and administerer of ever increasing doses of morphine to alleviate the pain of an old war wound of the General's.

On January 27, 1887, General Boulanger was elected to the constituency of the Seine by a stunning majority of 80,000 votes. That night France was his for the taking, virtually without opposition he could have established his dictatorship. In the Restaurant Durand, where he awaited election results throughout the evening, an enthusiastic mob was kept at bay with the iron shutters closed over the windows. Admirers urged him to act, to seize the government. Workingmen, students from Montmartre, aristocrats chanted "A l'Elysée! A l'Elysée!" *in the streets. Boulanger withdrew to a private room in the restaurant and consulted Marguerite. When he returned he issued orders that nothing was to be done.*

Sensing indecision and weakness on his part, the government set in train steps to arrest The Man on Horseback and General Boulanger fled wife and France accompanied by his mistress. A brief period of fashionable acclaim in English society followed, but the General was a spent force, an article for the shelf. In exile on the isle of Jersey, Marguerite fell ill while the General sat in front of a large portrait of Tunis.

The unhappy couple removed themselves to Belgium. There Marguerite died on July 16, two days after the date of the General's greatest triumph on the field of Longchamps. Several months later The Man on Horseback shot himself on his lover's grave. A large photograph of Marguerite which he carried under his shirt was so firmly pasted to the skin of his chest with dried blood that it had to be torn to be removed.

A horse can carry a man only so far and no farther.

Joseph Kelsey left home at the age of seventeen. For four years he attended the University of Saskatchewan, supporting himself with part-time jobs and scholarships. A Woodrow Wilson Fellowship took him to the University of Wisconsin. From there he went on to the University of Chicago and a Ph.D. in modern French history. While in Chicago he met and married Catherine Bringhurst, a medical student and a native of the Windy City. In 1974 Catherine completed her medical degree, Joseph took a job teaching history at Carleton, and they moved to Ottawa.

Each of these steps removed Joseph Kelsey a little further from his father, geographically and emotionally. Distance made visits more expensive and more infrequent. The world he lived and worked in now made the one he had departed seem impossible, at the very least improbable. Whenever he told Catherine stories of his childhood, of life in a shacky house, of a father and mother who never read a book, he felt self-dramatizing and false. The stories were true but in the alchemy of Catherine's imagination they were transformed and he became located in an unreal world of glamorous destitution. In rare moments of self-knowledge, Joseph Kelsey knew that this had always been his intention – to make his origins as romantic to her as hers were to him. His goal was a reciprocity of envy, something conceivable, given the mood of the sixties. Raised in an affluent suburb of Chicago by a doctor father and a psychiatrist mother, whom she addressed as Claude and Amelia, Catherine seemed inconceivably exotic to her young husband.

Joseph and his new wife made trips back to Saskatchewan twice in the years between 1974 and 1977. On both occasions they stayed in the local hotel at Catherine's insistence. Because Joseph's parents' house was so small, she didn't want Rupert and Mary disturbed by Andrew, a fussing baby on their first visit and, on their second, a small child in the throes of the terrible twos. Joseph didn't tell his wife that her middle-class consideration was interpreted by his parents as high and mightiness, a distaste for ordinary people and plain living.

Overhearing his mother refer to Catherine as "Dr. Bringhurst" confirmed for her son that it was a sore point with his mother that his spouse had retained her maiden name.

How Catherine reacts to this, or doesn't react to this – she is oblivious in the way the protected, privileged so often are, they cannot conceive of opinions except the proper ones, *theirs* – makes Joseph swell with a mild, chafing contempt. *She has no idea.* For her the man with the prematurely, fiercely lined face and the woman with the home permanent and tough, callused hands are salt of the earth idealizations; honest, kindly peasants like the ones first encountered in a suburban fairy tale, Chicago-style. Deep in her heart she assumes that they must admire her because that is what peasants do with princesses. (Catherine would be shocked and hurt if Joseph accused her of such an attitude.) But Joseph knows what his parents think of women who give their boy child a doll to play with, or hang on to their maiden names, or put up in hotels on family visits. Hoity-toity bitch, is what they think. So his son turns five before Joseph can bring himself to pay another visit home, before he and Catherine, his mother and Andrew find themselves standing in the IGA parking lot, watching the local Canada Day parade assemble. This year, like each of the fifteen before, his father, on horseback, is going to lead the parade and bear the flag.

It is not a good day for a parade. The morning is woolly and grey with a fine, misty rain, which recalls for Joseph the barely perceptible spray suspended in the air above the observation railings at Niagara Falls. He wishes it would piss or get off the pot. The day has the feel of a sodden Kleenex about to shred in his hands. He doesn't know why he should feel this, but he does. Maybe it's because Andrew, holding Catherine's hand and delightedly awaiting the commencement of the parade in a brilliantly yellow raincoat and sou'wester, seems to his father the only genuine patch of brightness on the scene, a patch of brightness soon to be eclipsed by disappointment. It's Joseph's guess that the boy expects a parade of pomp and magnitude, an Ottawa parade like he's used to. Andrew doesn't understand that all he is going to get is what is already collected in the parking lot.

That's the local high-school band whose uniform consists of the high-school jacket, nothing splashier, showier, or more elaborate. Also the local Credit Union, which has resurrected its perennial float, a six-foot-high papier mâché globe spotted with cardboard Credit Union flags to illustrate the international nature of credit unionism. The owner and parts man of the John Deere dealership are drunk and in clown costumes. The owner will drive a John Deere riding mower pulling a child's wagon in which the two-hundred-and-fifty-pound parts man will hunker, honking a horn and tossing wrapped candies to the children. The few remaining parade entries are of a similar calibre. Meanwhile the hapless drizzle continues, making everything fuzzier and murkier, wilting the pastel tissue paper flowers on the floats, frizzing the hair of the high-school queen and her attendants, painting a pearly film of moisture on the hoods, roofs, fenders of parked cars.

Buried in Joseph is the nagging realization that it is wrong to assign the feel of the day, the foreboding that it is about to fall apart in his hands, to any possible disappointment on Andrew's part. The real problem is his, adult disappointment. Because, ever since they arrived, grandson and grandfather have been stuck to one another like a new wooden rung glued into an old wooden chair. Joseph knows it is the horses. How can he compete with horses? Despite Catherine anxiously forbidding her father-in-law to carry Andrew wedged between his belly and the pommel of the saddle the way he once carried Joseph as a toddler, Joseph knows that hasn't stopped the old man when he's out of her sight: no woman is going to tell him what to do. And disobeying her has won him a friend for life.

Just now Andrew, all shining yellow, is standing riveted with admiration to the shining black asphalt of the parking lot, watching his grandfather show off for him on his horse.

There is no other word for what the old fool is doing but showing off and the performance leaves Joseph faintly disgusted. The pretence is that he is putting his mount through its paces, a sort of pre-parade disciplining, but in Joseph's books it is purely, simply, transparently, a pathetic ploy to impress a five year old.

The old man backs up the gelding across the parking lot, toes pointing outward in his stirrups, urging it backward with the pressure of his legs and firm tucks of the reins. Then he jumps it forward suddenly, swings it to the right in a tight, tail-chasing circle, the drooping standard shaking itself out from the flag pole in shuddering billows. Abruptly he throws the horse's head left, reversing the direction of the turn, rippling the flag with counter-spin. The slither of the gelding's hooves, the awkward, comic scramble of its back legs as they fight for purchase on the slippery pavement kick high-pitched laughter and skittish, excited hops out of Andrew. He's delighted with this cartoon.

Suddenly, in the midst of a spin, the horse's legs slip on the rain-slick pavement with a sound like a spoon scraping the bottom of a pot and shoot stiffly out, the horse going down, landing heavily on the old man's left leg, pinning him to the wet asphalt. For a moment, everyone except Andrew freezes. The boy, unable to judge the seriousness of the situation, continues laughing in shrill appreciation of the new trick until a squeal of terror from the fallen horse shocks him into silence.

Joseph runs through the rain. He sees the muscular arching of the horse's neck, the legs thrashing the air and pavement for a footing, his father clinging to the horn and heeling the horse hard with his free boot, urging it to its feet with shouts of "Hup! Hup! Hup!," the horse whinnying, straining to rise with this dead weight, this sack of guts and bone unbalancing it.

As Joseph reaches out to seize the bridle and help lift the head, the horse heaves, heaves desperately again, scrambles to its feet snorting and jerking, the old man sticking on for dear life, slung precariously from the saddle like a sidecar, bouncing and pitching with each convulsion of the powerful body, fighting to pull himself upright. Which he does, the horse dancing a nervous side-step across the parking lot, one rein dragging, the old man leaning forward, snatching for it and calling out, "Whoa! Whoa! Whoa, you son of a bitch!"

At last he grabs the rein and regains some control of the horse which stands blowing, snuffling, trembling, cornered eyes wary. People begin to crowd near, now that the danger is over. "I'm going to walk him out," says the old man to Joseph, ignoring the others, "to see he didn't bugger his legs." Horse and rider slowly circle the parking lot. Andrew leans against his father, bumps his head on Joseph's hip, and cries. Now that it is over, now that he has absorbed what has happened, the boy is finally frightened. As the old man passes them on his second circuit he calls out to his grandson, "Grandpa's okay, see? Look, Andy, Grandpa's okay." He grins hugely and strikes his chest dramatically with his fist to demonstrate his soundness. Grandpa making a joke on himself, Grandpa beating his chest wildly in this funny way, pitches the boy into no man's land, leaves him gulping tears, sucking back snot but also smiling with relief. Grandpa's all right. Grandpa's okay. He says so. However, a certain grim tightening about the mouth, the way the old man gingerly shifts his seat in the saddle contradict Grandpa's claim.

Reassured as to the horse's fitness, the old man asks Joseph to hand him the flag he dropped in the wreck. His son tries to talk him out of continuing but he'll hear none of that. Joseph knows it's injured pride, the shame of the apple cart upset in front of witnesses which prevents his father from withdrawing from the parade. Long ago he had said to Joseph, "Just like a box of Crackerjacks, there's a surprise in every horse." What went without saying was that Rupert Kelsey could handle any of those surprises. Now he is not going to let this surprise get the better of him, not with his grandson, his son, his daughter-in-law as onlookers.

Catherine is incredulous that Joseph won't stop him. "He ought to have medical attention! He's sixty-five," she says.

"You tell him he's sixty-five. You tell him he ought to have medical attention. You're the doctor, not me," says Joseph and walks away from her.

His father troops the parade all around the town with a grinning face as grey and wan as the day itself, then leads it back again to the parking lot. When he tries to dismount he discovers his left leg, the one crushed under the horse, can't bear his weight and he has to suffer the indignity of having Joseph support him while he bails out on the right side of the horse, the *wrong* side, like some know-nothing dude ranch cowboy. The left leg is, of course, broken and has swollen to fill his riding boot like sausage meat stuffed tight in its casing. When they cut the cowboy boot off him in the hospital he keeps sadly remarking, "Those are my show boots. Lizard skin. Expensive as all get out."

Joseph knows the difficulty of unlearning the things you were taught as a kid – he's been trying to do it for nearly twenty years. Still he backslides, caught in the current of his father's assumptions like a rudderless boat. Take the question of toughness, grit, physical courage. Joseph Kelsey's colleagues condescend to any such notions as the last refuge of the pitiably stupid and primitive, the resort of macho Neanderthals with brains the size of peas and exaggerated testosterone levels – football players or men like Oliver North and Gordon Liddy. They prefer moral courage, the variety of bravery on which intellectuals have a corner of the market.

Joseph has to concede that physical courage *is* inferior to moral courage. Nevertheless he often feels the need to play the devil's advocate, the devil prompting this reaction being his rooster-tough old man. Joseph wants to argue: But isn't physical courage sometimes a precondition of moral courage? Was moral courage in Hitler's Germany or Stalin's Russia possible without physical courage, without the guts to face the piano wire, the fist in the face, the boot in the groin, worse? When smug self-congratulation is in full spate in the faculty club lounge he is tempted to say, "Let's remember that it wasn't Heidegger who tried to blow up Adolf Hitler, it was army officers."

~

Nineteenth-century explorers reported of the bare-back riding Ankwe of the Kwalla district of northern Nigeria that they ensured themselves a sticky, adhesive seat on their horses by cutting a strip of hide out of the centre of the animal's back approximately eight inches long and several inches wide. On this raw, bloody surface the rider settled, gluing himself to his beast. The scab was scraped off and the sore freshened up with a knife whenever the horse's owner intended to go for a gallop.

~

Life went on. Joseph and Andrew paid annual visits to Saskatchewan; sometimes Catherine accompanied them, more frequently she did not. Her family medicine practice had grown to such an extent that it was difficult for her to get away. When she took time off, it was to see her own parents, both now retired and living in Florida. It was no secret that she wasn't missed by her in-laws.

The summer he turned fifteen Andrew trotted out a typical teenager's complaint. It was cruel and unusual punishment to be separated from his girlfriend and his buddies, trapped for ten days in a boring, geeky town where he didn't know a soul. Could he stay home this year? Joseph didn't put any pressure on Andrew to visit his grandparents because secretly he was glad that his son had proved to be as inconstant and disloyal as he had himself.

This was the August Joseph came home to find that his father had cancer. His mother was the one who broke the news to him, not the old man. That night, after supper was finished, the two men sat alone at the kitchen table with a bottle of rye between them while Mary Kelsey watched television in the living room. His father was not a drinking man, it was unusual for him to get drunk, but that night he did. For a long time neither Rupert Kelsey nor his son said anything. Joseph held himself sober, expecting the old man to raise the topic present in both their minds, but when his father did finally speak, it was to claim his innocence of crimes with which he had never been charged.

"One goddamn thing nobody could ever say about me was that I mistreated a horse," he suddenly said. "I never mistreated a horse. Am I right or am I wrong?"

Joseph looked at him with surprise. He said he was right. Nobody could ever accuse him of cruelty to a horse.

His father nodded to himself. "Every horse I ever owned was fat and happy. Nobody can say otherwise. I had horses that died of old age on this place because I wouldn't sell them to the likes of those that wanted to buy them. Died, mind you, *of old age and natural causes.*"

"Yes," said Joseph quietly.

"So, nobody, *nobody,*" the old man repeated with stark emphasis, as if challenging his son to dare deny it, "can say that Rupert Kelsey didn't do right by any goddamn horse he ever owned. And if they say he did – why they're goddamn liars. When there was money for nothing else around here, I saw to it my horses had oats. And nobody can say different. I never neglected a horse in my life!"

He continued on in a similar vein, justifying himself, offering evidence of his goodness, his kindness, his concern. Joseph wanted him to stop. It made painful listening. It put an ache in Joseph's chest, the kind that managed at one and the same time to feel heavy and sharp, the kind he hadn't carried around in him since he was a boy. It made him want to cry, the most inappropriate thing he could do in front of his father.

"Who's saying you did?" said Joseph. "Nobody's saying you did."

Rupert Kelsey picked up his glass with the calculated steadiness of the far gone in drink. "There's some," he said, "who I won't name, who would like to paint me in a certain light. They're wrong. I was never cruel. I never mistreated a horse in my life."

Joseph could not fathom what any of this struggled to express.

The following morning Joseph's father invited him to come for a ride. Because of the circumstances, Joseph couldn't see how he could refuse. It had been more than a dozen years since he had sat a horse and he felt ridiculous dragging himself aboard, feeling his ligaments tighten and burn alarmingly, his joints creak dryly as the horse plodded along.

His father led him down a little-travelled country lane, which was no more than the scar of old tire tracks. On either side of them the black poplars swirled masses of glittering leaves in the early morning breeze as birds hopped and sang noisily in the branches. A number of wrecked cars had been towed here to rust into the margins of the bush, shards of broken windshield grinning in the jaws of the frames with savage glass teeth. A woodpecker slashed by their horses' noses in the level, swift flight plan of its kind.

His father began to talk, not about his cancer, but in a different fashion from the night before.

He said, "You won't believe it but I had the same idea as you once – about getting out of here. I thought about going to South America, one of those countries there. Argentina. I saw this book with pictures, all open country, no fences, lots of cattle. Lots of horses. They live on the backs of horses there. I was twenty-one. I thought about going. But then the war came along." He paused. Joseph saw that in the morning light his father's face looked drawn, that in the light of day he looked sicker than he had in the electric light of the night before. "Who knows?" his father said to himself. "It doesn't matter. I likely wouldn't have gone. What do they speak there anyway? Mexican?"

"Yes," said Joseph, restraining pedantry.

"I wouldn't have been one for learning Mexican," said his father. "I didn't learn nothing much in my time."

They went along a little further in silence. The trail had dwindled away from lack of use. Chokecherry, pincherry, cranberry, and saskatoon bushes crowded in upon them. Tall grass, which had overgrown the tracks, feather-dusted their horses' bellies. The men were constantly fending off branches that threatened their faces, only a narrow channel of washed blue sky snaked above them. It felt to Joseph as if he were being swallowed up in a green dream.

His father said, "I had another chance to get away when you were about ten – you wouldn't know this. A fellow who was up here from Texas buying horses said I should come down to Houston and break horses for him. He had this operation outside the city where he sold saddle horses to doctors and lawyers and businessmen, rich people. Then he stabled the horses for them, got them coming and going, got them twice. He said to me, 'You can't live in Texas unless you own a horse. I got Jew dentists, come down from up north, never seen a horse in their lives, and even they end up owning horses. If they don't have to have one, their kids do. It's a fucking gold mine. You ought to throw in with me.' I ought to have. He needed a horse-breaker. He was offering good wages."

"And why didn't you?"

"Your mother didn't want to go some place strange." His father laughed. "You could have grown up a Texan."

"Just in time for Vietnam," said Joseph.

The grove of poplar was thinning, they came out into an opening in the bush, into the garish glare of prairie light unsifted by leaves overhead, rousting two large, rusty-brown hawks off the ground where they were tearing at a rabbit. The birds flapped into the air with harsh, indignant screams, inched up the sky steadily, one wing beat at a time, and disappeared from sight.

"I think we better turn back," said his father.

"You don't have to go back for me," said Joseph. "I'll pay for it in stiffness later, but I'm okay for now. You want to go on, go on."

"I ain't comfortable on a horse much any more," his father said. "I got this thing in my belly, after twenty or thirty minutes up on a horse, it hurts like a fucker. I been twenty minutes here. I got twenty minutes back. I don't have another twenty minutes in me."

To Joseph this was the only direct reference his father made to his cancer. Ever.

It takes him two more years to die. There are inexorable advances of the disease and inexplicable remissions. Joseph is there for the last and final stage, by his bedside. His father is unrecognizable, all the deft grace and assured power of the horseman has been wasted, worn away against the grindstone of illness.

His father has a recurring dream that he recounts to Joseph repeatedly. In the dream it is spring, early April by the look of it, patches of melting snow on bare ground, water running in the gutters, a persistent, pushing spring wind. He is enjoying the warmth, the returning sap of life, when a nagging disquiet surfaces to spoil his pleasure. There is something important he meant to do, has forgotten. Then he remembers. Last fall he'd failed to bring the horses in from the pasture, they have spent the entire winter out, endured blizzards and bitter cold without food and shelter.

The horses are waiting for him at the gate, where they have waited all winter. Skeletons with ribs like barrel hoops under the long matted hair of their winter coats, feeble legs with swollen knees bulging like coconuts, cracked hooves planted in the cold trampled mud, pleading necks stretched across the barbed wire, dull eyes staring.

Joseph tells his father that dreams like this are common, mean nothing. Yet in the last hours of semi-consciousness, in the delirious prelude to death, his father makes him promise, again and again, that he will save the winter horses. "Save the winter horses," is his last appeal, to anyone. "Save the winter horses," he beseeches.

Nine months after his father's death when it is late at night, very late at night, and Joseph is sitting in his study supposedly working on his fictitious article about Charles Maurras and the Action Française but really reading books on horses, he locates a memory, or a memory locates him. The yellow lamp-light loses its harshness, softens and deepens, signalling this is a memory situated in late afternoon, sometime around the supper hour. He is a small boy riding with his father, tucked behind the saddle horn in the way not so long ago his father used to carry Andrew, half-hypnotized by the horse's head nodding up and down against the sky in the regular rhythm of a metronome, tick tock, tick tock, lulled by the rolling gait. Full of a child's floating torpor, he is adrift, the tired, fumble-footed shamble of the horse rocking him, rocking him, his heavy-lidded eyes blearing the long grass rippling around him in a vibrant smear of endless green. The heat of the sun burns on his face and chest, the horse burns beneath him, the curve of his father's belly burns on his back. Golden, burning, he is carried off in what direction, where, he doesn't know. In his child's heart this journey is forever, this hour is a day, this day a week, this week a month, this is infinite, this is everything. He falls back against his father and he sleeps.

In Christian art the horse is held to represent courage and generosity. It is the companion of St. Martin, St. Maurice, St. George, and St. Victor, all of whom are pictured on horseback. In the catacombs it was, with the fish and the cross, a common symbol. No one is absolutely certain what its meaning was, although it is assumed it represents the swift, fleeting, and transitory character of life.

The Master of Disaster

THE SUMMER OF 1968. Norman Hiller and Kurt Meinecke, both dreamers, and me caught sticky between them, the jam in the sandwich. Norman was the flashy type, the guy who collected followers, collected them the way he did baseball cards and Superman comic books. I was seventeen the summer he collected Meinecke, old enough to have said something, to have warned my mild and innocent friend, but I didn't.

Kurt Meinecke and I had one more year of high school left, we were going back to the books in September. Norman Hiller, in a manner of speaking, was already done. In June of that year Principal Koslowski had handed him the grade-ten diploma he hadn't earned on the promise that Hiller would never again darken the classrooms and corridors of R.J. Plumber High. Which made Norman Hiller the Seventh Wonder of the World. Nobody but Norman would have dared to make such a larcenous proposal to old Cougar Koslowski. What's more, he drove the bargain through. Whenever any one of us asked him what he intended to do now, all he said was, "I got some irons in the fire. I'm waiting on developments."

Of the two of them, Norman and Kurt, Norman had the more remarkable imagination. The movies were partly responsible. Norman was always crazy about the movies. Our town had just one theatre, the Empire, and Hiller was always in it. Sometimes he would see the same movie, three, four, even five times. In the theatre he kept strictly to himself, was always alone. If any of us tried to sit with him, he'd tell us to piss off, he didn't need anybody yapping and yammering next to him, ruining the show. Twenty years after the fact I can still see him slouching down the aisle to his seat floppy-limbed, a tall boy with huge feet and hands and long, restless fingers constantly twitching in his pockets; a narrow, nervous face with hot, black eyes, which turned lukewarm and bored whenever the conversation slid off into anything he wasn't interested in, which meant practically everything except money, sports, and the movies. It was that look which made people, teachers in particular, think he was stupid. They never stopped to consider why, if he was so stupid, he was always managing to get the better of them.

There was a ritual he performed at the movies. Before draping his gangly legs over the seat in front of him, he loosened his laces so his feet could breathe. Next his baseball cap came off and was hung on the toe of one of his shoes. The cap coming off was like the Pope making a public appearance in shorts. The Empire was the only place anybody ever saw Norman Hiller without his baseball cap on his head; he even wore it in school. Every teacher who had tried to threaten him out from underneath it had failed. The baseball cap was non-negotiable. The only reason it came off was because it interfered with Norman's line of sight to the big screen. It says something about his self-possession when you remember the year was 1968, and, despite The Beatles and everything they meant, eighteen-year-old Norman Hiller could still wear a baseball cap winter and summer without risk of being laughed at.

When the screen lit up, retrieving the faces of the waiting audience from that fleeting, profound moment of darkness before the projector began to whir, Hiller was utterly changed. The scurry abandoned his eyes and the fidget was wiped from his face, leaving it pale, smooth, and shining.

What were Hiller's favourite movies? He had a list of them.

Norman was famous for his lists. "Okay," he'd propose, "name me the Top Policemen in the NHL, one to ten." Or rank the National League third basemen. It only followed that he had an All Time Greatest Movies list. By summer 1968 this list included *The Magnificent Seven, The Guns of Navarone, The Dirty Dozen, The Devil's Brigade,* and, in his opinion, the world's ultimo primo flick, *Cool Hand Luke.* These were the films from which Hiller absorbed the arts of scripting and direction which put Murph and Dooey and Hop Jump and Deke and me under his spell, a cast of misfits who could be persuaded to identify themselves with the screwballs who populated the movies Hiller loved. We were all reborn in Norman's imagination. He turned Dooey, an edgy little shoplifter, into James Garner. What was Garner famous for in *The Great Escape*? Scrounging. He could rustle up whatever you required, even in a Nazi prison camp. Norman constructed Dooey into a legend in Dooey's own mind, until he became the consummate booster, the guy who could steal anything. "Fucking Dooey," Norman would say, "nothing the guy can't lift. Dooey could steal Christ off the cross and not disturb the nails. Couldn't you, Dooey? Fucking right. Because he's the best. Dooey is *it.*"

If Cool Hand Luke gained undying fame just by swallowing forty hard boiled eggs, then wasn't glory in the cards for Hop Jump Benyuk? Because Hop Jump could stuff a whole baseball in his mouth. Encouraged by Norman, he even started carrying one around in his jacket pocket so he was always equipped to perform. "He ought to be on television," Hiller would exclaim. "How many guys can do what he can do? One in a hundred million? I doubt it. Maybe, just maybe – outside chance – one in two hundred million. The guy ought to be on Ed Sullivan."

And me, Bernie Beman, who was I? In the movies Norman admired I would have been the brain gone bad, the one the criminals nicknamed The Professor. Just possibly I was Donald Pleasance in *The Great Escape,* bird-watcher, egghead, forger. However, Norman was always a little bit uncertain of my dependability, my loyalty to the regime. He never forgot, or forgave me putting *Lawrence of Arabia* on my All Time Greatest Movies list.

"What!" he had cried, in open-mouthed disbelief. "A seven-hour movie about a bunch of camel-fucking Arabs?"

"Yes," I said, aware of Dooey, Murph, Deke, Hop Jump, all the other geeks, snorting their derision, already feeling the chill of exclusion.

"The only reason they had an intermission in that show was to go around and wake up everybody from the first half so's they didn't get bedsores. There something the matter with you, Beman?"

I didn't say. What was the matter with me was that I found it easier to identify myself with a tormented Peter O'Toole than a chiselled, brass-balled Charles Bronson or Clint Walker.

I pointed out *Lawrence of Arabia* had won a lot of Oscars.

"You ever think that those rug-riders didn't rig the Oscars?" said Norman. "Use your head. Those fucking Arabs are so rich their Lincoln, their Cadillac gets a full ashtray they walk away from it, buy a new one. I read that somewhere. They shit quarters and wipe their asses with ten-dollar bills. You think they couldn't buy themselves as many Oscars as they want? Even for such a loser as that?"

"There's no point in even talking to you, Hiller."

"No point in talking to me? No point in talking to you, Beman. No point in talking to *you.*" Which is what happened. Norman put the word out and nobody did talk to me. I was shunned, given the silent treatment for a month and a half before I managed to weasel my way back into Norman's good graces.

I was as susceptible to Hiller's manipulations as any of the others. When he was feeling magnanimous towards me, he made flattering predictions about my future as a lawyer (his choice of profession for me), extolled the notorious Beman vocabulary. With me as a lawyer, Hiller's clan would be untouchable, beyond the reach of the law. "How'd you like to be a lawyer and come up against a gunfighter like Beman there? Slinging those high words of his at you, words you hadn't even heard of? Fuck, the English teachers don't even know what Beman is talking about half the time when he starts firing off those yard-long words full of syllables. No shit, Beman reads the dictionary for fun. Don't you, Beman?"

"Yes." I couldn't help myself, I relished basking in the glare of Hiller's temporary spotlight, too. Just like Dooey or Hop Jump.

"Say one of your high words, Bernardo, my man."

"What?"

"Say one of those words no normal human being knows what they mean."

"Like what?"

"Come on, come on. A word, Beman. Give us one of those words of yours."

"Bastinado."

Hiller looking challengingly from Dooey to Murph to Hop Jump. "What's it mean? That word?"

Shrugs and sheepish grins.

"What'd I say? How you going to beat that man in court? How you going to argue against a guy when you don't even know what the fuck he's saying? Impossible."

Whatever I withheld from Hiller, whatever would have been unspeakable in the company of the others (like an affection for *Lawrence of Arabia*) was confided to Kurt Meinecke. Kurt and I had been friends since elementary school. What he listened to were secret, laughable ambitions. To be a journalist and report a war. To be drunk and cynical in a great city. To speak foreign languages like a native. With a patient, bewildered look on his face he heard me out nights as we tramped the dull, empty streets after the pool room shut, on the prowl until our knees ached, hoping against all previous experience that something exciting would happen and we would be there to witness it. But the only thing that ever happened was that a police cruiser would stop and the officers tell us it was three o'clock in the morning, get the hell home you two.

Kurt was possessed but he didn't look the way possessed people ought to, the way Norman Hiller did. Norman fit the bill because he was an exposed wire, sparking, jerking, snapping, hot with current. Kurt was the furthest thing from that. He was big and slow and solid. He walked like a man hip-deep in molasses, wading upstream against the flow of the current. But he was possessed.

Whenever I shut up long enough to give him an opening, he would jump in with something like, "I think I'll take up golf."

"Yeah?"

"Yeah. I think I'm suited to golf. All you need is hand-eye coordination and concentration. Concentration is my strong point."

"Sure it is."

"If I practised real hard I should do good. I got what it takes."

"Right."

Hopeless.

For as long as I'd known him, Kurt Meinecke had been in search of his game, the one that would prove what he knew deep down inside – that he was an extraordinary athlete. He was a Meinecke, which meant that he had the bloodlines of a champion. His father and all his uncles had been locally celebrated athletes, renowned hockey players and baseball players and players of every other game that idle, foolish men will play. It was even said that his Uncle Rudy Meinecke would have made the NHL if he hadn't caught his right hand in a power take-off which chewed four of his fingers off.

Kurt was a different story. It wasn't so much that he was bad at sports, only appallingly average. Yet his consistent failure to shine on the fields of glory did nothing to shake his bedrock, imperturbable self-confidence that he was destined for greatness. He always spoke of this as a given and obvious. And he tried everything, a hundred schemes to locate and free the springs of his talent. His batting problems would be solved if he switched from batting right-handed to left-handed. They weren't. He'd be a much better hockey player if he moved from forward to defence. He wasn't. A typical conversation with Kurt Meinecke might run something like this.

"It's too bad we don't play lacrosse around here. That'd be the game for me, you can get a running start and really pop somebody in lacrosse. That's my problem at football, from the down position I can't work up a good head of steam to pop anybody. I'm the kind of guy needs a head of steam to be effective."

There were times when this serene absence of self-doubt worked on my nerves terribly, festered until I believed there was no help for it, I was going to tell him. Of course, I never did. Truly sweet and gentle souls never get told what the rest of us do. Kurt Meinecke was so incorrigibly innocent that whenever I rehearsed the cynicism and world-weariness I intended to adopt when I was loosed upon the great cities of the world, he would smile uncomfortably, duck his head, and waddle along just a little bit more quickly in that goofy, toes-turned-out walk he had, as if seeking to put distance between himself and the nasty things being said.

Norman and Kurt weren't strangers, our town was too small for that, but they never had much to do with one another. Hiller wasn't interested in collecting the likes of Meinecke, someone who, on the surface, was as dull as ditch water and twice as murky. But then one afternoon Norman sensed a possibility, leaned over, peered into the ditch and saw all the way down, clear to the bottom. I was there when it happened.

Kurt and I were planted on a bench in the pool room. Meinecke was droning on and I was pretending to be preoccupied with a couple of senior citizens shooting a game of blue ball so I didn't have to wax too enthusiastic about Kurt's next adventure in the wide world of sports. That's when Norman Hiller slouched over to pay us a visit, jabbing his thumb in the direction of the pool table and delivering a typical sample of Hiller wit. "You know why they call it blue ball, eh? Because that's what the old farts who play it got dangling between their legs." Having delivered this line, he dropped down on the bench beside us and started to beaver a toothpick for all he was worth.

I laughed, but Hiller's sally only caused Kurt to blink a couple of owlish, solemn blinks before resuming his monologue. "I was thinking I'd go out for the wrestling team this year," he said. "I ought to be a pretty decent wrestler. I mean I got real strong fingers" – he held them up and flexed them under my nose – "and they say strong fingers are a must. I think I ought to make an okay wrestler."

I didn't say anything. Hiller did. He always had an opinion when it came to sports. "You don't want to wrestle," he said. "Wrestling is a homo sport, guys dry humping each other all over a mat. There are more queers in wrestling than there are in figure skating. Little known fact. You want to take up the personal combat line – go into boxing, Meinecke."

"Boxing?" I said. There was no boxing club in our town, nor any boxers that I knew of.

"Yeah, well, look at him," said Norman turning to me. "Look at the fucking neck on him. The guy's got a fucking neck like a tree trunk. Neck like that – works like shock absorbers on a car. You hit a guy with a neck like that, no way you could knock him out."

I cast Kurt a sidelong glance. I could see he was listening intently. Hiller could see it too.

"Neck and hands," continued Norman confidently. "That's what makes a fighter. Kurt here has the neck but does he have the hands? That's the sixty-four-thousand-dollar question. Let's have a peek at the mitts, Meinecke."

Kurt showed the mitts, self-consciously displaying them on his knees where they lay immense, red, chapped, ugly.

Norman prodded the knuckles with his index finger. "Look at them knuckles, Beman!" he urged. "Like fucking ball-bearings. These are lethal weapons we're looking at. Stand back! Stand back!" he shouted theatrically, recoiling in mock alarm. "You don't want those exploding in your face!"

Apparently Kurt had it all, neck and hands. To hear Hiller talk we were in the presence of greatness. And greatness believed it. Norman shifted position on the bench and slipped his arm around Meinecke's shoulders. "Ducks were made for water," he said. "And you were made for the ring, Meinecke. You are a natural raw talent just waiting to be developed."

"But how? How do I get developed?"

"You got to have like a manager, a trainer. Somebody to get the best out of you."

"But who?" said Meinecke. "Who's a trainer around here?"

I knew. Before answering, Norman leaned a little closer.

The Meinecke training camp's headquarters was established at Deke's. Deke's daddy had disappeared about the time Deke turned fourteen, three years before, and the mattress which Deke's Mom had drunkenly set on fire while smoking in bed, and which his father had hauled smouldering through the house to heave into the backyard, was still there, a map of interesting stains dominated by the charred, blackened crater whose flames Mr. Deke had extinguished with the garden hose that fateful day. Shortly after this incident Mr. Deke had taken off for parts unknown and Mrs. Deke, down in the dumps and remorseful over the turn her life had taken, fell prey to Jehovah's Witnesses and converted. Despite all these momentous changes, nobody got around to hauling the offending mattress off to the nuisance grounds and three years later it still lay where it had fallen. Which was convenient for Dooey, Hop Jump, Murph, and the rest of us because it provided a spot to loll about on while watching Hiller put Kurt through his paces. There amid the yellow grass, the run-over tricycle with the sow thistle growing up through the spokes of a twisted wheel, the greasy patch of lawn which Mr. Deke had killed by draining the oil from his car onto it every change, there amid all the other symptoms of neglect – scattered gaskets, a picket pulled from the sagging fence by Deke's brothers and sisters, a lid from a paint can, shards of vinyl from a broken record, a torn plastic diaper, a discarded hot plate whose two rusted elements seemed to regard the scene with blood-shot, whirling eyes – the training of Kurt Meinecke went on in a blistering July heat wave.

Meinecke jumping rope in the hottest stretch of the afternoon, Hiller roaring abuse and ridicule at him. "Knees higher! Get them knees up! No pain, no gain! I still see titty bouncing there! Bouncing boobies, Meinecke! Shame! No fighter of mine goes into the ring looking like he needs a brassiere! Knees up!"

Road work was even more brutal. Hiller conned Kurt into allowing himself to be tied to the bumper of Murph's reservation beater Chev with twenty feet of rope. The car was then driven at exactly six miles an hour down two miles of deserted country road with Kurt flailing along behind in the dust. If Meinecke didn't keep up he'd be dragged. When I protested, Norman said that it was the only way to get Meinecke to put out, he was such a lazy fuck. Anyway, boxing was survival of the fittest.

"But what if he trips and falls?" I asked.

"He's got no business tripping," said Norman.

The really bizarre thing was that Meinecke seemed grateful for the opportunity of being leashed to a bumper and towed up and down country lanes. "Like Norman says," he explained to me when I told him he was crazy, "'no pain, no gain' and another thing – which Norman also says – 'you don't know what you can do until you have to do it.' Couple of times there on the road I wanted to quit awful bad, but when you know you can't ... well, you don't. And then you're the better for it."

"Yeah, and after that fucking lunatic ends up dragging you a couple hundred yards behind a car, then you'll say you're the better for the skin graft too."

Norman was a genius of the stick-and-carrot school of psychology. For Meinecke, the carrot was the rapturous commentary which Hiller provided to accompany Kurt's daily thumping of the heavy bag dangling from Mrs. Deke's clothesline pole. There was no doubt about it, Meinecke could punch. Even with Murph clinging to the bag, bracing it, Meinecke could rock them both with one of his awesome right hands. A little praise from Norman and Meinecke looked like a cat full of sweet cream. "That's a boy, Kurtie! Look at that! That boy's what you call a banger. Your classic body puncher, your get down and get dirty George Chuvalo kind of fighter. Jab! Jab! Stick it in his face! Set it up! Go downstairs now! Hit him with the low blow! Crack his walnuts! All's fair in love and war, Kurtie, my man! You beauty, you!"

A typical July afternoon.

Each of Hiller's boys had a role to play in the making of a champion, nobody was left out. The pattern was the same as in *The Magnificent Seven, The Great Escape, The Dirty Dozen,* where each contributed according to his talents. Dooey was our equipment manager, shoplifting vaseline, adhesive tape, gauze, iodine, Q-tips, copies of *Ring* magazine – all the props – from the local drugstore. Murph and his beat-up '57 Chev towed Meinecke through his road work. Deke's yard was our training camp. I was delegated corner man and masseur. To Hop Jump fell the honour of being appointed Meinecke's sparring partner, a seemingly perverse choice since the Hopper was notorious for his cowardice. This he cheerfully acknowledged with the frequent declaration, "I'm a lover, not a fighter." The truth was that he was neither, but everyone instinctively understood poetic licence and what he was getting at. Hiller was implacable; no amount of whining and pleading on Hop Jump's part got his sentence commuted. For the rest of us seated on the pulpy mattress, swigging Cokes and puffing cigarettes, the sparring match was the highlight of the day. We jeered and hooted "Beep! Beep!" as Hop Jump, the human roadrunner, ducked and dodged and scrambled all over Deke's backyard, dust puffing up out of the dead grass around his sagging white socks, Meinecke in awkward, earnestly determined pursuit.

Up and down, back and forth, from corner to corner, from pillar to post, around the clothesline pole and the smashed trike they went, Meinecke occasionally unleashing a looping roundhouse which nearly always missed the mark, or at best, landed a glancing blow to Benyuk's shoulder or back, pinching a squawk of terror out of him and spurring him on to swifter flight.

When I asked Hiller about this strange pairing, inquiring why he had assigned Meinecke a sparring partner whose one aim was to avoid an exchange of blows at all costs, he gave me a long, steady look before answering. "I don't want Meinecke getting used to getting hit – and Hop Jump isn't going to hit him. I don't want Meinecke hitting nothing but the bag – nothing human – and Hop Jump sure the fuck isn't going to let nobody hit him. Perfect," he concluded enigmatically.

Meanwhile, the changes in Kurt were growing more and more pronounced. It was bad enough that he did exactly what Hiller told him to do when Hiller was there, but now he went even further, obeying his instructions to the letter even when Norman had no way of checking up on him. Hiller had ordered him to get lighter on his feet and now Kurt minced along on tippy toes. Walking home with him was like taking a stroll with Liberace. It didn't stop there. Each night he poured half a box of Windsor salt into the bathroom sink filled with water and soaked his head in it because Hiller had told him that fighters who cured their skin in brine toughened it, making themselves harder to cut.

Kurt may have been having the time of his life, but for the rest of us, the novelty began to wear off soon enough. Even Hop Jump's scampers around the backyard weren't as funny as they once were. We'd seen too many Road Runner and Coyote cartoons, they'd begun to pall. Nobody said it, but all of us were thinking it. What was the point?

Norman, with his exquisite sense of timing, broke the news just when interest was nearly dead. "Having just concluded extensive and lengthy negotiations," he reported, "I am pleased to reveal that I have signed Meinecke for a fight."

"What?" I said. "You negotiated Hop Jump into a phone booth? Because that's the only way you'll get a fight going between those two."

Everybody laughed. Everybody but Hiller.

"I got him a fight with Scutter," he said flatly, in a tone that judges in the movies use to hand down a death sentence.

Nobody spoke. We all avoided looking at Meinecke. A kind of deadly hush embraced the seven of us.

"Nothing to worry about," Norman said calmly. "Scutter's a street fighter. This is way different. If Scutter can't flash the boots he ain't much – and he can't flash the boots in a boxing match. Never fear. He's soap on a rope. Our boy's got the training, our boy's got the know how, our boy's got the neck and he's got the hands." Hiller gave us a significant look. "Our boy's got the *team*."

The team didn't say anything, the team was thinking of Blair Scutter. Scutter was unquestionably the most dangerous of the local psychopaths, a square, stocky kid with acne so bad that his head looked like a gigantic raspberry perched on a cigarette machine. When he was twelve he had given up terrorizing contemporaries and started picking fights with teenagers; when he was a teenager he graduated to brawls with miners at dances in the community hall. When Blair Scutter walked down one of the humanity-choked corridors at R.J. Plumber

High, an avenue opened in the congestion, everyone shrinking back against the lockers so as not to risk brushing up against his brutish shoulders. Brushing up against Scutter was like rubbing shoulders with death.

Hiller could see we weren't convinced. "Everybody heard what I said?" he demanded. "I said we got the team. And the team backs Kurt here a hundred and ten per cent. We all *think* positive. We all *do* positive. As President Kennedy said, 'Ask not what Kurt can do for you, but what you can do for Kurt.' Right?" He looked at each of us in turn, gouging out of us grudging nods of agreement. What we were thinking went unvoiced.

I felt compelled to speak to Norman and hung around until everybody had left that afternoon.

"What is this?" I said to him. "You know he hasn't got a chance."

"He does if he does what I tell him," said Norman. "But the rest of you got to back me up. No fucking with his head, putting doubts in it. A right attitude is a winning attitude. Anybody gives him doubts is a traitor in my books." It was clear whom he was thinking of when he used that word. "Anybody's a traitor in our camp better watch out."

I left that alone, tried another tack. "But why Scutter?" I asked. "Why start him with Scutter?"

"Box office," said Norman abruptly. "You promote a fight you got to have a draw. Scutter's a name attraction. I got a hall to fill."

Things were moving too fast. "What do you mean hall? What hall?"

"Kingdom Hall. That Jehovah Witness place a mile out of town. Deke's old lady has the key to it because she cleans it. So Deke'll steal her key and we have the fight out there on a Thursday night. It being out in the country it won't attract too much attention if we borrow it a couple of hours. If somebody drives by and sees cars and lights they'll just figure the

Jehovahs are having one of their singalongs or circle jerks or whatever they do out there."

"You're going to throw a fight in a *church*?"

"Hall," Norman corrected me. "The place is called Kingdom Hall. It isn't a church."

There was no debating with Hiller. Arguments with him were conducted in a twilight zone where normal mental operations were suspended and invalid. I switched tracks. I wanted to know what was in this for Scutter.

"Twenty-five bucks," said Norman. "I guaranteed him twenty-five to fight and fifty if he wins. But no sweat. We can charge two bucks a head at the gate for a fight like this. And there's no problem getting a hundred guys in there. I got Murph to drive me out so I could look in the windows yesterday. They don't have pews. Just those tin stacking-chairs. We can clear a space easy. It was made for us."

"And what about Kurt?" I asked. "What are you paying him? What does he get out of this?"

Norman gave me one of his dangerous stares, the kind in which his eyes went flat, unreadable. "Don't play stupid with me, genius. You fucking know as well as I do what Kurtie gets. He only gets what he's been begging for all along. Nothing else."

"So tell me, what's he been begging for?"

"Just what he's going to get," said Norman.

Maybe at seventeen I was already as cynical at heart as I hoped to be in those future haunts – London, Paris, Vienna, Rome – which I imagined for myself. When Hiller unveiled his fight plan naturally I assumed Meinecke was being set-up, jobbed. Norman claimed that the way to beat Scutter was to blow his mind the way Paul Newman had blown George Kennedy's mind in *Cool Hand Luke*. How had he done this? By absorbing all the punishment that Kennedy could hand out while proving that it was not enough to break him. This totally fucked a guy's head when he was giving you his best shots and you were laughing at them. "Meinecke will not even think of throwing a punch until he gets the nod from me," said Hiller. "Meinecke will let Mr. Hardass wear himself out hitting him. He will inform Mr. Hardass that his sister can hit harder than that. He will Cool Hand Luke him. He will be trained for this. He is going to show Scutter that when you got the tree trunk neck, when you got the Floyd Patterson peekaboo defence, when you got the team behind you – then you are unstoppable. *You* are the hardest ass in town, none harder. You got the plan to twist all the bolts and nuts loose in Scutter's head. Once they are good and rattling I will turn Meinecke loose. He will execute."

I didn't point out the obvious to Kurt – that being forbidden to hit back in a boxing match is a handicap. I was busy trying to convince myself that he was asking for whatever he got. I felt disgust for his naked need, for his gullibility, for the soft, accommodating clay he had become under Norman's hands. In one of Hiller's favourite movies, *The Magnificent Seven*, a ruthless bandit, who has been robbing and terrorizing poor peasants, poses a question to Yul Brynner, the gunman who has become their protector. He asks: If God did not wish them to be shorn, why did he make them sheep?

A sheep myself, I still managed to muster contempt for the others in Hiller's flock, for their stupidity if nothing else. Didn't they know what was going on? When Hiller made his speech about how we ought to show team spirit by each handing over to him five bucks to bet on Meinecke, I knew what was up. The bet wasn't going on Kurt, it was going on Scutter. And when Scutter pounded the snot out of Meinecke those morons would believe their money was lost because Kurt had lost. Sure, lost. Lost in Hiller's pockets. Still, I didn't break ranks. He got my money too.

Five days before the fight Meinecke was christened. Hiller explained to us that his research proved there had never been a great fighter who didn't have a great ring name. Check it out.

Archie Moore? The Mongoose. Beautiful. Jack Dempsey? The Manassa Mauler. A one. Robinson? Sugar Ray. Sweetness itself. Ingemar Johansson? The Hammer of Thor. You had to love it. Joe Louis? The Brown Bomber. Outstanding.

For days now, he confessed, he had been racking his brains to come up with a moniker that would elevate Meinecke into the same class as Robinson, Moore, Dempsey, etc. And now he had it.

There was a stir of anticipation. I glanced at Kurt who looked like he was about to come in his pants.

"Yeah?" said Murph, unable any longer to contain himself. "So what is it?"

"Gentlemen," said Norman, making a sweeping gesture of introduction, "let me present, Kurt Meinecke, The Master of Disaster!"

Enthusiasm was unanimous. "Right on, like a mouse's ear!" "Fucking, aye!" "Leave it to Hiller." "The Master of Disaster! It's pissing!"

Kurt beamed.

I did not bother to point out that the meaning of Master of Disaster was ambiguous. English Composition was never Norman's strong suit. Psychology was.

The big night arrived. As Murph headed his Chev out of town for Kingdom Hall, the streetlights were flickering feebly into life and then, one after another, exploding full strength in the failing light. Norman sat up front beside Murph. Kurt, in running shoes, shorts, and boxing gloves, was in the back seat wedged between me and Hop Jump like a prisoner under escort. Nobody said anything during the short drive, although Meinecke kept nervously clearing his throat and striking his gloves together, one muffled pop after another. Deke and Dooey had gone on ahead to open the hall and sell admissions to what Norman predicted would be a standing-room-only crowd.

Hiller was correct, the turnout was prodigious. Forty-five

minutes before fight time and the parking lot was already crammed with cars, many with their engines running and their headlights left on to provide light to party by. When we pulled into the lot, guys with beers in their hands were lounging on fenders, perching on bumpers, saluting and insulting one another, drifting about from one milling, jostling gathering to the next. Nosing a car through the throng wasn't easy. Norman stuck his head out the window and began to shout, "Make way! Make way! Fighter coming through! Out of the way, peckerheads!" Every couple of seconds he lunged impatiently across Murph to knock peremptory blats out of the horn with the heel of his hand when people didn't hasten out of our path quickly enough for him. Slowly we crept around to the back of Kingdom Hall, pale, excited faces with bottles tipped into them looming out of the swiftly falling darkness; dust swaying and shaking like smoke in the white-hot tracks of high beams; figures doubling over to gape through the windows of the car at Meinecke huddled up between Hop Jump and me in the back seat. As we edged along they thumped the hood of the car, gave ear-splitting whoops and hollers, chanted a variation of Hiller's announcement: "Corpse coming through! Make way! Dead man coming through!" Hiller had been wrong about one thing. No one passing by would have mistaken this congregation for Jehovah's Witnesses.

At last Murph got us clear of the mob and drew the car up to the back door. Norman gave everybody orders to stay put in the vehicle and wait, except for me. I was to accompany him. Inside, the hall was filling rapidly, growing warm with the funky, animal heat of packed bodies; blue with cigarette smoke and yeasty with the smell of beer. Like any promoter worth his salt, Norman immediately made for the box office to check the take. As he peered over Dooey's shoulder into the shoe box holding the money, Deke began to gripe and bitch about the behaviour of the crowd. Who had stolen the key? Who was going to take any of the shit coming down if the premises got damaged? Him. Deke. "They won't stop smoking," he said to Norman in a whiny voice. "You got to lay the law down to them, Norman. I mean Jehovahs don't smoke. You think they aren't going to smell stale smoke and wonder how it got here? And somebody spilled a beer on the floor. Already the place stinks like a fucking brewery. You got to do something with them, Norman ..."

Norman wasn't listening. He turned to Dooey. "How much?"

Dooey gave a shake to the box. "Close to a hundred and twenty so far," he said.

"All right," said Norman. "Shoo those assholes in the parking lot in here. That fucking carnival out there is going to attract attention. I want this show on the road." Norman had an afterthought. "And, Dooey, remember. No sticky fingers in the till. Sticky fingers are broken fingers."

"Norman ..." Deke began mournfully, trying to steer the conversation back to his complaint, but Hiller was moving off, double-time, flipping a roll of electrician's tape from hand to hand. Lugging a plastic pail and a brown paper shopping bag stuffed with a corner man's supplies, I trotted after him.

In the centre of the hall Norman commenced laying out the boundaries of a ring on the floor with the black tape. There were no ropes or posts, but he explained that if the crowd stood flush to the tape that would keep the fighters hemmed in. I set up chairs in opposing corners and unpacked the medical supplies Dooey had shoplifted: sponge, gauze pads, Vaseline.

Meanwhile Hiller had completed his chores and was on the prowl like a caged beast, pacing back and forth, jacking himself up on his tiptoes to scan late arrivals over the heads of the thick mob, muttering to himself. Scutter hadn't shown yet. Donald Broward, half-drunk, wandered over to get instructions from Norman. For a six pack Hiller had hired him to referee, not because Broward knew anything about boxing, but, a lineman on the high school football team, he was big enough to pull Scutter off Meinecke and prevent a homicide if things got out of hand.

The multitude suddenly stirred and then there was a surprising drop in the volume of drunken noise. Scutter trooped into the hall, flanked by his brother and some other bad actors. As he advanced on the ring, a swell of encouraging murmurs trailed after him, accompanied by several shy pats to his shoulders and back which he, supremely indifferent, accepted without acknowledgment.

I heard Hiller whispering to himself as we watched him approach. "Yes," he said. "Yes. I've got you in my sights now."

From this point on, everything went forward in a dizzy rush. Hiller ordered me off to collect and ready Kurt. As I swung open the back door I heard him throwing himself into his highly coloured impersonation of a Madison Square Garden ring announcer.

"Tonight, from Kingdom Hall, Norman Hiller Productions presents the fight extravaganza of the century. The Collision of the Titans – ." The closing door had choked him off.

In the last half hour all the headlights had been extinguished, night had overtaken us, and the yard was thick with darkness. After the brightness of the hall, it was difficult to see. All I could make out was the car parked at the bottom of the steps, more solidly black than the blackness which lapped it. I cast my words into this blackness, like a line into a pool. "Kurt, they're almost ready for you." There was movement near the car, a wrinkling of the skin of night. Then Hop Jump proclaimed, "He's just finishing up losing his cookies. Be with you in a sec." I waited. My eyes were becoming more and more accustomed to the darkness, I could make out Murph and Hop Jump now, their pale shirts focusing whatever light the dim air contained. Then Kurt stood up behind the car, his nakedness a white ghostly blur. Back in the hall, the din was increasing, growing stronger, more frantic, more violent.

"Hurry up," I said. "It's time."

The three of them filed up the steps, Meinecke wiping at his mouth with the back of a glove. Striking a match I looked in his face. "Are you okay?" He nodded. "You're sure?" He nodded again. Even in the flare of the match his face had that dirty, grey-white colour that a sink in a public washroom acquires with time.

"All right," I said. "You know the drill. Let's do it right, just like Hiller wants it, just like we practised it."

They bumbled into place. Murph in front, Kurt in the middle with his hands on Murph's shoulders, Hop Jump behind him. I draped a towel over Meinecke's head, just the way Sonny Liston had worn his towels, so as to give his face a hooded, menacing look. Then I took up my position, point man, three steps ahead of the procession. From inside the hall we heard an overwhelming roar, Scutter's introduction was climaxing. I dodged catching Kurt's eye, stepped quickly to the door and opened it a crack so I didn't miss our cue. Norman's voice came drilling into the night, strident, straining to clamour above the bedlam it had incited.

"Please welcome, in the red trunks," he was shouting, "the challenger, your favourite and mine." I hustled into the hall, Murph and Meinecke and Hop Jump shuffling forward just the way Hiller had taught them, hands laid on the shoulders of the man in front, eyes lowered. "Kurt Meinecke!" Hiller screamed. "The Maaassster of Diiisssassster! The Maaaass-ster of Diisssassster!" And right on cue, also as rehearsed, Deke and Dooey began to chant at the top of their lungs, "MASTER! MASTER! MASTER!"

I flung myself into the melee, shoving and pushing, cleaving the pack for the three scuffling behind me in tandem. Ahead of me, Norman was hopping about the ring like a fiend, pounding the air with his fist, urging the crowd to join the chant. Here and there about the hall it was being taken up with a jokey, aimless excitement. "Master! Master!" they cried. And then more added their voices, on every side of us the crowd began to sway to the dull thunder of the refrain. "Master! Master! Master!" And there was Hiller, striding up and down the ring, grinning triumphantly, eyes glittering as he flourished his fist, whipping them into an even greater frenzy.

We fought through the crush and gained our corner.

Kurt seemed in a daze, a trance, he looked as if he scarcely knew where he was when Hiller took him by the wrist and led him like a child to the middle of the ring to be introduced to his opponent. Scutter had stripped off shirt, shoes and socks and was wearing only his pimples and blue jeans. While the referee stumblingly repeated what Norman had coached him to say, Scutter, who couldn't hold a cigarette with boxing gloves on his hands, kept jerking his head at his brother, signalling for a drag on his. Each time his brother held the butt to his mouth for a pull, Scutter inhaled deeply, then expelled the smoke in Meinecke's face with a thin-lipped smile.

Broward ended his little speech. "Let's have a good one, boys," he said.

"Yeah," Scutter said, "let's have a good one." Even from where I stood it was unnerving.

The preliminaries done, Hiller led Meinecke back to the corner and pushed him down into the chair to wait for the bell. "Get him loose," he said to me, gesturing impatiently. "Can't you see he's tight?" I proceeded to massage Kurt's neck. It was like kneading banjo strings.

"Okay," said Norman fiercely to Meinecke, "you know what to do. We've been over this like a thousand times. Scutter's a street fighter. How does a street fighter go?"

"He does a couple of dekes and then takes a run at you," said Meinecke reciting from memory. "He tries to knock you off your feet."

"And you go?" coaxed Hiller.

Meinecke didn't reply. He was staring across the ring where Scutter was cutting up, kicking out his bare feet right, left, right, left, as if he was booting somebody's knackers off. His supporters were falling all over themselves laughing.

"Are you fucking listening to me or not?" demanded Hiller.

Kurt looked up at him, bewildered.

"You go how?" repeated Norman. "How?"

"I cover up," said Kurt.

"That's right. Elbows in tight to the ribs, chin down on the wishbone, gloves up high like Floyd Patterson," said Hiller, illustrating. "Be a bomb shelter. No way that dink can hurt you. And don't hit back," Norman emphasized. "Not until I say. You hit back – what happens?"

"I open up the defence."

"Right. And peckerhead there puts your lights out. So remember our number one rule is – no hitting!"

The bell rang. Kurt stood like a zombie. "And don't forget – laugh at him. Cool Hand Luke the fucker," was Norman's last bit of advice.

It happened just the way Hiller said it would. Cocky Scutter grinning, feinting, pecking at Meinecke's gloves, skipping on his bare feet. Then the kamikaze rush. Meinecke ducking low to meet it. A storm of wild blows raining down on his back, his shoulders, uppercuts smacking into the forearms protecting his face, a punch skidding off the crown of his tipped skull. And then the fifteen-second flurry was spent and Scutter was left panting, momentarily winded.

Meinecke slowly straightened up, gingerly flexing his arms and revealing splotches of fiery red on his back and shoulders where he had been hit. There was an expression on his face I'd never seen before, a sort of puzzled exasperation, annoyance.

Norman was screaming his lungs out. "Defence! Defence!" A brief moment of hesitation, or regret, and then Kurt obediently lifted his gloves high and settled warily into the Floyd Patterson peekaboo crouch that Hiller had been coaching him in during the past week. For the remainder of the round he grimly and obediently followed Hiller's fight plan, stayed a punching bag. At first Scutter was wary and cautiously circled Meinecke, flicking out jabs which bounced off Kurt's forehead and bee-stung his ears. But realizing he had nothing to fear, Scutter went to work, throwing short, vicious hooks in behind the elbows (not quite kidney punches but close) which Kurt kept stubbornly pinned to his ribs the way Hiller had taught him. Every blow he absorbed screwed Meinecke's mouth a little more crooked, drew his eyes into tighter slits. He was paying a price.

Kurt's performance was not going down well with the

crowd. Their mood was changing, the chant of "Master! Master!" died away as disappointment seized them. Someone yelled "Fight!" and someone else, "Chickenshit!" When Dooey clanged on the pie plate to end the round, Kurt Meinecke's return to the corner was greeted, here and there, with boos.

Norman was all over him as soon as his ass dropped on the chair. "Goddamn it," he hissed, "you aren't Cool Handing him. Laugh at the fucker! Tease him! Tell him he hits like a homo! You're forgetting what I said. What'd I say? 'Ninety per cent of boxing is mental.' You're overlooking the mental. Laugh at him!"

"You can laugh at him," said Kurt, probing his rib cage with the thumb of his glove. "You got no idea how hard he hits."

Norman slapped the glove away. "Stop that!" he said. "He's watching you." It was true. Scutter was pointing in our direction and making smirking asides to his brother.

"Look at him," Kurt said, brooding. "Acts as if I'm nothing. Thinks he's so smart."

Dooey beat the pie plate. Norman caught Meinecke by the hairs on the nape of his neck as he was rising. "Remember," he said, tugging them for emphasis, "Cool Hand Luke him. And no hitting back! I'm warning you, Meinecke, no hitting!"

For the next three rounds Kurt did exactly as he was told. There was plenty of hitting and none of it was done by him. When Scutter did his ham-handed Ali imitations, dancing circles around Meinecke, inviting attack, parading and flaunting his jaw within easy range of the Master of Disaster who inexplicably declined to strike, this incited the bloodthirsty mob into more taunts and jeers, the cue for Scutter to stop dead in his tracks and pepper Meinecke with a storm of punches.

Each time Kurt came back to the corner, he added another injury to the catalogue, a mouse swelling under the left eye, a cut inside the mouth that kept him drooling pink saliva into the plastic bucket, a raw lace scrape on the side of the neck, knots and eggs popping up all over his head.

It was the humiliation that worked the change in him. He began to beg, really beg Hiller to let him hit back. Kurt had always been so mild, nice was maybe the word for him, that I would never have guessed he had the stuff in him to hate. But the look on his face told me he'd found it, or, rather, Hiller had found it for him. He was like one of those neglected dogs tied in a backyard which you know has taken one kick too many and wants to sink its teeth into somebody. Kurt wanted a bite, too, but Hiller wouldn't give it to him. He kept telling him to do what he was told, stick to the plan, and Meinecke kept asking when, when, when do I get to hit him?

By the end of the seventh round Meinecke was in bad shape, blood leaking out of both nostrils, an eye swollen shut, a split lip. I put my mouth to his ear and said, "Get it over, Kurt. Next time he hits you – drop. Fuck this noise."

"I got to get my chance. All of them laughing at me. It isn't that I don't *want* to hit him. If Norman would just let me hit him. When Norman says – then look out." He was staring across the ring at Scutter.

Norman shoved me roughly to one side. "How many fucking times I got to say it!" he shouted at Meinecke. "You're supposed to be lipping him and you stand there like a goddamn dummy! Yap at him! Tell him he's a pussy! Do something!"

"I can't. I get mixed up. It's the noise. I can't remember what I'm supposed to say," Meinecke said, on the verge of tears. "Just let me hit him, Norman."

"You got to earn the right to hit him," said Hiller. "I want you to be professional. You think I invested all this time in you so's you can go out there and make me look like a loser? You get him mad, really mad, I'll let you hit him. For Christ's sake we got a plan here." He paused. "Be a fucking man, Meinecke."

Meinecke went out and took another battering. He stood there with his gloves up, elbows clamped down hard on his ribs, chin ducked into his chest, and took his beating. Wobbling and staggering, he took it. He was flinching now before he was even hit, out of fear of being hit. But he didn't try to run from it. And when the bell rang and Scutter turned to stalk back to his corner he tried more. There he stood with his arms hanging helplessly at his sides, his mouth working. I knew what he was doing. He was trying to take hold of those things that Hiller wanted him to say and fling them after Scutter, but his rage and his shame were obstacles to his finding them. Or perhaps he didn't have mean, dirty taunts in him, only blind, suffocating rage. He stuttered, he stammered. "Yyy-ou," he said. "Yyy-ou ..." But it was useless, hopeless. The crowd was whooping and caterwauling. "Pardon me?" they shouted. "Come again?" "Take a seat, harelip!"

Defeated, he blundered back to the rest of The Magnificent Seven in conference in his corner. Norman was not sympathetic. "I couldn't believe my ears," he said. "Who holds your fucking hand when you cross the street, Meinecke?" Kurt didn't say anything. He dropped on the chair and covered his face with the gloves. I could only guess what was going on behind them. The sight of Meinecke sitting there with his face covered was quieting the hall.

Norman exploited the hush for his own purposes. "Hey," I heard him shout across the ring to Scutter. "Meinecke says for you to pull all the stops out. Either that or get a dress. He says you're a pussy puncher, Scutter! And he eats pussy!"

Scutter squinted, the mask of acne darkened. "Yeah?" he shouted back. "Yeah?"

"Fucking right." Hiller poked Meinecke. "Do I speak the truth, or do I speak the truth? Is that pussy over there, or is that pussy over there?" Meinecke slowly raised his face from his gloves. He scanned the hall with glazed eyes. "Pussy," he said in a quiet, muffled voice.

Hiller cupped his hand behind his ear. "What's that? I'm not getting that."

"Pussy," Meinecke said, loudly this time. "Definitely pussy."

"You heard it from the horse's mouth," shouted Hiller. "Go home and put a rag on, Scutter. Get ready to bleed."

"That flabby fuck is dead," Scutter said. "Right where he sits he's dead."

But Hiller wasn't listening. Already he was squatting down directly before Meinecke, hands on his fighter's knees, looking up into his face, speaking urgently. "Listen, he's mad. We got him mad. The bell goes, he's going to take a run at you. Just like round one. Take four steps into the ring and then wait. Wait for him. He's coming on, he's coming on hard, and you cold cock him. Same as hitting the heavy bag. Same punch. He's bowling in, he doesn't expect nothing, and you stiff him. Understand?"

"You mean hit him?" Kurt asked. He didn't seem to understand he was finally getting the green light.

"Not *hit* him," said Norman. "*Kill* the fucker."

Meinecke thudded his gloves together. He'd got it.

I was holding my breath. I let it out when Dooey clanged the pie plate. Scutter was coming in, hard. Kurt stopped, braced himself per instructions, swung. Swung like he'd done a thousand times at the heavy bag, one of those economical, sweet punches with the hip and the shoulder behind it and something added to the physics of it – pure hate. All that and Scutter collided right in front of my eyes. I heard a sound like knuckles cracking, saw a head snapping back, the whites of eyes flashing as they rolled in their sockets, heels skittering, and down he went, head bouncing off the floor with a leaden clunk.

You could have heard a pin drop. Scutter rolled over, got his hands and knees under him. Dark red drops of blood splashed onto the floor from his nose, swept back and forth in a fine spray when he shook his head, trying to clear it.

"Count! Count, fuck face!" Norman screamed at Broward. He did. The first two numbers into a stunned silence; the next two into the kind of hysterical uproar occasioned by the death of one god and the birth of another. At five, Scutter began to creep about on all fours like some old blind dog trying to find the scent home. He crawled over to Broward's legs, clutched one, and shakily started to pull himself up.

Scutter was reeling, one arm clasped around Broward's waist, when Meinecke stepped in and chopped two hard, desperate blows into his temple, sending him crashing. It didn't quite stop there either. The Master of Disaster, sobbing uncontrollably, kept pounding Scutter where he lay on the floor until Broward, Hiller, and me managed to drag him off.

For months afterward Hiller told and retold the story of how he had engineered the greatest upset in boxing history since Cassius Clay whipped Sonny Liston.

"I trained him perfect," he'd say. "I brought him along just so. As soon as I seen him hit the heavy bag, well, there was no question but he could hit. The problem was making him *want* to hit. Fucking guy was too nice for his own good. So I took the mental approach because if he seen the damage he could do hitting somebody – he wouldn't want to hit people any more. That's where Hop Jump came in. Somebody to dance the night away with because no way, Jose, was Hop Jump going to let himself get hit.

"Scutter I was worried about. For him I designed the Cool Hand Luke defence. After a couple of rounds of that, Scutter figured he didn't have nothing to worry about. And Meinecke – the pounding he was taking – that had to get to him, that had to piss him off. And everybody laughing at him, that twisted him, and me sitting on him, not letting him hit, that twisted him more. Psychology. He had to blow. I loaded him, I cocked him, I pulled the trigger."

Kurt was never the same guy after the fight. Deke, Hop Jump, Murph, everybody in Hiller's gang began to notice that he was avoiding them. He avoided me too. No more long conversations late at night after the pool room closed down, walking those empty streets and talking about how, just around the corner, things were going to fall into place for us. When we ran into each other, we nodded, said a few words about nothing, and then edged away from each other like people who share a secret they would sooner forget.

There were other changes. His hair grew longer. He quit the football team, didn't bother to go out for wrestling. He began to hang around with strange types, two or three assholes who had published poems in the yearbook about Vietnam and babies crying in Watts. Deke said he had heard that Meinecke was taking acoustic guitar lessons. Hiller said, "Fuck him. You can drag a person up to your level but if they don't make an effort they'll sink back to where they naturally belong." Meinecke and his new friends cut a lot of classes and spent afternoons at the house of a girl whose mother worked, listening to records, smoking grass. Finally, with only three months of school to go before graduation, Kurt dropped out.

The last that was seen of Kurt Meinecke he was standing at the edge of the highway at five o'clock on a Sunday morning with his thumb stuck out. When those that had spotted him passed that way again a few hours later, he was gone.

Ray

IT WAS RAY'S WIFE WHO WAS responsible for planting in him the notion that something had been askew in his childhood, wrong in his upbringing. He didn't want to believe this was true and Pam's persistence in claiming it was led to their first fight as a married couple.

"What about the train and the cards and all that?" she said. "You can't seriously suggest there was anything the least normal about that." He wasn't sure what his young wife meant. He had told Pam the anecdote intending to amuse her, but she had taken it all wrong.

Ray's story concerned the year he was ten. It was 1961 and his father was building a rec room in the basement. Just then rec rooms were all the rage, everybody on the block had one, or was building one, and his father didn't want to be left behind. That was the kind of man Ray's father was, always worried that somebody was stealing a march on him. Every night he came home from the mine where he was a shift captain underground, ate his supper hurriedly, without a hint of relish or appreciation, and then plunged downstairs into the basement to continue with his improvements. Only many years later did it strike Ray that his father had seen scarcely more than a few minutes of sun all that autumn. If he wasn't deep beneath the earth ripping out potash, he was down in his basement playing handyman in the artificial glare of a naked light bulb.

Most evenings Ray crept down the stairs after his Dad and put himself quietly in an out of the way corner to watch him renovate, an awkward boy with embarrassingly heavy thighs, plump behind, and a mild, trusting face that led his teachers to smile at his infrequent, small misdemeanours and always think the best of him. Ray resembled his mother but it was his father he admired. In particular he admired the way his father looked, strong, lean, and rangy like the cowboys on his favourite television shows. Like those cowboys, his father seldom spoke and was inclined to stare away questions rather than answer them. Ray didn't ever ask him much, although by nature he was a curious boy. He would have liked to have been let in on the secrets of construction, to have understood how his father commanded and directed water and electricity to do his bidding, but he knew better than to make himself a bother and risk getting sent upstairs. Usually his father neglected to notice that Ray was even in the room with him, although once or twice in the course of an evening he would summon him to perform some simple task, to hold the end of a tape measure, to pass nails, to sweep sawdust. These rare occasions justified Ray's announcing to the kids on his street: "Me and my Dad are building a rec room. We want to get it done by Christmas, for the parties. It's an awful lot of work."

Ray was agog with excitement over the anticipated Christmas parties. His family had not been in this particular town long, had never been in any town long because the nature of his father's profession kept them moving. An ore body played out, the bottom dropped out of a metal market, his father wrangled with a foreman, and the family pulled up stakes and moved on. For young Ray, the building of a rec room promised changes, the introduction of gaiety and permanence in their lives.

In the past Ray had heard his mother speak of a time when she and his father had "entertained." Whenever she talked about this his father stared at her, unblinking, until she stopped. If there ever had been such a time it went back far beyond Ray's recollection, back perhaps to when his brother Kenny was still alive. Ray understood, without resentment, that he was some sort of replacement for this dead brother. When he was six he overheard his mother say to a neighbour lady, "We just had to have another baby as soon as possible. It's the only way Ted could have got over it." And then she added, as an afterthought, "I felt the same way, of course." It always gave Ray a queer, unsettled feeling to think that he, too, might die one day and his place be usurped by a shadowy, unimaginable brother waiting patiently for his chance, in the wings.

By the end of October work on the rec room neared completion. Unlike anyone else who renovated, Ray's father had refused to invite the neighbour men over to drink beer and help. He said most of them couldn't be trusted to do the simplest job properly. He knew that much from watching them operate at the mine. Let them waste the company's time, not his.

Ted Matthews was a perfectionist, it was the word his wife relied on to describe him to strangers. The walls of imitation walnut panelling lining the recreation room were seamlessly fitted. There was tile laid on the cement floor and carpeting on top of the tile so that the cold wouldn't rise up in the winter and numb the soles of your feet like it did in so many other houses where people didn't care to do things right. At the end of the long, narrow room his father installed a wet bar and a second-hand fridge to keep beer and soft drinks cold. The refrigerator was the only item second hand. The chesterfield, the half-dozen wicker chairs, the pole lamp bought at the Saan Store mightn't be of the highest quality but they were new and not the junk and cast-offs which other people tried to pass off as furniture, stuff you looked twice at before you sat down on.

The only thing left to be done was run track for the railway. The railway was the crowning touch to the rec room, a bit of ingenious engineering that would allow Ray's father to speed drinks directly to his guests without ever having to step from behind the bar. It ran the length of the room, supported on brackets screwed into the wall panelling.

"What'll they think of that?" Ted kept demanding of his wife and son.

Ray was convinced his dad had to be just about the smartest dad in the world to come up with such a plan. Yet there was something about the railway he didn't completely understand. Several years before, Ray had been rooting around in his parents' closet and he had discovered track, a selection of railway cars, and a wonderful black locomotive packed away in a cardboard box. But when his father found him playing with it, Ray got the worst licking of his life, with an extension cord. His mother, trying to explain why to him later, said that because the train set had been Kenny's favourite toy his father couldn't bear the thought of it getting broken. "He wants to keep it just as your brother left it," she said. "That's why it must never be played with." Ray had accepted that, the way he accepted everything concerning his father. But now he was bewildered. What had changed, making it all right to use the train set?

The approach of the Christmas party not only got Ray excited, it got his mother all a-flutter too. Packing one-gallon ice-cream containers with homemade Nuts 'N Bolts to be frozen for the party one afternoon, she began to happily reminisce about his brother. "Kenny was such a people person," she said. "Your brother just loved people. When we entertained I used to put him to bed early but there was no way of keeping him there. Out he'd come in his pyjamas and start passing around the peanuts or whatever to the guests. He was so polite and cute. Everybody loved to see him playing the little host. He was definitely a people person, your brother Kenny."

The last week of November arrived and Ray's mother asked his father for a guest list. He said he was thinking on it.

During the first week of December she warned him that it was getting late, he'd better make up his mind soon. He said he'd make up his mind when he was good and goddamn ready to make it up and not before. Anyway it was a christly hoax, Christmas and the whole chiselling season.

"Now why do you say things like that?" Ray's mother asked. "Don't you remember how you used to enjoy Christmas? The parties we used to have?"

"Shut up about the parties we used to have!" his father cried.

One evening in mid-December his parents had a fight at the supper table. Ray's mother said, "If you don't want to have a party just say so. If that's the case I won't bother knocking myself out getting all the stuff ready for something that isn't going to happen, the food, the decorations, the rest of it." Ray had never seen her look as she did then, wild, barely in control of herself.

His father didn't trouble to answer her. He just stared at her across the table.

"Don't you give me that look of yours," she said. "Give me an answer. Are we having the party? Yes or no?"

"No," he said. "We aren't."

"And why not?" she cried. "After all these years, why not? What would be wrong with a party? What harm would there be in it?"

"It wouldn't be right," his father said. "That's all."

Then his mother did something Ray would never have dreamed she would do. She got up from the table and put on her coat and scarf, leaving the scattered dirty dishes, the left-over pork roast just as they were.

"Where do you think you're going?" his father demanded.

"Out. To a movie," she said.

"Well you aren't taking the car," he said. "It's blizzarding out there and I've got no intention of paying for a tow truck to pull you out when you get yourself stuck."

"I'll walk," she said, slamming the door behind her.

His father sat without twitching a muscle and Ray did likewise. Neither looked at the other. Then his father slowly pushed back his chair from the table, stood, and walked out of the kitchen. Ray heard feet on the stairs and knew that his father was going down to the rec room.

Ray wasn't sure how to behave. Nothing like this had ever happened before. The unusual sight of food abandoned on the table frightened him, as did the sound of the wind, suddenly loud in the quiet kitchen. He got up and tiptoed after his father.

Ray found his dad sitting on one of the wicker Saan Store chairs. His father lifted his eyes from the floor and arrested Ray in the doorway with his gaze, held him there for several seconds, then nodded permission to enter. Ray ducked into the room and scurried to a chair across from his father.

"I guess you and me are bachelor boys for the night," his father said.

"I guess," said Ray.

"I don't forget how it used to be. I don't forget as easy as all that," said his father. "Piss on parties and piss on people who have to have them."

"Yeah," agreed Ray.

His father lit a cigarette, flourished the dead match at him. "There's ashtrays behind the bar," he said to Ray. "Be a good boy and fetch me one."

No sooner had Ray gained the bar than his father came up with a better idea. "Hey," he called, "ship it down on the train. And while you're at it, put a rye and coke on the freight." He paused to glance at his wristwatch. "Put a rye and Coke on the 7:17 and we'll baptize the son of a bitch. We'll make a wet run."

Ray could scarcely credit the honour being done him, his rare good fortune. He wedged the ashtray securely in a coal car, balanced the tumbler of whisky on a flat car, and sent the train swaying cautiously down the line. When his father offloaded the freight, Engineer Ray backed up the train to the station at the bar. A dime lay on the flat car which had borne the whisky. His father saluted him with glass lifted high. "A lesson for later life," he shouted from down the room. "Always tip the bartender and you'll get what you want, when you want it. Remember that, Ray. Now mix me a vodka and orange juice, plenty of ice."

To be privileged to run his brother's train and serve his father was all Ray could ask for. Because Ted Matthews sat in the farthest corner of the room, isolated in the light of the pole lamp, it appeared, by a trick of perspective, that the train had to traverse a great distance to reach him. For an hour the locomotive crossed and recrossed this daunting span without mishap or incident, exchanging drinks for pocket change and empty glasses.

With four or five belts in him, Ted grew increasingly talkative and noisy, addressing Ray in an unusually loud voice. "You're all right, Ray," he said. "You may look like your mother but you think like me. So you can't be all bad, you goddamn little fifty-per-center, can you? I still had something left over after making Kenny, didn't I?"

"Sure," said Ray, laughing at the funny things his father said. He was settling the next drink, vodka and tomato juice, on the train with great care. His father hadn't requested the same drink twice.

"You've got a good heart, Ray," his father said. He attempted to pluck the Bloody Mary from the train before it came to a full stop and slopped a little of it on his wrist. "But you're not all that likeable. If I had one bit of advice to give you, it's this – work on your personality. Being good doesn't take you very far in this world."

Ray nervously bobbed his head.

"And always look both ways, twice, before crossing the road, and up, once, in case anything's falling out of the sky."

Ray laughed at this but his father sternly said, "Be serious. I'm giving you serious advice here."

So Ray composed a serious face and listened closely to all

the advice his father started to expound. He must never marry a woman who dyed her hair and he must make sure to keep insurance policies in a safety deposit box. If he ever needed a lawyer, hire a Jew. Last of all, avoid leukaemia. "That was your brother's biggest mistake," he said. "He caught leukaemia and it killed him, the dumb little fuck."

Having emptied himself of advice, his father relapsed into his customary stony silence. When Ray persisted in trying to talk to him, his father curtly ordered him to scare up some cards. Drunk as he was, he cleaned Ray out of his tips. When Ray had no more money to play, that was the finish of blackjack. "Money talks and bullshit walks," was all his father would say. Ray was disappointed – not over the money – but because losing the money brought an end to this momentous evening. His father abruptly got to his feet, stumbled up the stairs, and fell into bed drunk.

The next day his mother cleared the supper dishes and did not go out to a movie as Ray hoped she would. His father offered him no more advice. The railway disappeared mysteriously from the rec room, although the screw holes were there in the wall for Ray, a doubting Thomas, to touch with his fingers.

Years later, Ray was convinced that the best explanation of himself he could ever give his new wife was hidden in the events of that evening. Yet when he attempted to relate the story he could not find the words to express how rich, how moving that strange memory was for him. Losing his nerve, he offered a trivial version which he struggled to make hilarious. A small boy milked his father for pocket money by running drinks to him on a preposterous toy train and then got his comeuppance by losing it all in a card game.

Pam's harsh reaction to his story surprised him. She didn't find it funny at all. The word she used was "sick."

"What's sick about it?" Ray wanted to know.

"For starters, what man in his right mind would insist that his kid play bartender and make him a witness to such a sickening spectacle? And what about winning all your money back and keeping it? That sounds to me like a pretty cruel thing to do to a ten year old."

Ray disputed all this, which was unusual. He seldom disputed anything Pam said. He hated disagreements.

"If you ask me, Ray," Pam said, "your father has never treated you very well."

"Why do you say that?"

"You're not a very good reader of human nature, are you?" snapped Pam.

Ray supposed he wasn't. People were always seeing subtly shaded motives where he only saw black and white. Maybe when it came to judging people he suffered from something akin to colour blindness. Living in the university-student residence he had been everybody's favourite mark, continually beset by practical jokers, borrowers and plagiarists begging for a peek at his assignments. He was always taken in.

Nevertheless, he instinctively avoided any of those subjects (philosophy, psychology, sociology) which purported to grapple with the puzzle of human behaviour. A modest talent with numbers saw him safely through the College of Commerce, although the compulsory first-year English course was a close shave, throwing him utterly at sea whenever the complicated motives and actions of bizarre characters were confidently probed and analyzed. Ray never forgot one of the questions on his first English quiz. The professor wanted to know why it was significant that the rescue boat in *Lord of the Flies* was a warship. Ray couldn't detect any significance unless it was that the navy was the logical branch of the armed forces to effect a rescue at sea, rather than, say, the army. So that was what he had answered. But that wasn't right. No, the significance lay in the irony of the boys being saved by a warship, symbol of the murderous impulses responsible for crashing them on the island in the first place, and of the murderous impulses which destroyed their idyllic paradise. Of course, once it was all explained, Ray grasped the professor's point. And all along he thought Mr. Golding only wanted him to feel sorry for poor Piggy.

Although stubbornly defending his father against Pam's charges, an irritating speck of uneasiness was introduced. He could not deny he had been wrong about this or that person before. Yet when Pam drew unflattering comparisons between his and *her* father, Ray couldn't help feeling it was unfair, like comparing apples with oranges. One was khaki work clothes. The other, white shirt and tie. A prosperous businessman could pet, indulge, and dote upon a beloved daughter. Boys needed a different preparation for the world. Maybe his father kept the money won in the card game not out of any meanness, but to teach Ray a useful lesson about the world. That was all.

If criticism of his father had come from anyone but Pam, it's likely Ray would have shrugged it off. But he genuinely admired his wife (perhaps even more than he did his father) and found it difficult to dismiss any of her opinions. Ray was convinced of her superiority to him in every respect.

It was this capacity for admiration that had brought Ray and his wife together in the first place. The daughter of the Ford-Mercury dealer, and mayor of a town of 800, meant Pam was small-town royalty, raised with the conviction that she was special. And it could not be denied that she was a reasonably attractive, reasonably intelligent young lady. Unlike other girls in town, Pam's hair was permed regularly at the beauty parlour, her dresses purchased in the city instead of from the catalogue, and she drove her own car, a 1965 Ford LTD convertible. The car alone would have made her somebody special.

In such a tiny parish, with its limited pool of talent, she passed for extraordinary. Pam was the perennial female lead in the Drama Society's productions, she sang the solos in the Glee Club, and played clarinet in the school band. Three times she was crowned Snow Queen at the Winter Carnival and it would have been four if there hadn't been a stupid rule against freshies competing. Her senior year she was unanimously chosen class valedictorian, as she knew she would be. Pam Ferguson was the planet around which her satellites gratefully arranged their orbits.

University had come as a dreadful shock to her. Suddenly she found herself demoted to ordinary. The professors did not listen respectfully to her opinions in class the way her high-school teachers had, and the boys favoured her with perfunctory attentions. In residence, on her floor alone, there were two girls better dressed than she was. At the end of two months, Pam was so desperately unhappy that she seriously considered returning home to let her father arrange a job for her in the local bank.

Then an acquaintance took her to a house party. Within an hour of arriving, the acquaintance was picked up by an engineering student and disappeared, leaving Pam to fend for herself. As she ranged through rooms plugged with strangers, looking for a familiar face, Pam bumped into a shy-looking boy with a gentle voice. This was Ray and he swiftly put Pam at ease by appreciating her the way she was used to being appreciated. In no time at all she confided to Ray her father's foolish insistence that all her Best Actress trophies be lined up on the mantel for the whole world to see. It was so embarrassing! He was also treated to a blow by blow account of her troubles editing the high-school year book. The evening flew by for both of them.

There was nothing much attractive about Ray. His rear end was still too big, his thighs too plump, and his face too innocent to be appealing to any woman under the age of forty. But his fervent devotion outweighed these handicaps and gave Pam a new lease on life. She found it possible to continue. They dated through all four years of university, although several times Pam broke it off. On each of these occasions Ray begged her to take him back and she consented – without Ray she felt common, plain, neglected. A month after they graduated Ray landed a job as a government accountant and she agreed to marry him.

Pam harboured ill will against her father-in-law from the start. The size of the cheque he presented as a wedding gift struck her as insulting. Added to that there was the annoyance of Ray having to repay a student loan.

"Why is it that your father didn't help you through university?" she asked Ray one day.

"Why?" Ray said. "Because he hasn't any money. He's just a working stiff."

"But I thought you mentioned he bought his R.V. while you were going to school."

"I guess he did," said Ray.

"It's nice he had his priorities straight," said Pam.

Ray began to wonder if there mightn't be something to what Pam said. He became less eager to phone his parents long distance when Pam called attention to the fact that it was Ray who always called, never his dad. Other sore spots developed. When Ray got a promotion after three years of work with the government he looked forward to impressing his father with the news. The old man interrupted him in mid-sentence and commenced his own story about how an expensive piece of machinery had been wrecked by the carelessness of a young miner. "The young ones are no damn good," he concluded. "I'm sure it's the same in your business." Ray would never have stopped to think that he, too, qualified as a "young one" if Pam hadn't pointed it out to him.

These insights of his wife's sometimes made him sad, but Ray was not a man inclined to dwell on the gloomy side of life; he consoled himself with his good fortune in having a woman like Pam to love. It was true that life was not always a bed of roses with Pam, she sometimes caught the blues and Ray had to do his cheerful best to raise her sinking spirits or keep her from turning sour. When she complained that her anthropology degree made her unemployable, condemned her to housewifery, Ray suggested perhaps she would like to return to school. When she charged six years of marriage with causing her to gain forty pounds, Ray assured her that she was every bit as beautiful and desirable as she had ever been.

"Can't you see how upsetting it is to me?" she would scream at him. "I'm not beautiful. I'm fat. You only say I'm beautiful so you won't have to talk about my problems with me. You're just like your father, Ray. You don't care about anybody but yourself. You'd tell me anything in the hope it would shut me up. You're selfish and uncaring – just like him."

It had been hard for Ray to accept Pam's view of his father but now that he did, he felt no hatred for him. Instead, he felt an odd shame, like the man who discovers he has been invited to a party because there was no way of *not* inviting him. As much for his father's sake as his own, Ray began to avoid him.

Shortly after Ray and Pam celebrated their seventh wedding anniversary, steering clear of his father became easier. His parents, two old gypsies, moved again, to Pine Point in the Northwest Territories. The distance between them, a distance compounded by bad roads and the horrors of winter driving, gave Ray a plausible excuse for paying fewer visits. This was a satisfactory solution for a time, then Ray began to be plagued by mysterious premonitions of a disaster about to befall his father. As a small boy, he had known children whose fathers or brothers had been killed in mine accidents, and the possibility that one day the mine would slay or maim his father had always been there. Now it came forward and took possession of him. He imagined electrocutions, catastrophic explosions, cave-ins, entanglements with machinery. Whenever the imagined scenes became too real, too horrific, he would phone Pine Point. If he got his mother, he would speak. If his father answered, he simply hung up, comforted to know he was all right. Pam began to question him about the phone bill. "Five calls to Pine Point in two weeks? Why Ray?"

Two years after his parents moved north, the news Ray had been dreading broke. It didn't matter that his father wasn't killed in an accident at the mine but had drowned in a boating mishap, Ray couldn't shake the guilty feeling that somehow his dark reveries had dragged his poor father down through fathoms of icy water to his death.

Pam reminded Ray that life goes on and waits for no man. That he was responsible for managing his loss. But every time Ray made a step in that direction he suffered cruel setbacks. The worst was his mother's treachery. He encouraged her to move south after the funeral but she refused. The beauty of the north was in her blood, she said, Pine Point was home, she was perfectly happy where she was and knew her own mind, thank you very much. Not long after the first anniversary of his father's drowning Ray discovered what had really got into his mother's blood – a mechanic at the mine. In a tremulously defiant voice, she told Ray over the telephone that she and this man were getting married. Ray was not a person to be rude and cutting to anyone, let alone his own mother. But he was shocked and hurt by what she was doing – for his father's sake.

According to Pam he was acting like a child. "If you ask me," she said, "you ought to be glad your mother is getting married. At least she has someone to look after her and save you the worry. Besides, everyone deserves a chance at happiness."

Ray demanded to know what that was supposed to mean.

"Oh, nothing. Except that you never really saw how it was with your parents. You know, your mother was never happy with him."

"What do you know about it?" said Ray, using a peevish tone of voice Pam seldom heard.

"I know habit is only habit. It isn't love."

Ray credited two things – Pam and the grind of his professional life – with keeping him in balance. He was thankful for both. For nine years he had worked in government service, slowly and steadily riding a wave of modest promotions. There was no man better suited to the task he was called upon to perform than Ray; his unflinching doggedness and diligence were bywords in the office. The most recalcitrant accounting foul-ups were turned over to him to solve, tough nuts that never yielded to a single blow but only the most persistent knocking and rapping. He worked calmly and methodically on all problems, often remaining at his desk long after he had cheerfully waved his colleagues out the door. He did not begrudge the extra hours in the least, except for the inconvenience they caused his wife. To make up for this, Ray was always ready with small gifts, flowers, and dinners out in expensive restaurants.

It was at Ray's prompting that Pam renewed an old interest from high-school days and joined an amateur theatre group. To Ray's delight, his wife came to life, seemed happier than ever before. She enjoyed her new circle of friends and even shed twenty-five pounds so that she could get a crack at better parts. As she said to Ray, "It's difficult to play Blanche Du Bois tipping the scales at one-sixty."

What particularly gladdened Ray's heart was the revelation that his wife could really act. Of course, he didn't rely on his taste to come to this conclusion, Ray realized that he didn't know beans about good acting. But from the way she was treated at cast parties, or at the readings sometimes held in the living room of their home, he could see that everyone respected Pam, even deferred to her. She was on her way to becoming a star in the small world of local theatre. Now it seemed she was out more evenings than he was himself, always at rehearsals, attending productions of the local professional company, or taking part in something curiously called workshops. Her happiness was proclaimed by a more flamboyant style of dress and the variety of accents in which she spoke to him, English, Irish, even German. When she said she was on her way to becoming a new person, Ray could well believe it. Sometimes he didn't know her himself.

Then she got her break, the artistic director of the city's one professional company offered her a role. It was a small part, the nurse in *Equus*, but for the first time in her life Pam would be paid to act. *Equus* played for two weeks, and during the course of the run, Ray attended four performances. He joked to the other accountants that if he went to all fourteen, he still wouldn't know what the play was supposed to be about, he was that dense.

At the end of those two weeks, Pam left him. Ray came home late from work and found a fat envelope resting on the kitchen table with his name on it. The long letter inside explained that it had nothing to do with him and everything to do with her. The last two months of auditions, rehearsals, and the show itself had been a process of awakening from an interminable, dreary sleep. At last she knew what she must do with her life. She must act.

What was important for Ray to understand was that this was nobody's fault. Their marriage had been doomed from the beginning because it had linked two incompatible natures, the practical and the artistic. Only the suppression and denial of her true, artistic nature had permitted the marriage to survive. She did not blame Ray that this relationship had nurtured him while she withered like a plant denied light and water, nothing was to be gained from finger pointing. But now they must go their separate ways. The cruellest thing he could do would be to try to dissuade her from "following her bliss." There was more in the letter, dealing with the practical matters that were supposed to be his specialty. Pam had withdrawn half of the money held in their joint account and suggested that the house be sold as soon as possible so the proceeds could be divided. She could not see him but he must promise to take care of himself.

Ray took this badly but also, as was his habit, very quietly. In private he sometimes grew frantic, turning this way and that in his mind, seeking a way out, but his gaze always came to rest on a blank wall. When he studied a column of figures or read a newspaper or made himself a meal in the tiny bachelor apartment he rented after the house was sold, the wall was there, forcing its blankness upon him. Ray's face grew haggard and grey from twisting his neck in a futile effort to see beyond and behind the wall, to wherever Pam had gone. In time, this failure turned his stare apathetic and rubbed the innocence out of his face.

Nobody knew his wife had left him. If he had a friend, Ray would not likely have said anything to him anyway, because he could not believe this was happening to him. He would get Pam back. People in the office saw very well what was happening to him, that he was losing weight and making mistakes at his work that no one would have believed Ray Matthews capable of. Most of all, they noted the haunting change in his face.

When things were at their worst, he heard Pam's voice in the kitchen one morning when he was shaving. It was months since he had seen or heard her and the sound of her voice made him shake so violently that he had to lay his razor down so as not to slash himself. Then it came to him what it was. Pam hadn't come home to him. She was being interviewed on the local CBC morning radio show.

Ray stood absolutely still, intent, and as he listened to the disembodied voice of his wife, something strange began to happen. He heard the electrical whir and chatter of wheels speeding over flimsy rails, the clink of ice rocking against the sides of a tumbler, his father shouting funny things to him in a raw voice, the laughter of a small boy who could not guess or imagine the harsh territory his father had crossed to find himself standing where he stood that night. Ray could guess now, having been on a similar journey, now completed.

Pam's voice returned from the other room, talking about some man called Ibsen. Over all the months of separation her voice had changed, or his way of hearing it had. Coming out of the void, how false, how insincere it sounded, how *actressy.* It struck Ray that the owner of such a voice might not know all there was to know. Something more *had* passed between him and his father, borne on his dead brother's train, than a mere exchange of drinks and loose change. What, was for him to decide.

With that thought, Ray picked up his razor and set about uncovering his face.

New Houses

1957 WAS THE YEAR the Americans arrived. The men came first, engineers, accountants, managers, shift captains to organize and oversee the construction of the mine. Their wives and children would follow later, when proper, suitable houses had been built for them.

Del Cutter, his wife Marge, and their son Sammy were the Americans' closest neighbours and saw all of it, from the beginning. In the time before the Company, an open field had faced the Cutter place, a three-room house sided in imitation brick they had lived in ever since Sammy was born. Then the Company bought the field opposite for a housing site, earth-moving equipment roared and rumbled, tracing roads, crescents, bays. Next the water mains were laid. By June the basements were dug and the old pasture where Sammy had wandered about collecting burrs and fox tails in his socks was dotted with heaps of brown earth thrown up by the excavations. Concrete for the basements was poured and the carpenters started framing the houses. The shriek of power-saws, the hammering, the shouting of men back and forth went on for as long as there was summer light to work by. Only on Sundays was the site deserted and quiet. Sundays, the Cutter family crossed the road to admire the new houses.

They would walk the hard-packed dirt roads and gaze at the Americans' houses, split levels and ranch-style bungalows mostly, the kind of houses their owners had grown accustomed to in New Mexico and Texas. Time after time Sammy's mother would halt dead in the middle of the road, shade her eyes with her hand and stand motionless, staring at the unroofed frame through which the sun could be seen sinking, burning between the ribs of the skeleton house like a fiery heart. Then she would fold her arms underneath her breasts and walk on to the next house like a woman moving from picture to picture in a gallery, deep in contemplation.

On these outings Sammy sensed something strange in the air. He couldn't put a name to it but the feeling was like the happy expectancy that came with waiting for Christmas. Perplexed by his excitement, he ran about, showing off, scrambling up the big piles of dirt, screaming "I'm the king of the castle," then crazily tearing down, arms pinwheeling, an avalanche of clods and stones bouncing at his heels. Or he'd quietly burrow his hands into the sand which was dumped in driveways to be used for mixing concrete, working his fingers past the dry, hot crust, deeper and deeper until the sand grew cool and surprisingly moist to the touch. And whether he was noisy or silent, his mother paid him not the slightest attention, but walked the raw, empty streets as if she were half-asleep. Sometimes she asked his father questions.

"When do you think they'll come?"

"Who?"

"The Americans."

Her husband always squinted his eyes when considering a question, in the fashion of country people. "Beats me," he said.

Not until they had gone up and down each street once, sometimes twice, did they turn back to their own house and beds.

What people said was that Del Cutter was a hard man to figure. He was a dandy worker but it didn't do him much good because he never took go-ahead jobs. Winters he was the caretaker at the rink and an acknowledged wizard at pebbling a sheet of curling ice, none better. But almost any job would have paid more than caretaker at the rink. Summers he mostly worked out on farms. If a farmer got behind with his seeding, or fencing, or summer fallowing, Del Cutter was there to give him a week's worth of solid work before moving on to the next man who needed a hand. But it was the same thing all over again. It didn't pay. Still, Del never complained. The job at the rink suited him because there was nobody over him there; he was his own boss. And the way he worked summers suited him because with so many bosses he could always tell one to go fuck himself if he felt like it. Cutter was a proud, hot, touchy sort. He preferred not being tied to any one man's pleasure or displeasure. Don't put all your eggs in one basket was how he reasoned.

One morning, up early to get a few poplar sticks from the wood pile to kindle the breakfast fire in the woodstove, Marge Cutter paused and studied the men outlined against the cloudless blue sky, roofing the houses. Later in the day, while pumping water at the well to do her laundry, she overran the bucket and soaked her shoes because she had forgot what she was about, mechanically driving the handle up and down while studying the New Houses. That was how she spoke of them now, with capitals in her voice. She could hardly wait to see them finished, everything of the very best, clean and bright and shining.

The following Sunday, on their tour of the New Houses, Marge up and entered one of them, without so much as a by your leave. Del was taken quite aback because it was not in Marge's nature to be a forward woman, with anyone else but him she was shy and retiring. Although steps to the front door weren't installed yet, she'd reached up, clutched the door jambs, pawed at the threshold until her foot caught a purchase, and then boosted herself through the doorway. "That's trespass," Del had called after her, watching her disappear. He called out to her again and when she failed to reply he waved Sammy into the vacant house, looked doubtfully up and down the street, and then sprang up after his wife and son.

The house was still nothing more than a shell, outside walls and a roof, rooms partitioned off. Del hardly recognized the voices of Marge and Sammy echoing in the back; the hollow house made them entirely different, the voices of ghosts and strangers. He tracked their unfamiliarity through several doorways and discovered wife and child in the kitchen, Marge holding forth on the layout to the boy as if she had drawn the blueprints with her own hand.

"And this is the counter," she said, pointing, not looking at Del when he came in. "And these holes here are where the double sinks will go in. And over there, in front of that big window is where the stove'll go. Electric." She brushed past Del, Sammy trailing after her, and turned into a hallway. Her husband hesitated and then followed the two of them. "Here's the indoor toilet," she said to Sammy, "and it'll have everything, a sink and a bath. All that." She trooped them through the three bedrooms, talking in a high-pitched, nervous, eager way that Del hadn't heard before.

"Look at the size of it!" she exclaimed to Sammy when they entered the master bedroom. Sammy said it didn't look so big to him but his mother explained that was how an empty room always appeared. It was a funny thing, the more you put into an empty room, the bigger it seemed to get.

She ended her guided tour in the living room, counting off on her fingers. "Kitchen, three bedrooms, bathroom, living room. How many rooms is that? Six, isn't it? Six rooms. And the kids' bedrooms are nearly the size of my kitchen," she said wonderingly. She took her son by the shoulders, steering him directly in front of the enormous rectangle cut in one of the living-room walls. "You know what that's called, Sammy?" she asked. "That's called a picture window. It gives you all of outside to look at, the whole big picture. Just look at that view."

The three of them regarded solemnly and reverently a vast open expanse, the same view that they had been able to enjoy from their front yard before these very houses had been raised to stand between them and what they now admired. But neither Sammy nor Marge remembered this. Standing where they stood the landscape was changed, was charged with an unfamiliar, heart-rending beauty. A limitless stretch of brome grass billowed in the evening breeze, the slanting rays of the evening sun glinting upon it each time it bowed down before the wind. When the wind ebbed, the grass sprang upright again, swaying and shuddering, a deep green tide surging against the dam of pale sky. And here and there, isolated amid the grass, islands of red willow turned a sad, dusky rose in the dying sun, and poplar bluffs were crowned with swarming, shimmering light.

"How would you like to look at that every day of your life?" Sammy's mother asked him. "Wouldn't that be something? Sit in your easy-chair and look at that?"

And Sammy nodded yes because he knew his mother wanted him to, which was enough for him, always had been.

His mother had been very particular about getting the number of rooms in the house she had clambered up into correct. Six. Sammy could recall very clearly how she had counted them off, concluding with the thumb on her right hand, which was the living room. It surprised Sammy that he had never thought of their own house in such terms before. Now he pondered the matter long and hard. Kitchen, living room, bedroom made three. Sammy did not have a bedroom of his own. He slept on the sofa in the living room. Three rooms. If he stretched things he could get five by counting the attic and the dirt cellar which you could get into by a trap door in the floor of the kitchen. But if he did, then it was only fair to count the Americans' basement and that gave them seven rooms. No matter how he worked it, Sammy came up short.

He wondered why he had never thought of their house this

way before. Was it because he had been too little to consider such things? Now that he was thinking of it, he realized that there always had been better houses in the town than his, but he hadn't realized this was so. Maybe because though better, they were still old and shabby. He had heard his mother say that there hadn't been a new house built in their town since before the Depression when the money evaporated. Now, all at once, there were twenty-five or thirty new houses going up right under his nose.

Try as he might, Sammy could not imagine what kind of people lived in such fine, modern, beautiful houses. He could not imagine them in some far-off place, waiting to be called to come and take possession of their handsome residences. He could not imagine the towns they waited in, or how these people talked, or how they looked. And because all of these things were impossible for him to imagine, he was made uneasy at the prospect of their coming.

The contractor's foreman paid a Sunday visit to the building site to satisfy himself that everything had been properly stowed away and left shipshape for Monday morning. As he cruised the crescents he glimpsed a young boy running around the corner of one of the houses. Suspecting mischief, he parked the company pick-up, got out, and went behind the house to investigate. What he found around back was Del Cutter, his wife, and their boy. Being a local man, the foreman knew Del by reputation and, despite Cutter's embarrassment at being discovered there, he knew Del was an honest man and not likely to be sniffing around looking to pinch tools.

"Hello, Del. Hello, Marge," he said.

Del nodded uncomfortably and plunged his hands deep into his pockets. The boy edged a little closer to his mother. The foreman didn't have a clue what the three of them were up to. "You folks looking for something?" he asked.

Del and Marge glanced at each other. "Just window-shopping," said Marge hurriedly when she saw her husband didn't intend to offer an answer. Then she gave a brittle yelp of laughter.

"Window-shopping," repeated the foreman. "That's a good one. Window-shopping."

"We better get along, Marge," said Del.

For a second, it looked to the foreman as if Marge Cutter might refuse to budge. Her mouth opened, as if to issue a protest, and then closed again.

Only when the Cutters started to move off did it come to him what they had been doing. Likely hunting for scrap wood to burn in their stove.

He called out to Cutter. "Hey, Del," he said, "if you was looking for odds and ends to use in your stove that's okay by me. Not to worry. Take whatever you can find."

Cutter paused, turned slowly around. The foreman smiled. The Cutters weren't the lazy, shiftless kind, just people who worked hard to no effect. Letting them walk off with a few butt ends of two-by-fours, or scraps of cedar shingle for kindling took nothing out of his pockets. "Help yourself," he said swelling with easy generosity. "It'd be a hand in keeping the area tidy."

He got no thanks from Del Cutter. "I buy my wood," he said in a quiet voice. "I ain't a scrounger."

The foreman almost retorted, If you ain't a scrounger, then what the hell are you hanging around here for? But on weighing the heat in Cutter's eyes and his small, hard, terrier's body, he didn't. People said Cutter wasn't anybody to trifle with, not if he was mad.

"Suit yourself," is all he dared to say.

The Americans were not the only strangers to come, or promise to come. A trailer court mushroomed on the outskirts of town, rows of mobile homes propped up on cinder blocks, vehicles parked every which way on straggling streets, plenty of mud and pot holes and sagging clotheslines flapping laundry, a maze of rusty-coloured snow fence to prevent babies from wandering off yards of beaten, trampled grass. An encampment of itinerants, shaft-sinkers, electricians, mechanics, steel workers, their women and children.

The trailer court gave Marge Cutter an idea that wasn't clearly hopeless. One night at supper she said to her husband, "What do you think we could afford in the way of a mobile home?"

Del looked up from his plate. He'd been mowing hay all day under a hot sun and his face was the colour of fire brick. For the first time in their married life, the red face and faded ginger hair struck Marge as sly, maybe even slippery.

"What would we want a mobile home for?" he asked.

"To live in," said Marge quietly, giving a little hitch to her chin.

"A tin house," Del said. His father winked at Sammy, making him wince. The boy knew that his mother was deadly serious, even if his father didn't. "What would that make us? Spam in the can?"

"They've got running water out at the trailer court and septic tanks," said Marge coaxingly. "Those mobile homes all have indoor toilets."

"You seem to know everything they got," said Del. "What else they got?"

"You buy a mobile home," said Marge, "and it comes complete. Furniture, beds, cupboards, electric stove and fridge, propane furnace for heating. Everything in one package, all built in."

"We got furniture," said Del.

"Nothing stopping anybody selling furniture."

Marge watched him go shifty-eyed, a fox cornered. "I don't see the percentage in selling perfectly good furniture," he said. "You never get what it's worth."

"I don't see the percentage in some things either," announced Marge. "I don't see the percentage in knocking myself out in an uphill battle to keep this shack clean. An old place like this – the doors and windows don't fit proper. The wind blows and there's dust under every sash. In the winter I got to keep a rug under the door just to keep the snow from sifting in on the floor. The linoleum won't polish because it's worn clear through to the backing in places. Look," she said, indicating where the pattern had been scuffed away. "I've got to haul wood to cook and water to wash and in the winter I got to empty chamber-pots. I take up Sammy's bed in the morning and I make it up again at night. He ought to have his own bedroom and his own bed. I'm tired of carrying this wreck of a house on my back. Times are changing. They aren't what they were. Why can't I have something that isn't broken, that the dirt isn't ground into?" she said with longing in her voice. "Something new."

Del didn't have a ready answer to her question. In his mind he was willing to grant that she was entitled to what she wanted, that Marge, so long uncomplaining, deserved consideration. But he did not know how to say so, did not see how it could be brought to pass, so he shrugged hopelessly and muttered something about money.

Marge stared at Del and Del at Marge. Sammy knew what the look on his mother's face meant. It was the look she got whenever Sammy pushed her too far, past her breaking point. Once his mother said something, or stated an intention wearing that face, she never took it back.

"They're paying a dollar an hour out at the mine site," said Marge. "You don't make near that kind of money now."

He hadn't expected that. Del scooted his eyes back down to his plate. Like Sammy, there were things he couldn't imagine. One of them was crawling about under the earth, working like a maggot in the black guts of an animal. "I don't know nothing about that kind of work," he said. "It's not in my line."

"They're training men. Dollar an hour to learn."

"Dollar an hour to learn to be a worm. I ain't a worm."

Unlike Sammy and Del, Marge's trouble came from what she could imagine, not from what she couldn't. She was not prepared to surrender these imaginings. Bitterly, she said, "You aren't a worm and you aren't Spam in a can. What the hell are you?"

"I'll tell you what the hell I am," his father said. "I'm the goddamn boss around here, that's what I am." But Sammy could see that the brave words didn't match his father's expression. The look on his face belonged to a man hurt and frightened, the mouth shamming hardness while the eyes begged.

Sammy could recall bad times between his parents before, times when they had turned the air cold and thin in a room. But it had never gone on for so long, the irritable, flesh-crawling silences, the flashes of dogged, stupid bickering. In the past, one or the other of them had forgotten or pretended to forget, but what had passed between them now was unforgettable, with too much at hazard for even gentle pretences to be possible. So Sammy and Marge paid visits to the new houses without Del. Ever since the foreman had insulted him by supposing he and his family were scavenging – like some sort of tribe of bone and rag pickers – Del Cutter wouldn't have been caught dead on the Americans' property.

It was an entirely different story with his wife. He had made it plain that he wanted her to stay off the place too, but she ignored him and returned again and again to roam the empty houses. The only difficulty was that the nearer the houses came to completion, the harder they were to get into. Now they had doors which could be locked. Here Sammy came in handy. He had inherited his father's lean, compact body and could wriggle through windows carelessly left open. Cat-like, he squeezed into basements or, standing on his mother's shoulders, slithered through bedroom and bathroom windows left ajar, dropping to the floor and padding off to unlock the door and let her in.

Always, there was something new and noteworthy for his mother to show him. "See, they're putting in a fireplace now. She'll have fires in the winter. She'll put her chair so. It'll be night and she'll turn out the electric lights to watch the fire all the better. Her shadow will be big on the back wall across there. She'll have carpet all through. She'll be able to walk from the living room to the bedroom in her bare feet and never have them touch anything but carpet, never chill them on linoleum."

"This baseboard trim is mahogany," she told him. "You're looking at the best. She'll have a mahogany mantel on the fireplace too. These walls she'll have painted cream to set off the trim. She'll have it lovely once she's done."

They went into the kitchen. "She'll have all the cupboards mahogany too – with a dark stain. There'll be a Lazy Susan to keep all the spices, coffee, tea, sugar, and such, convenient at a spin. She'll have a hood and fan over the stove to suck up grease and smoke. The kitchen curtains will be white with green trim – not plastic curtains but linen."

"This'll be the boy's bedroom," she said, standing in the centre of the vacant room. "She'll buy him a captain's bed – a bed with drawers underneath for his clothes. He'll have a bulletin board where he can pin up pictures of his favourite hockey players. She'll buy a desk and lamp for him so's he can do his home work and not be bothered and interrupted while he studies. She'll paint his walls blue, a boy's colour. He'll have a chest to keep his toys. Can't you see it?"

Maybe not, but he could see her face.

They were going at it again, in their new way. Not yelling, not storming as once they had, but teasing in a vicious, cold-blooded fashion, biting at one another. He had moved to the kitchen but his stomach didn't hurt any less, he could still hear them.

His mother said, "Maybe it's wrong to offer you encouragement. Maybe what they say is true, maybe old dogs can't be taught new tricks. Maybe we'll die in this kennel."

His father wasn't as good at this as she was. "Well, if I'm an old dog what does that make you? You've got two years on me."

Sammy got to his feet and went out, careful not to let the

screen door slap shut behind him. It was getting late and he shouldn't have been going out, but he couldn't take any more of it. For a moment he stood absolutely still, waiting for a voice to order him back inside. It didn't come. They had no ear except for the wicked things passing back and forth between them.

He crossed the road to the new houses. The sun was going down, shedding an odd, orange light. Many of the new houses wore a fresh primer coat of white paint and when the sun touched them they glowed copper. The first time his family had inspected the houses the setting sun had burned amid their ribs like a fiery heart. They had all three been together then. Now the burning was outside, on the paint.

He walked slowly up and down the roads, sizing up the houses. The angrier he got, the more slowly he prowled, slower and slower. He stopped in front of a split level. A roof, shingles, paint, siding, concrete driveway. Sammy went up the walk, tried the front door, then circled around and shook the back door. It was locked too but all the windows looking out on the yard stood open. He found himself a pair of sawhorses, a board to stand on, and pulled himself up and through a bedroom window. When he dropped to the floor he realized his palms were sticky and the front of his shirt smeared with paint from sliding down the wall. The smell of paint was very strong in the house and he understood immediately why all the windows had stood conveniently open for him. He held his shirt out from his chest and examined it. He was in trouble with his mother.

Sammy started to wander aimlessly through the house, opening doors to rooms, to closets, to cupboards. Each time he pulled open a door he jerked it a little more cruelly, slammed it a little harder. Running out of doors to open and close, places to seek answers, he went into the living room. There a canvas tarp was anchored to the hardwood floor with buckets of paint and a roller tray that held several brushes soaking in turpentine. A cluster of curls, wood shavings planed from a door, were swept into a pile at the edge of the tarp.

Sammy sat down on the floor. This house was all but finished and now he could feel it waiting for one of the American ladies to come and claim it. He knew nothing at all about such ladies. They were scarcely real to him, scarcely to be believed in. He struggled to see them clearly. He strained to catch their voices. Nothing came to him except a picture of his mother, drifting through these rooms. What he heard over and over was his mother talking. *She'll this, she'll that. She'll this, she'll that,* his mother repeated in his ear.

The sun finally sank, like a stone. The sky framed in the picture window was a soft, mindless grey.

Again he followed his mother, watched her hands darting, pointing, her voice urging him to appreciation. *She'll this, she'll that,* he heard his mother say. After all these months, this trouble, who did it belong to?

The room had gone dark and a little scary. Sammy fumbled in his pockets for the matches he carried to light his mother's stove. A match blazed in the cup of his hands and he held it, staring at the flame, seeing his mother walk the hard-packed road that day the sun had burned in the ribs of the houses, back then before all they could think of was houses, houses, houses.

The match scorched his fingers and he dropped it. He struck another and began to nuzzle a solitary wood shaving that lay beside the pile with its flame, watched the shaving catch and writhe under the caressing blue tongue. He rubbed out the last poor sparks with the toe of his running shoe, examined the smear of black ash on the floor.

He lit the last match, let it drop, went out into the street.

For long moments the fire rustled in its dry nest of shavings like a mouse, scurried aimlessly up and down the frayed borders of the canvas, floated a few fat drowsy sparks about the room. Then the turpentine popped and a blue quaking light which resembled the glow of a television ran flickering up the walls. The dull thumps of rupturing paint cans could be heard.

An unexpected breeze sighed the length of the dark deserted street. The front door which he had neglected to pull firmly closed behind him swung slowly and invitingly open.

The house drew a long breath, exploded.

He saw it once again, the burning sun, a picture in a picture window.

Teacher

1.

Never before, and never since have I hated anyone as I did then, with a ten year old's insulted and seething heart.

2.

Her name was Mrs. Dollen and she taught grade six at R.J. Hewitt Elementary. I would place her in early middle age in 1961. Dark complexioned, monumental, she was easily the most physically imposing teacher in the school, two inches taller and twenty pounds heavier than Alley Oop, our principal, who liked to give expression to his power by cracking and shelling walnuts with his fingers as he strolled the school corridors at recess. Of course, poor Alley Oop's hands paled in comparison with Mrs. Dollen's, which were emphatically more prodigious and mannish.

Mrs. Dollen favoured lace, frills, and chiffon blouses, perhaps to counteract the impression created by the size of her shoulders and hands. Like all teachers, she had a distinctive, identifying odour. Hers was feminine enough, a mingling of eau de cologne and dry-cleaning. There was nothing specifically eccentric about her appearance, no flamboyant costume jewellery, no laddered and sagging nylon stockings, no radical and abrupt changes of hair colour like Miss MacDonald, the grade-one teacher. Nevertheless, there was something unnerving about the way she looked. Now I see what it was. If Chief Sitting Bull had been permed at our local beauty parlour he would have borne a strong resemblance to teacher.

3.

What was it that people in our small town said about Mrs. Dollen? The chairman of the local school board liked to note that the life span of a set of textbooks was five times longer in Mrs. Dollen's classroom than in any other. Put plainly, they lasted. Nobody dared rip a page, or draw a picture in one of *her* books.

Exasperated mothers used to threaten their kids: "Just you wait until you're old enough for grade six. Mrs. Dollen will put an end to your smart alec lip!"

In the janitor's opinion there wasn't another teacher like her in the whole school. Her pupils lined their shoes up at the back of the room and sat in their stockinged feet. No black scuff marks on the floor, ever. No mud. You didn't even have to buff the tile after a waxing, students did it for you with the soles of their socks.

What did my father say? He said the reason Mrs. Dollen got the job teaching was the condition of her husband, because of the shape he came back in after the war. Mr. Dollen didn't work, scarcely put his nose outside the door, and was reported to suffer from an undefined ailment. Contracted, my father liked to add, from germs found only inside certain bottles.

My father was known to be a character, and the owner of a maliciously sharp tongue. As he cut their hair at the barber shop, his customers encouraged him to pass his famous opinions on acquaintances and neighbours. The louder they roared, the more bloody-minded and funny he became. What he never realized was that walking home after, the laughter forgotten, they all turned sour pondering what he might have to say about them when they went out the door. My father was never as popular as he assumed himself to be.

One of his most celebrated comic turns involved the Dollens. Holding his scissors aloft, the blades nervously snicking back and forth, he would propose the theory that the reason Ernie Dollen was never seen outside the house was that he was kept chained up inside, garbed in silk pyjamas, Mrs. Dollen's "personal love slave."

4.

Entering Mrs. Dollen's class I was aware of her reputation. It was just that I saw no reason to personally worry. Since beginning school I had always been the pet, the darling, more the ally of the teachers than their pupil. They knew that when the school superintendent came sniffing around on his inspections I could be depended upon to politely volunteer answers to his questions, drawing fire away from more unreliable and erratic scholars.

Both Mrs. Dollen and I had reputations, although mine was minor and hers major. The seed of mine was that I arrived in school able to read, something highly unusual for that time and that town. After my mother died when I was three, my father took me with him to the barber shop. In one corner of the shop he erected a barricade out of a scrap of old snow fence which he put me behind when he was busy (to keep me out of the hair on the floor) but when things were slow the two of us sat in the big nickel-trimmed barber's chair and looked at the ragged magazines stocked for the amusement of his patrons. I learned to read from *The Police Gazette*. My father liked to call attention to this, in a manner he imagined self-deprecating, but wasn't in the least. "He never got his brains from me," he used to declare. "I've still got mine!"

Then, when I was six, my grade-one teacher discovered me in the school library reading a grade-twelve history text. Actually I was only looking at gory illustrations representing the Battle of Marathon but the incident contributed to a growing suspicion I might be "academically gifted." When the Department of Education appointed an innovative superintendent and Alley Oop saw it might be wise to portray himself as a progressive principal, I was the one selected to be "accelerated" through several grades. All this relentless promotion meant that, already undersized for my age, I started grade six a full two years younger than the rest of my classmates.

5.

A description of a school photograph of me taken at the age of ten:

> Glasses and freckles, a rigid smile, western shirt and western bola tie. (My father loved Zane Grey.)
>
> A *very* good haircut.

6.

On my first day in grade six I claimed a seat where I always had, directly in front of the teacher's desk in the first row. Unspoken rules guided me there. It was the place for someone like me, just like the back of the room was the place for retards like Wayne Leszinski. The world ordered itself that way in those days.

So it came to be that two legends, myself and Mrs. Dollen, were separated by less than four feet when she opened the register and proceeded to call the roll.

"Deborah Atkins."

"Here."

Without lifting her eyes from the register, Mrs. Dollen said: "People in my room answer properly when I call the roll. In my room 'here' is not acceptable. The proper response is, 'Present, Mrs. Dollen' or 'Present, teacher.' Is that understood?"

"Yes, teacher."

"Deborah Atkins."

"Present, teacher."

"Robert Bing."

"Present, teacher."

And so it continued until she came to me.

"Myles Rampton."

"Present, Mrs. Dollen."

For the first time that morning, Mrs. Dollen directed her attention away from the register and towards one of her students. She stared at me with eyes so expressionless and dry that mine began to itch in sympathy. "So," she said at last, "here I am, face to face with the Boy Wonder."

I beamed a smile back at her, never imagining that this was anything but a compliment. I was accustomed to being complimented by teachers.

"I wouldn't smile if I were you until I had something to smile about," she said, meaning it. Laughter burst at my back.

7.

I was in the right place, at the front of the room, but nothing else was right. If Mrs. Dollen asked a question and I put my hand up, she never called on me. If it didn't go up, she did. On the first Friday afternoon that it was too rainy to go outside for phys. ed. we had a spelling bee and teacher kept me standing uncomfortably at the blackboard while she thumbed through the dictionary searching for my word. She settled on "anaclisis." I was the first one knocked out of competition.

Mrs. Dollen made a discovery. The first three pages of my Social Studies notes were written in ballpoint pen. Only fountain pens were permitted in her classes. Surely we were all big enough to use a proper pen at our age. I was set recopying these notes using a proper pen. And then recopying them once again because I had used peacock-blue ink and Mrs. Dollen would countenance only blue or black. Neither of these rules had ever been announced.

8.

I could not understand this passage from privilege to persecution. Possible reasons for it were:

a. The weakness evident in my face. I neglected to mention this when describing my school photograph. The face is humble, it asks only to please.

b. A woman like Mrs. Dollen was bound to resent other teachers' enthusiasms being thrust upon her. She would pick and choose her own favourites, thank you very much.

c. My father.

Certainly this list does not exhaust possibilities, lists never do. It is only a beginning. At the time, however, I did not even have a beginning. I sought very hard for a reason that Mrs. Dollen should dislike me and could not find one. It was a useful lesson teacher taught me, that to demand misfortune make sense is futile.

9.

What this seemed to be was what my father referred to as a "misunderstanding." He used the word frequently since his life was rife with them because of his satiric urges. I took it upon myself to clear my misunderstanding up, to prove to Mrs. Dollen that she was wrong and that I really was a model student. Throughout every lesson, throughout every hour of the day, I wore an alert and interested face. I was modest, unassuming, diligent, and cooperative. I volunteered to wipe blackboards, pound chalk dust out of erasers, and run messages to Alley Oop's office. All of which only seemed to stimulate her disdain.

10.

Behind my meek demeanour I fantasized revenge.

What if I telephoned her, claimed to be a former student, and threatened to break into her house with a butcher knife, seeking revenge for the wrong she had done me years ago?

Two or three times I made a dry run, dialling Mrs. Dollen's number with the receiver resting in the cradle so that her telephone couldn't possibly ring. But I lost my nerve and dropped even that mild, pale rebellion. I couldn't shake the feeling that she knew the game I was playing and would answer despite my precautions, *could* and *would* answer a phone that hadn't rung.

11.

October was devoted to Noxious Weeds. Mrs. Dollen turned our classroom into a rogues' gallery of the weeds named in the province's Noxious Weeds Act, hanging illustrations of twenty of the most noxious on the bulletin board. We had orders to find specimens of each, press them, label them, and mount them in a scrapbook. For three weeks I spent every spare moment combing ditches, fields, and my father's neglected garden patch for Russian thistle, fox tail, creeping Charlie, leafy spurge, chickweed, wild oats. Teacher had made it perfectly clear that seventeen or eighteen, even nineteen weeds would not be good enough. It was all twenty or nothing. We sweated in pursuit of the rare, uncommon ones. Mrs. Dollen's students bartered weed specimens the way other, happier children traded baseball cards.

"I'll swap you a wild oats for a wild mustard."

The weekend before the Monday we were supposed to hand in our scrapbooks I was still short a plantain and so overwrought that my father gave up his only day off, Sunday, to help me on my weed hunt. This was a considerable sacrifice since he looked forward to spending his day of rest ridiculing everything offered on CBC television. He had been born in Duluth and although he had moved to Canada at the age of two, he thought of himself as an American and liked to disparage everything north of the forty-ninth as pitifully second rate. He always made a great show of scowling and grumbling when forced to his feet for the singing of "God Save the Queen."

All afternoon I tramped worried circles over the countryside while he ambled along behind, complaining of the varicose veins which, along with haemorrhoids, were what he called the "barber's curse." Every now and then he would pluck a bit of vegetation and present it to me for inspection, hoping that at long last he had found his ticket of release and could get home in time to mock the sanctimonious performers in "Hymn Sing."

"Do you think?" he'd ask.

And I would roll my eyes in wild despair and cry: "No, no, no. *Plantain!*" And my father, growing cold because he never bought himself a proper jacket (since the only weather he ever got was stepping from his car into the barbershop) muttered: "Well, how the christ am I supposed to know? They didn't make farmers out of us when I went to school. We studied the three R's, we got an *education*!"

12.

Nineteen noxious weeds lovingly mounted, protected under Saran Wrap, their names painstakingly stencilled in coloured pencils, a beautiful job, did not cut any ice with teacher. She wanted to know where plantain was.

"I looked and looked," I said, "but I couldn't find any. Honest I couldn't."

"I can just guess how hard you looked," said Mrs. Dollen in a manner meant to make it clear that she believed I was a liar. "You've got a pretty high opinion of yourself I don't doubt, skipping those grades. But if I was you I wouldn't be so quick to turn up my nose at practical knowledge. Not everything is learned out of a book. There are plenty that go lots further than the likes of you because they don't think themselves too good to learn everyday useful things. Like weeds."

13.

I noted this about teacher. She liked to be asked questions. Not the sort of questions a boy like Wayne Leszinski asked, who was dumb as a post, but the sort of questions asked by girls who got solid B's and wrote in their exercise books with concentrated, lip-chewing exactitude. Girls who, in Social Studies class, fretted over how provincial capitals should be marked on their study maps, with stars or dots. Please, teacher, which?

Salvation might lie in questions of this ilk. "Mrs. Dollen, how do you spell Charlottetown?"

Teacher wondered aloud to the class how a boy who had managed to take two grades in one year didn't know how to spell a simple, ordinary place like Charlottetown.

"I know how to spell *Charlotte,*" I said with emphasis, "and I know how to spell *town.* What I don't know is whether it's one word or two."

Unfortunately, the sands of patience had run out for both of us at the same time. Mrs. Dollen leaned across her desk and waved a forefinger the size and colour of an uncooked sausage in my face. "Don't adopt a tone with me, young man. You might have got away with blue murder in other places and other times but this is here and now. I've had my eye on you for weeks and I don't like your superior airs and your habit of carrying your nose aloft. You seem to think I've got nothing to teach you. Since that's the case you better pick up your desk and cart it off to the back of the room where I won't be in your hair. Set it down beside Mr. Wayne Leszinski. Like you, he seems to know all he'll ever need to know. The two of you are welcome to each other."

14.

A description of Wayne Leszinski as he appears in the school photo he gave me at the end of the year which he signed, "Your friend, Waynie":

A stocky, moon-faced boy of fifteen with wavy blond hair, already showing signs of premature thinning, and a long upper lip that appeared slightly swollen because it was pulled down to hide bad front teeth. No proper shirt, just a white T-shirt, despite the fact that the itinerant school photographer always arrived to take pictures at R.J. Hewitt Elementary in January.

When I set my desk down beside Wayne's, he had already been parked on that spot for two years and was beginning his third. No other teacher had ever held Wayne back in any grade for more than two years, but Mrs. Dollen was a woman of principles. If you couldn't pass her exams you didn't leave. So Wayne was stalled in grade six until he gave Mrs. Dollen a stroke, or had his sixteenth birthday and the law said he could quit – whichever came first.

I was righteously indignant at being bracketed, yoked, paired with the likes of Wayne Leszinski. I could feel him watching me in the way embarrassing and stupid people did, without disguising their curiosity. I could hear him breathing in an embarrassing and stupid way also.

Then he spoke to me. "Now you're one, too," he said.

"One what?" I whispered angrily. "One what?"

15.

Everyone was aware that Health was teacher's favourite subject, perhaps because as it was taught then, it was made up of entirely practical knowledge. We learned Canada's Food Rules, the circulation of the blood, and tips on personal grooming. Wayne was a useful example when it came to grooming, which was a popular topic with Mrs. Dollen. If you used too much Brylcreem and didn't wash your hair regularly you could expect to go bald by the time you were twenty-five, which was what Wayne was going to be by the looks of him already.

She would also order Leszinski to hold up his big, cracked, chilblained paws as evidence of what you could expect if you dressed with an eye on fashion rather than weather conditions.

"And you've all seen Mr. Leszinski's ears," she would add, while Wayne swept the room with a challenging grin.

We had all seen his ears. Wayne was famous for ignoring the cold. All winter he slithered about in ordinary leather street shoes, in a light nylon windbreaker, without gloves, without a tuque. His frostbitten ears were tattered with peeling skin, curled like birch bark. Brylcreem froze in his hair on his way to school and dripped down his neck when it thawed in the muggy warmth of the classroom. What teacher did not grasp was the pleasure that Wayne Leszinski took in being singled out in Health class. It gave him status.

16.

The back of the room was not my place. Everything seemed to be happening too far away. There were times I could almost believe I had caught some sort of infection from Leszinski, just from sitting near him. I could no longer concentrate, or remember what had just been said, or even do things I had always known how to do. One day I was overcome with a chilling panic when I discovered that, no matter how hard I tried, I could not recall how to multiply and divide fractions.

My grades began to drop. If this could have been attributed to Mrs. Dollen's prejudice in marking, I would have been less shaken and anxious. But even in subjects such as Arithmetic, where an answer was either right or wrong, I went from an A the previous year to a B and then to a C.

The only things that I could seem to learn were the things

that Wayne was teaching me, the things I did not want to learn. I did not want to know that girls bled once a month from between their legs. I found it horrible to imagine them all sore and sticky, bleeding the way Wayne said. Even though I dismissed him as a moron, he could make me feel even dumber than Mrs. Dollen could. When Wayne said he'd like to share a French safe with Sharon Stottlemyre, I took this to mean that Wayne wished to share some fabulous treasure with the equally fabulous Sharon, a treasure so valuable that it had to be lodged in a very secure safe, a special kind only obtainable in France. When later I learned that the treasure this French safe was meant to hold was what Leszinski called "Wayne's wiener," that thick, coarsely-veined stump he liked to flaunt and waggle in the bathroom to over-awe the rest of us who as yet only had what he disparagingly referred to as "winkles," I felt slightly ill.

17.

Before my relegation to the back of the room I used to look forward to examinations, but now the little excited butterfly of anticipation which used to flutter eagerly sank like a cold, heavy lump of lead in the pit of my stomach.

God knew what was in the pit of Leszinski's stomach when he wrote a test. First he printed his full name, Wayne Martin Leszinski, at the top of the test paper, taking great pains with each of the letters, a different coloured pencil employed for each. Once his name was a rainbow, he didn't even bother to glance at the questions but laid his head down on his desk to wait out the remainder of the hour just like he was stoically waiting out the remainder of his sentence in Mrs. Dollen's room. I wished I could renounce the desire to recover my old self, and do likewise.

Was it the struggle between my old self and my new self that caused my confusion of speech, my stutter? Now whenever teacher asked questions in class I would stare at my hands and beg God, someone, I didn't know who, not to let her call on me with my dry tongue and thick spit, not to let the words which used to come so easily and naturally and confidently, jerk and stumble their way from between my lips, my thoughts whirling and my eyes furiously blinking. There were giggles and heads began to slyly turn to greet the show whenever my name was called.

I suffered stomach cramps and diarrhoea, my palms were always clammy.

18.

Why didn't I involve my father in my troubles at school? Because I had arrived at the age that a child convinces himself his father is a fool. Mostly this had to do with the way he looked. He did not dress like other fathers who were farmers, mechanics, carpenters. He did not dress like fathers who were lawyers, businessmen, doctors. The cheap, short-sleeved white shirts and clip-on bow-ties he wore to the barbershop made him resemble the mild, kind hosts of children's programs. What use was Mr. Dressup to someone in my predicament?

19.

I was luckier than Wayne because teacher didn't lay hands on me. Leszinski she hit. Most often it was a flurry of open-handed slaps, although once, when he ducked down and hid his face in his arms, she pounded on his back with doubled-up fists.

What always drove her to let fly was Wayne's sudden barks of laughter when she was speaking. Teacher always assumed his outbursts were calculated displays of disrespect for her authority. It might have been much worse if she had detected the real reason for his amusement. Wayne couldn't help snorting and braying whenever he heard her say anything into which a reference to sex could be read. Mrs. Dollen had only to say: "Make sure you have a period at the end of your sentences" and Wayne would be helplessly doubled-up with laughter, hopelessly convulsed.

After a hammering, Wayne would dismiss her with contempt. "Her?" he'd say. "That old cunt can't hit for nothing." His old man, he liked to brag, now *he* could hit. Nevertheless, on the heels of a beating a look crept over Wayne's face, a suggestion that what was at issue was not the strength of blows but something more inexpressible, more difficult to calculate.

20.

An article in *Reader's Digest* outlined how to escape from a submerged automobile. I put Mrs. Dollen in her ugly maroon Ford and ran it off the bridge. Standing at the smashed guardrail I watched the car slowly sink while she beat her hands on the windshield, her mouth forming soundless cries for help.

Too bad she hadn't read the article I had. Maybe people who read got more practical knowledge which carried them further in the world than you'd think. Especially under forty feet of water.

21.

November brought more distress. By then, Wayne had come to assume that our enforced association was the same thing as friendship, that we were best buddies. To my horror, he insisted on walking home with me each day after school. Didn't he know how ridiculous we looked together? He a full head taller than me, shambling along, hunched up in his shirt against the bite of the wind, his hands clamped in his armpits. And I, encased in parka, fleece-lined boots, visored hat with ear lugs, pelted along at a furiously indignant pace intended to get me to my front door as soon as possible and separate me from my mortifying companion and his mortifying suggestions – that we go to his house and play with his tabletop hockey game, that we watch Yogi Bear and Boo Boo cartoons, or look at the hot rod and skin magazines he had five-finger discounted from the drugstore.

His mother worked at the dry-cleaner's until six. "Nobody's home," he would confide, seeing this as an irresistible attraction. "Nobody'll bother us. We can just give'r."

He did not understand I did not want to give'r with him.

22.

Christmas that year meant an escape. An escape from Mrs. Dollen and an escape from Wayne. It meant two weeks without stomach cramps or sweating hands, two weeks free of being hounded by one or the other.

You have all seen the movie. The one in which the long-term con is keeping his nose clean while he serves the last days of his sentence. Hours before he is granted parole there is a prison riot, destroying his hope for release. From that point on you know it is inevitable that when the cell block is stormed by state troopers, he will be killed.

All December I sniffed the air for riots.

23.

On the afternoon of December 23, the last day of school, we had our class Christmas party, a tobogganing outing. Shortly after one o'clock Mrs. Dollen trooped us out of R.J. Hewitt Elementary and marched us across a mile of dazzling snow to the golf course where the ninth hole provided a perfect run. From the elevated tee we could go whizzing down three hundred yards of steeply sloping coulee. Three-quarters of the way down, where maximum speeds would be reached, a ramp of packed snow had been shovelled up by older boys from the junior high school and provided, by the generous contributions of their bladders, with an incredibly slippery glaze of yellow ice. The grade-eight boys had named it Piss-Ice Death Jump and only the most crazed kamikaze tobogganers, legendary nutters like Ernie Kunkel and Morris Fellows, ever took it at full speed, putting eight feet of air between them and the earth when they shot off it with blood-curdling screams of "Banzai!" Teacher needed only one glance at old Piss-Ice to declare it out of bounds and expropriate it as an elevated traffic island from which she could supervise our fun. No sooner had she unsteadily clambered up on it than she began to wave her arms, blare warnings and threats.

"What did I say, Donald? What? Down coming keeps to the right side of the hill. People pulling toboggans up the hill stay to the left. I don't want to speak to you again. Is that clear?" From where I stood on the tee box, at a distance of two hundred yards, her jerky gestures, her thin screechy voice made her seem like a cranky puppet. "No walking up the hill abreast! How many times do I have to tell you? Get in single file before one of you gets hit and killed! That's my last warning. If you people don't decide to start listening, I'll pack us up right this minute and we can go back to school and get started on next term's work right this minute. Am I making myself clear? Am I?"

Everybody but me went flying down the hill with abandon, red-faced and whooping. The sun burned with the intensity of a camera flash. Scars on the white bark of the naked poplars in the coulee were black as ink. The glare of the snow stunned aching eyes and made the landscape bobble. Skidding, tumbling bodies chipped sparks of snow from the slope, and runaway sleighs ran smooth and empty to the bottom of the hill.

I tried to negotiate this bedlam as inconspicuously as possible. By now creeping and slinking had become second nature to me. I eased down the slope with all due care, stuttering the toes of my boots in the snow to brake my descent. I cautiously and conscientiously ascended the left side of the hill, as per teacher's instructions.

24.

Wayne didn't own a toboggan. All he had to scoot down the hill on was a piece of cardboard, but teacher wouldn't let him use it.

"What if you were to hit a rock riding on that?" I heard her demand, as I plodded past Piss-Ice. "You'd be killed and who'd get blamed? Me. Not on your life, Mr. Leszinski."

I avoided Wayne like the plague, knowing he would expect to be invited to ride with me. With only a couple of hours more to get through, I had no intention of doing anything to draw the awful wrath of Dollen, and that included carrying freight with a talent for attracting her lightning.

25.

One of the saddest sights is the sight of someone lingering hopefully. Leszinski stood at the top of the hill, shivering in the thin nylon jacket, trying to catch my eye, but I kept my eyes elsewhere.

Neglected, Wayne began to make a nuisance of himself, turning vaguely menacing as he strutted aggressively up and down the cowed line of "winkles" waiting their turn for a run down the hill. "Anybody looking for the ride of their life? Let Waynie steer. Waynie'll give you little chicken poops a thrill. Who wants a thrill? How about it?" He halted in front of me. "Let's us do it," he said quietly. "You ain't scared."

But I was.

There was something genuinely humble and patient about the way he waited for his answer.

"No," I said.

"Why?" Wayne wanted to know. "You got a nice big one. You could easy ride two. Why?"

I turned away from him and squinted at the low winter sun scraping through a tangle of leafless poplar branches. Because you're bad luck, I wanted to say. Because just sitting at the back of the room with you has made me stupid. But I only shrugged.

"Why?" persisted Wayne. "You got a real nice one, a tin one. We could go real fast on a tin one."

"Aluminum," I said.

"Them tin ones fly," he continued doggedly. "You and me could really fly."

"Take it," I said. "You want to really fly – just take it."

"Why, Myles? Why don't you want to ride with me?"

I threw the tow rope at his feet. "You want to fly, go ahead. Take it. Just leave me alone."

"I got one year to my driver licence," said Wayne, sliding his eyes away from me and down the hill where Mrs. Dollen stood with her back turned to us, haranguing a miscreant from the vantage of Piss-Ice Death. "One year and I could drive you anywhere you want to go, Myles."

He waited.

"All right," he said at last, stooping down and savagely snatching the toboggan to his chest. "Fuck you, Myles." For several yards he ran furiously down the slope, lurching blindly from side to side, the toboggan held up in front of him like a glittering shield. Then he flung himself upon it and shot off down the slope.

26.

We were both turned in the same direction, Mrs. Dollen and I, both facing the rule-breaker who stood yards beyond Piss-Ice Death where the slope of the coulee began to level. There was no time for a warning. At the last possible moment Wayne slung his weight violently to one side and the toboggan veered sharply left. It ran up the ramp, struck Mrs. Dollen with terrible force in the back of her ankles, popped her up into the air, shot underneath her, and flashed over the lip, disappearing before she came twisting awkwardly down in a heap, a game bird dropped on the wing.

27.

Pressing in around the body, staring at her legs poked out of rucked-up coat skirts at stomach-turning angles, we wanted the noises she was making to stop. We didn't like it that an adult whimpered, panted, groaned open-mouthed, face down in the snow. We gave her pinched-face encouragement to try and be herself.

"Teacher, are you okay?"

"Teacher, are you hurt?" Eileen Kerning had found Mrs. Dollen's glasses lying several feet from their owner in the snow. She dangled them above the prostrate figure and said, "Here's your glasses, teacher. They aren't broken."

"My back," said Mrs. Dollen in a scary, smothered voice. "My back, my back."

We looked uncertainly at one another. "My back, my back, my back," teacher shrilled at us.

Something had to be done. Suddenly the sky and snow grew dull, as if one were the pewter image of the other. Perhaps it was this draining away of the light which quickened us, bringing home the lateness of the hour. A toboggan was pulled up alongside her and Harvey Whiteside, who was a patrol leader in Boy Scouts and had a First Aid badge, issued directions for rolling her onto it. Mrs. Dollen did not submit to this manoeuvre calmly. At the critical moment she shrieked once again, "My back, my back, *my back*!" Her face was a match for the tired grey of sky and snow.

28.

There was something thoughtful, almost meditative in the quiet, subdued fashion with which we drew our burden back to school. Without discussion we had all decided that dumb silence ought to surround this incident. Everybody that is except Wayne. Clearly pleased with himself, he fell into step beside me and began to sing "The old grey mare, she ain't what she used to be," giving knowing winks and grins to anybody who looked his way. Nobody appreciated this. People began to drift further and further away from us, until we were quite alone.

"If I were you," I said to him, shaking with anger, "if I were you, I wouldn't act so smart."

He laughed.

"It was my toboggan," I reminded him. "You used my toboggan. You had no business acting smart with my toboggan."

29.

We returned from Christmas vacation to a surprise. Instead of Mrs. Dollen we found a substitute teacher, Miss Clark, an elderly lady familiar to some of us as the ineffectual conductor of the United Church Junior Choir. In a faint, tremulous voice she reported on teacher's medical condition to the class. At first, the doctors had thought that Mrs. Dollen had ruptured a disc and would require an operation, but now this was ruled out. What she had done was strain a group of large muscles in her back. After another week of bed-rest it was believed she would be able to resume her duties in the classroom.

Miss Clark exhorted us to try and be on our very best behaviour when teacher came back to us because, as we could all imagine, Mrs. Dollen hadn't spent a very happy Christmas laid up in hospital. It was up to us to try and make it up to her by being especially kind and good and considerate for the rest of the year, so that every single day would feel like Christmas for our dear teacher.

Last of all, Miss Clark said that although she knew many boys and girls would have sent Mrs. Dollen Christmas and Get Well cards (puzzled glances were exchanged at this bizarre notion) it might be encouraging to teacher if we all took a little time now to write her a short note telling her how much we missed her. Miss Clark held up a packet of envelopes and happily announced: "I have an envelope for each member of the class so that our communications with Mrs. Dollen remain private and personal. I shall pass these out now."

It took me all of thirty seconds to compose my private and personal communication to teacher.

> Dear Mrs. Dollen,
>
> I hope your back gets better soon. Grade six is not the same without you.
>
> Yours sincerely,
> Myles Rampton

That chore taken care of, I turned to scratching the rash on the backs of my hands, which had coincidentally appeared twenty-four hours in advance of school re-opening.

30.

Wayne wanted to know what he was supposed to *do*. Anything that wasn't routine, anything the tiniest bit out of the ordinary always threw him badly.

"Myles, Myles," he hissed across the aisle at me, "what should I write?"

At that moment my father's blood flowered darkly in me. I grabbed a pencil and savagely scribbled the sort of thing I had been hearing him entertain the barbershop peanut gallery with for years.

> Dear Old Scrag,
>
> I only wish you were paralyzed from the neck down and had to spend the rest of your life being fed corn mush with a rusty tin spoon and having your bum wiped for you.

It took Leszinski a little time to wade back and forth in this message until he got the gist of it, but when he did he gave one of those barks of delight that usually coincided with Mrs. Dollen mentioning the word "period," or her asking the class whether we had caught the author's "point."

31.

Suddenly I found myself wildly scrawling on sheet after sheet of paper, shaken by a reckless, silent laughter.

> Dear Mrs. Miserable,
> Wishing you to get well in about a thousand years, if not later.

> Dear Mrs. Fart Sucker,
> You'll be glad to hear I stood up for you the other day. Somebody said you weren't fit to eat a shit sandwich and I said you most certainly were.

And much more of the same.

Then, without warning, Alley Oop appeared in the doorway and Miss Clark was clapping her hands to attract our attention and piping at us in her benign, frail, old lady's voice that we must hurry and finish our letters because the principal, who was on his way to visit Mrs. Dollen in the hospital, had dropped by to collect and deliver our good wishes. I could see Alley moving up my row, gathering envelopes, and I scarcely had time to thrust the incriminating letters into my desk and seal my own good wishes to teacher before Alley Oop's big-knuckled, hairy hand was impatiently extended to receive my envelope.

32.

That very day, going through my desk I found the letter which should have gone into the envelope intended for teacher, the one which said:

> Dear Mrs. Dollen,
> I hope your back gets better soon. Grade six is not the same without you.
>
> Yours sincerely,
> Myles Rampton

Reading and re-reading the words, I tried to will them away and onto the sheet of paper that had journeyed with Alley Oop to the hospital. But the words stubbornly remained where they were and they stubbornly insisted on saying what they said and nothing else. Worse, I knew it didn't matter that the note I had sent wasn't signed, she would recognize the handwriting. Teachers always recognized your handwriting.

33.

The following Monday Mrs. Dollen returned to school walking with a stiff limp, leaning on a cane. We watched her make her way across the front of the room to her desk with the sort of awed silence that must have greeted Lazarus's first turn around the graveyard. When she laid her stick across the desk top it was with the restrained menace of a gun man placing his revolver on the bar-room table. I could hear the clock on the far wall ticking clear across the room. "Thank you for your letters," she said. "I read them all."

34.

The day of the accident Wayne had sung "The old grey mare she ain't what she used to be." This was and wasn't true. For a start, Mrs. Dollen showed her old form when she gave Leszinski a couple of brisk cuts across the shins with her cane for leaving his legs out in the aisle, declaring as she did: "We've had one too many accidents around here lately. There won't be any more."

On the other hand, her second day back, in the midst of working through an arithmetic problem at the blackboard she lost her train of thought, her eyes suddenly brimmed with tears, and she flung the piece of chalk in her hand to the floor, crying out, "What's the use! What's the *point*!" and left the room, not to return until after the mid-morning recess.

I knew teacher had read my letter. I knew this because two

or three times a period she would appear beside my desk and stand there for a full minute or so. At those times I could not shake the feeling that she was about to speak, would speak, if I so much as looked her in the face. For this reason I kept my head lowered and my gaze fastened on the red rubber tip of the cane until it moved off, squashily punching the floor.

35.

Mrs. Dollen took to smiling at me. She smiled each time she called my name off the roll, a strange contortion of the lips. It had been months since she had called on me in class, even for purposes of humiliation, but now there were questions for me again, easy ones, accompanied by the smile. She smiled at me coming in and going out of class. There was something coaxing in it, something that made me feel I was being lured out into the open the easier to be torn apart. And each time she smiled I shrank a little more, waiting for the coming of my just desserts.

36.

Teacher had been back about a week when she put it to me. This time she stood a little longer by my desk than was usual and in the end touched me on the shoulder, forcing me to look up, blinking, into her face.

"I've been thinking that you would like to move back up to the front of the room," she said. "Would you, Myles? Would you like that?"

Across the aisle Leszinski was tensely listening.

I did not answer her.

"What you have to understand, Myles, is that I put you back here so that you could learn something. And I think you have, I'm sure you have. Have you, Myles?" She smiled and suddenly I recognized it for what it was. The false smile of the coward, the very one I had offered her so many times in the past months to disarm contempt.

"All I want you to say, Myles, is that you have learned your lesson and you can go back to the front of the room. But I can't know you've learned your lesson unless I hear you say that you have. That's only fair, isn't it? That you let me know you've learned your lesson?"

I did not answer.

"Do you understand, Myles? All you have to do is let me know that you've learned your lesson. Just say it. Just say, 'I've learned my lesson' and you can go back to your old place."

37·

It didn't matter how nicely she wheedled. It didn't matter how hard her blunt fingers tightened on my shoulder, how hard she shook me, slapped me, I would not say it. The child could never go back.

Fraud

EVERY MORNING WHEN THE ALARM went off sharp at eight o'clock, Mrs. Cora Rook swung her skinny legs out of bed, snatched the binoculars from the bedside table, and in a state of dread rushed out of the bedroom and into the living room in her fuchsia negligee. There at the window of her tenth-floor condominium she pursed a mouth smeared with the lipstick she had forgotten to wash off when she had gone to bed drunk the night before and offered up a silent, panicked prayer as she struggled to focus her field glasses on the Bank of Montreal branch on Second Avenue. One of Mrs. Cora Rook's myriad fears was that overnight the bank would burn and all the money she had on deposit there would go up in flames, bankrupting her. Thank God! It was still there!

Cora's understanding of financial questions was rather shaky. Her husband Len, owner of a successful chain of six dry-cleaning outlets which he had sold shortly before his death almost two years ago, had been the money expert. While he was alive she had simply abdicated all control to him. "Oh, interest and taxes – I don't want to get involved in all that."

But now the situation was changed. Now it was her money to worry about – not Len's – an onerous responsibility, a weight on her mind. What made it worse was that unlike some of the other widows she knew, she had no children to lean upon for support and advice in her hour of need. All alone as she was in the world, who could she turn to? It was difficult for her to forget Len's stories of what a dog-eat-dog world it was out there. How often she had heard him say, "The cleaning business is the dirtiest business in the world. Everybody is out to cheat you. If I wasn't on my toes a hundred per cent of the time, the bastards would have put us in the poor house ages ago."

If Mrs. Cora Rook was sure of anything, it was that the poor house was one place she did not want to go. She did her best not to put herself there, acting on whichever of Len's economic principles she might be able to recall. "Buy in quantity. There's always a saving in bulk," had been one of his favourites. It was the reason she always purchased her scotch by the case load rather than the bottle. Writing cheques had always thrown her for a loop so Len had given her an allowance in cash and out of habit she continued the former cash-only policy, going to her bank three or four times a week to make withdrawals. When the tellers saw her come sailing through the doors they gave each other significant looks to which Cora was oblivious.

Reg Stamp couldn't believe how hot it was for ten-thirty in the morning. Heat always made him edgy. He couldn't keep still. His restless hands kept flitting about, tugging at his cuffs, tightening the knot of his tie, stroking his shirt front. Every few minutes he walked to the florist's window to anxiously inspect himself.

What the glass reflected was a middle-aged male retaining a little of the surly insolence of someone once very attractive to women. But that had been a long time ago, in the days before the Beatles when Ricky Nelson and Fabian were the beau ideal, soft-looking, baby-faced men – "cute" was the word girls used back then to describe them. Cute does not always wear well. And Reg Stamp was badly worn. His dirty-blond hair was thinning, his swollen face was an alarming pink. Troy

Donahue drowned, bloated, washed up on a beach. However, Reg was blind to his puffy desolation, he was gazing approvingly upon the grey three-piece recently purchased at Bay Day. The pen in the breast pocket was pure brilliance, the telling detail which inspires confidence in the beholder. The shoes were great too. Like the suit they were new, but he had polished them anyway, then propped his toes up against a wall and flexed them a hundred times to crease the leather and give them that used, lived-in look. A lot of guys disregarded the small particulars, arguing: Who ever notices? But Reg sincerely believed that you couldn't make a convincing pitch unless you were prepared to climb into the skin of the person you said you were. And that meant living the part right down to broken-in shoes and a pen in the breast pocket of your suit. He had even read a book about it called *An Actor Prepares*. He prided himself on his professionalism. He knew what he was doing.

Despite his thoroughness, Reg's nerves were acting up dreadfully. This was happening more and more frequently of late. Since the bank had opened its doors at ten o'clock, he had let at least a dozen prospects go by. Furious, he put the blame on the hot weather. Along with a rash on his ass, it always gave him second thoughts.

But when he saw *her*, no more second thoughts. She was what a hanging slider is to a hitter in a bad slump, the dippy old broad in the turban sort of hat with a brooch the size of a small hub cap pinned to the front of it. And a cape. Who the fuck did she think she was, Super Senior? "Head 'em up and move 'em out, Reg," he whispered to himself. "Corral that loon." He put on a smile as big as the great outdoors and glided up to her. When he caught a whiff of her breath he knew he was in like Flynn. Whisky. At ten-thirty in the morning.

For sheer sordidness, Mrs. Cora Rook had never heard the like. Dear, clever Len had been righter than right, the world was filled with the "grifters," "hyenas," and "vampires" she so often heard him curse, drink in hand after a hard day's work.

Cora was rather pleased with herself for guessing which one was the ring leader: the rude girl with the big boobies who had made excuses about not wanting to fill out her withdrawal slip for her a number of months ago, claiming that the sign clearly said Commercial Teller and that she was holding up the line. The true nature of those types was apparent to anyone with eyes in their head.

Of course, she didn't quite understand it all, the ins and outs, the whys and wherefores, all the computer flibbertigibbet of money transferred out of one account and into another and then, finally, into someone else's pockets. What she understood perfectly was that it involved stealing her money, the money that Len had worked so hard to leave her. The bank investigator had left no doubt on that score.

The bank inspector was a charming man, so simpatico. Sitting in the donut shop drinking coffee, it had seemed the most natural thing in the world to tell him how difficult it was to be widowed and childless and how distressing it was to learn that the people you had put your trust in, bank people, were fleecing you. Even if she hadn't had a personal interest in the case she would have been inclined to help such a nice, agreeable man. Tomorrow, when she took delivery of the incriminating bills that had been marked with invisible ink so that the embezzlers could be traced and identified, she was sure she would feel a little bit like Mata Hari.

Reg had suggested that she hand over the money in her apartment. No way did he want to be seen receiving a wad of bills in a donut shop from a batty old broad. Eleven o'clock found him in a phone booth located across from the bank. He watched her come out. As far as he could see nobody was tailing her.

Now he was on his way to grandmother's house and still half-expecting to meet up with the wolf. He was also kicking himself. Yesterday, when she had asked how much she should take out of her account, he had quoted the usual – a thousand. In his experience that was the old girls' upper limit, even a measly thousand often gave them serious second thoughts. You suggested any more and they developed circulation problems, came down with a case of cold feet. So naturally he had gone with standard operating procedure.

She hadn't batted an eyelash. It would have been all the same to her if he had asked for two thousand, maybe three thousand. He had no one to blame but himself for misreading the situation. That's what came from not paying attention. Paying attention counted in this business. The cape and the weird headgear had thrown him – naturally he hadn't associated big money with someone who looked like a refugee from the church rummage sale. The upshot was he hadn't spotted the rings on her fingers until he'd already made the suggestion she withdraw a thousand. Seven rings. *Serious* rings, lighting up those gnarly old fingers like a Christmas tree, sparking and winking whenever they moved in the light.

Reg paused outside her building. He had to collect himself, was finding it hard to catch his breath. What was happening to him? He was turning into a bona fide shell-shock case. Last night he had hardly slept for speculating on what might go wrong. For the last five or six blocks he had been glancing over his shoulder every few seconds, to see if he was being followed. But if they wanted to nab him, ten to one they were waiting inside. With that happy thought he began to drip sweat, *rain* sweat for chrissakes. Sure as shit, he was working up an ulcer. His stomach hurt. Maybe worse than an ulcer. Hadn't he read somewhere that you could give yourself cancer, bottling up your emotions?

He stood on the sidewalk looking up at the tenth floor, vacillating. Walk away, he said to himself. It's still not too late.

When she opened the door to him, Reg warily studied her demeanour and sniffed the air. Immediately he brightened.

His instincts told him everything was copacetic here. Brightening up did Reg a world of good in more ways than one. When he was cheerful, residues of the old good looks and charm surfaced, like flotsam from a shipwreck. His old feeling of confidence and control returned as he calmly spread his props out on the coffee table, a receipt he had typed up the night before on his Olivetti portable and a zip-lock plastic sandwich bag labelled "Evidence." The receipt was a useful delaying tactic with the Alzheimer Annies. Give them an official-looking piece of paper and the hens would sit quiet on the roost long enough for the fox to clear out of the hen house. Depositing the money in a plastic bag and sealing it before their very eyes also lent the whole exchange a bureaucratic air which they found reassuring.

Once Mrs. Cora Rook produced the cash, Reg went through the drill, carefully counting the money, recording the amount in the blank space on the paper with the forged signature of somebody called J.J. Tolman (Reg's old high-school principal) and presenting her with the receipt. Then he put the evidence in the "Evidence" bag, sealed it, wrote "$1,000.00 (One Thousand Dollars)" on the label, and explained that now the money would not be removed from the bag for *any reason whatsoever* until the trial date. It was in government safe keeping.

Mrs. Cora Rook could hardly wait for him to finish his explanation so she could suggest they have a small drink to celebrate the conclusion of their mission. Which she did. Reg agreed there was no harm in one drink. The way things had shaken down he was feeling pretty pleased with himself. What did it hurt to have a snort with a lonely old girl? Besides, some of the effects of his earlier brush with the heebie-jeebies still lingered. A drink might be exactly what the doctor ordered.

Mrs. Cora Rook produced a bottle of single malt, the Glendronach she ordered by the case, and splashed it generously around in a pair of tumblers. Reg leaned back, stretched out his legs, sipped and savoured. Very good whisky. He patted the chesterfield on which he sat. Very good furniture. Now that he was relaxing after a job well done and taking in his surroundings, he realized the old dame had changed her outfit sometime between leaving the bank and greeting him at the door. She wore mules and apricot satin lounging pyjamas with a gold brooch shaped like a pretzel pinned to them. The salt on the pretzel was diamond chips.

Mrs. Cora Rook positioned herself on a chair in front of the picture window, insuring that she was back-lit and her profile was turned to her guest. At seventy she was elegantly emaciated in the style of the Duchess of Windsor and Isak Dinesen in their old age, women who expected clothes and men to hang well on them.

She took several brisk, bird-like nips at her whisky. She knew that it was a lady's duty to be entertaining but she wasn't sure what a bank inspector would find amusing. So she decided to conduct the conversation along customary lines. She asked Reg what his last name was.

Reg said that he was not allowed to divulge that for security reasons – it was a rule with bank inspectors.

"In that case," she said, "you'll have to stop calling me Mrs. Rook and call me Cora. First names both. It's only fair." And much nicer too, she thought. Reg had the same pleasant feel on her tongue as Len had. The names were remarkably similar. Three letters each. Reg, Len. Len, Reg. She leaned across the coffee table and clutched the whisky bottle in her be-ringed fingers. "Let me top that up for you, Reg," she said.

"Only if you'll join me, Cora," said Reg. You only live once, he reminded himself, this was thirty-five-dollar-a-bottle whisky. "It'd be criminal to refuse," he said, barking laughter.

Cora laughed too, although the joke didn't mean to her what it did to him.

By four o'clock in the afternoon Cora was finding it uncomfortably warm being back-lit by the blazing July sun. She rose and, drink in hand, swayed to the air-conditioner, turned it on full blast, and swayed back to her chair to resume the conversation where she had left it suspended in mid-sentence.

"– and I'll tell you another secret, Reg, no fooling, you remind me of my deceased husband – "

"Leonard Darwin Rook," interjected Reg. Yesterday he had thoroughly cross-examined her on her family situation. Now he dug up the name more or less to prove to himself that he wasn't drunk yet. Far from it. Miles off.

Cora wobbled with whisky and astonishment. In a voice that had slurred and deepened with cigarettes and scotch over the course of the afternoon, she declared that, "You, Reg, have an *amazing* memory."

She wasn't going to get an argument out of Reg. "In my line of work – you have to. If you don't – one slip and its game over."

"Figures," said Cora.

"What?" Len was having some difficulty concentrating. He put it down to all that hot sun shining in his eyes.

"Figures," repeated his hostess. With her index finger she wrote several numerals in the air – 3, 8, 10. "In your line of work you have to be able to remember figures."

"Of course," said Reg, finally catching what she was getting at. He raised his drink aloft. "This is my sixth glass if I don't stand corrected." He pointed his finger at her. "And I don't, do I?"

"Who's counting," said Cora. "Not little old me. I have a terrible memory for numbers." She smiled a small, helpless smile. "But I never forget a face or a pleasant moment. And I just want to say, Reg, that I have seldom spent a more congenial moment than the congenial moments that you and I have passed this afternoon. They are congenial moments that I will recall in days to come with much pleasure."

"Very enjoyable, very enjoyable," Reg muttered into his glass.

"I'm not afraid to say it, Reg. I am one of those women who have always preferred the company of men. I have always believed in the mingling of the sexes. Don't you agree that we only present our best sides when we have someone of the opposite sex to present them to?"

"There's something to be said for that opinion, Cora."

"Does your wife feel similarly? Women most often do."

"I never married," said Reg. This was not strictly the truth, not if commonlaws counted.

"How sad," said Cora.

"Yes," said Reg doubtfully.

"Since Len passed on I haven't been the same," Cora confessed, skinning her palms along the slippery satin encasing her thighs. "I miss the *companionship.*" Reg failed to respond so Cora adopted a more elegiac tenor. "He always brought out the best in me. Men do that for women, you know. I dressed only for my man!" She indicated her outfit. "This was a favourite of his." She sighed. "But I'm afraid grief has led me to neglect my appearance."

"Cora," said Reg, "if every woman neglected herself the way you do, men would have no reason to complain."

"Reg, you have no idea how I appreciate that."

Reg didn't appear to have heard her. He was staring at the face of his watch trying to decipher the time. When he did, he lurched abruptly to his feet. "I'm late," he said.

At the door Cora did what she could to delay his departure. "I've enjoyed working with you. I'd do it again in a minute," she said, propped up against the door jamb.

"You handled yourself like a real pro," said Reg. "You handled yourself beautifully."

Cora was reluctant to let the moment pass. "What if there are more of them in on it? I could go back and do it again. Just to make sure."

"I see where you're coming from. One bad apple can spoil the barrel. Right?"

"Exactly," said Cora.

Reg aimed his forefinger between her eyes. "I get you. The rot spreads." He paused. "Why the hell not? Let's do it again."

"Tomorrow?"

"Without question or comment. And this time, pull two thousand." He stooped over her, breathing a confidence down into her uplifted face. "Because you know, Cora, the more they steal, the longer the sentence they get."

In the next week Cora made three more trips to the bank, withdrawing two thousand dollars each time. It was thrilling, the adventure of a lifetime. In early afternoon Reg would arrive to collect the evidence and Cora would serve drinks and snacks and they would have long, intimate conversations. She could feel the strength of their regard for one another growing day by day. A difference in age was no impediment to mutual respect and affection.

Reg was sweet in an irresistibly boyish sort of way – she couldn't forget how he had pretended to resist when she had coaxed him into dancing with her to Perry Como on the stereo. A bachelor's shyness. Whatever he might have said to the contrary, Cora was sure that dancing had done him as much good as it had done her. It had made her blissfully happy.

Reg was not happy. Despite having seven thousand dollars in his pocket, his stomach hurt. After three thousand dollars, he'd told himself That's enough, pack it in, get while the getting is good. He'd told himself the same thing after five thousand and seven thousand but he couldn't stop. He knew the longer he hung in, the greater the risks he ran. If he kept on with this life – aspirins for tension headaches and whisky to take the kinks out of his neck – his guts were going to end up Swiss cheese.

Wasn't this always the way? A man gets to the very peak of his career, he's conducting some old broad like she was an orchestra, and still he can't shake the queer feeling that he's had ever since he laid eyes on her – that he's losing control of his own life.

"Reggie," said Mrs. Cora Rook, stretching her arms out to him, "let's dance." Andy Williams was on the stereo.

"I don't want to dance," said Reg. It was true. He didn't like the way she felt under her caftan when he held her in his arms. It was like steering a bundle of sticks and twigs.

"Reg," said Cora, "a gentleman does not refuse the invitation of a lady."

"The middle of the afternoon is the wrong time for dancing," argued Reg. "Have another drink instead."

"No, it isn't. Len and I often had a dance in the afternoon."

"Well, I'm not Len."

Cora pouted, held out her glass for him to fill. "I'm feeling gay and Mr. Growl Bear is being a poop." She had started calling him that in the past couple of days. He didn't like it. But what was he going to say? She had volunteered to go to the bank again which put him under some obligation to be nice to her. Come to think of it, maybe it was only wise to dance.

He did. Cora crooned "Moon River" in his ear the whole time.

Reg developed a theory about Cora. After four drinks she got unpredictable and could go one way or the other, sunshine or showers. One afternoon she rained on him for hours, telling him how hard her life was.

"There are some women – I won't mention names – who like being widows. But not me, because if you have a loving heart you want to share it. Len used to say to me, 'Dicky bird, I'm the happiest man alive and I owe it all to you.' And truer words were never spoken. I gave myself completely to that man's happiness – his slightest wish was my command – but the way I look at it, that's the least a woman owes a man who takes charge of all the more sordid details of life. I don't think a woman wants to be involved in the sordid details of life, money and taxes and bank accounts and all that sort of rigmarole. That life isn't for me, Reg. I don't know who is cheating me and who isn't. A very masculine type of woman could maybe manage this, but I was not made to be bumped and bruised. Len used to say to me, 'Honest to God, dicky bird, you were not made for this world.' If he knew the heart-ache his money has given me, I'm sure Len – even though he was a very jealous man – would want me to marry again. Marry a man with a little business expertise, a man with financial experience like yourself, Reg, who could take over these things and relieve my mind and make me happy again. A man for who I could be Queen of the Home. Do you think I'll ever find a man like that, Reg?"

Reg walked for hours that night, up and down darkened streets. It was clear to him that there was no future for him in his present occupation. Years of preparation and effort and what did it get him? A stomach in knots, a case of nerves you wouldn't believe. And yesterday, diarrhoea. What did it count that he was twice as intelligent as anybody else in his field of endeavour, that he had taken the trouble to make an analysis of it, read books and try to improve himself, always pay attention to the smallest details? Who else had come up with plastic sandwich bags and receipts? Not those other schmucks, those snatch and grab goons. And yet they still did as well as he did – *better* – despite being dumber, despite falling far short of his charm and *savoir-faire* and good looks and *je ne sais quoi* – all qualities that were supposed to be at a premium in this line of work. Which only went to show you a man was only as good as his luck and Reg Stamp's had always been bad. If he'd been born into the right family, given a proper start, he was sure that a man of his abilities could have been every bit as big a success as the famous Len. He, too, could have been the owner of six dry-cleaning outlets and up to his ass in clover. But when it came to luck, he'd been short changed.

And now his nerve was gone. Without it he was nothing, less than nothing. When the nerve went, jail was just around the corner. Jail was not his cup of tea, to tell the truth it scared the holy shit out of him. Of course, the ignorant general public would never understand the difference between him and your usual run-of-the-mill criminal who lacked Reg's sensitivity.

He'd been in twice. The first time he'd got one year less a day. The second time he was sentenced to thirty months. He had barely survived the longer sentence with his sanity intact. The problem with the pen was the kind of people you found there, very low-rent, very crude individuals. Nobody was noisier than a criminal, always shouting threats, slamming cell doors, screaming in their nightmares, playing their radios full throttle, showing absolutely no consideration for their neighbours, none. Reg hated noise. It interfered with his reading magazines and books from the prison library.

And they were violent. If there was anything Reg hated more than noise it was violence; he lacked a drop of violent blood in his veins. Regardless of any other complaints they might have had about him, several of the women he had lived with in the past had commented on this remarkable aspect of his character – no matter how mad he got he never hit them. A gentleman at all times.

Really, he could hardly be considered a *criminal.* Not if the word meant anything. Who had he ever really hurt? Okay, he had received money from people who should have known better. But in what way was that different from what so-called honest, respectable businessmen, so-called pillars of the community, were doing every day of their lives? And what did it amount to, the money he had taken? Peanuts. A thousand dollars from this one for aluminum siding, a thousand dollars from that one for a burial plot, a thousand dollars here and a thousand dollars there. Nobody could tell him that they hadn't been able to spare it either. What a bunch of crap. *If they hadn't been able to afford it, they wouldn't have parted with it!*

It was the unfairness of it all that got him down. He had met a guy in the Prince Albert Pen who had murdered three people, two of them children. With an axe. And he was never sick a day in his life, ate like a horse, slept like a baby. But Reg Stamp, who had never done anything much worse than a sort of practical joke, a complicated prank, *he* couldn't sleep, couldn't eat, couldn't find a second's peace.

He would be fifty-three years old in six months. If he continued on this way he might never see another birthday, the stress and strain of this life was going to kill him. Other men in precarious health could fall back on disability pay, draw on company pension schemes. Not him. Other men could look forward to a secure retirement. Not him.

There was nobody to take care of Reg Stamp but Reg Stamp himself. In his current dilemma, he couldn't see any way out except to marry her. At least it was legal and most likely a shorter sentence than he'd get if he were convicted again. How long was an old lady like that likely to last, abusing herself with alcohol the way she did? To put it in perspective, all you had to tell yourself was that it was like waiting for a Canada Savings Bond to come due. While he waited he could relax, take life easy, rebuild his health. If he made like he'd given up a promising career as a bank inspector to manage her affairs she'd be delighted, eternally grateful. She'd probably even buy him a classy present.

And the beauty was it was all legal, no financial hanky-panky involved. Good fortune made him feel generous, magnanimous. He expected to give something in return, that was his style. He knew what these old ladies like Cora wanted – a little care and kindness. So what if she went fishing for a compliment once in a while, he'd give her one. It was no skin off his ass. So what if she wanted to sit and drink Glendronach in the afternoon, he wasn't averse. So what if she wanted to have a little dance now and then, he didn't mind dancing. After all, keeping her happy today would ensure his happiness tomorrow.

~

They were married ten days later, a whirlwind romance. Reg argued for a private wedding, by which he meant secret. "Let's surprise our friends," he urged, overlooking that he had none. Reg didn't want someone meddling and queering the deal at the last minute. The ceremony was performed by a marriage commissioner, the witnesses were the caretaker of Cora's building and his wife. Reg gave them twenty bucks a piece.

There was some confusion in the beginning because the marriage commissioner kept trying to pair Cora and the caretaker together, assuming, because of their ages, they were bride and groom. When it finally got sorted out, with much shuffling and shifting and switching of places, Reg was pretty peeved because he had been made to feel ridiculous. Also, the commissioner giving him the hairy eyeball all through the service didn't do anything for Reg's increasing bad humour either. And Cora insisting on playing the blushing bride and carrying an enormous bouquet bristling with baby's breath just topped it all off. Every time Reg looked over at her he asked himself, "Who does she think she is? Doris Day?"

But he pecked the bride and it was mercifully finished with, the happy couple returning to the apartment to order Chinese food and drink the two bottles of champagne that had been left chilling in the fridge. Cora giggled a lot over her new name, Mrs. Cora Stamp, slamming her foot to the floor every time she said it. She hadn't had much time to get accustomed to it because she had learned it only after Reg had proposed and security restrictions were lifted because he was quitting his job. Reg bridled inwardly whenever she laughed because he didn't see anything funny about his name. Of course, when Cora got drunk she could find paint on the wall hilarious.

After they polished off the two bottles of champagne they uncorked a bottle of Glendronach from the case she kept stashed in the linen closet. An hour or two later, Reg, seeing that Cora was getting into pretty bad shape, suggested she go lie down for a while. Cora, who thought she knew what he was hinting at, got unsteadily to her feet, went into the bedroom, put on her filmy fuchsia negligee, freshened up her lipstick, and lay down on the bed to wait for her new husband to come to her.

Reg sat in the living room with a glass in his hand, a man of property. He looked around him. That bottle of whisky was his whisky. That chair was his chair. That stereo was his stereo. Once these things had been Len's but by the simple act of obtaining a marriage licence they had become his. Which only went to show you that in the end he had a step up on old Len, was miles ahead of that supposed financial wizard. To keep these nice things, all he had to do was be kind to an old lady, carry her grocery bags for her, help her into taxis, put her to bed when she was too drunk to do it herself.

Finding this very funny he laughed, poured himself another drink, stretched out on the sofa. He didn't know where he was going to sleep tonight but *pas de problem*. In the course of such an eventful day there had been no time for a discussion of domestic arrangements and for one night he had no objection to roughing it on a soft sofa. He'd slept worse places in his day. Tomorrow he'd have her buy a water bed for him; he'd always wanted one of those, but his former life had made one impractical. You couldn't skip about the country the way he had with a water bed.

And he needed a new suit. He had the feeling that part of the marriage commissioner's evident contempt for him was the way he was dressed, in a Bay Day suit. Reg continued to count off items on a lengthening shopping list as if they were sheep until, all at once, he was asleep.

Mrs. Cora Stamp lay in bed awaiting the groom for a long time. He did not make an appearance. Several times she called out in an enticing voice, "Mr. Growl Bear? Mr. Growl Bear?" but got no answer.

Reconnoitring, she found him asleep on the chesterfield. The dear boy really was handsome, handsome in a more refined way than Len had been. She gazed at him fondly. What a picture of innocence! Leaning over, she kissed his brow and quite by accident one of her breasts grazed his cheek, provoking him to stir. She continued.

Reg Stamp woke in confusion from a dark dream of treachery and deceit, shouting: "Fraud! Fraud! Fraud!" in a terrified, accusing voice. He had no idea who he was indicting. Whether it was Reg Stamp, or the blurred, wet red lips he felt dabbing at his neck and face, it all came to the same thing. All he knew was that life, the old whore, had tricked and cheated him once again.

Home Place

IT WAS EARLY MORNING, so early that Gil MacLean loaded the colt into the truck box under a sky still scattered with faint stars. The old man circled the truck once, checking the tail-gate, the tires, and the knot in the halter shank, tottering around on legs stiff as stilts, shoulders hunched to keep the chill off him. He was sixty-nine and mostly cold these days.

A hundred yards behind him one window burned yellow in the dark house. That was his son Ronald, asleep under the bare light bulb and the airplanes. Whenever Ronald fled Darlene, the woman Gil MacLean referred to as the "back-pages wife," he slunk back to his father's house in the dead of night to sleep in a room lit up like a Christmas tree. To her father-in-law, Darlene was the back-pages wife because Ronald had found her advertising herself in the classified section of a farm newspaper, right alongside sale notices for second-hand grain augers and doubtful chain-saws.

Dawn found the old man in a temper, a mood. It was the mare he had wanted when he rattled oats in the pail and whistled, but it was the gelding which had been lured. The mare, wiser and warier, had hung back. So this morning he had a green, rough-broke colt to ride. There was nothing for it, though. He needed a horse because his mind was made up to repair Ronald's fences. They were a disgrace.

Generally that was the way to catch what you wanted,

shake a little bait. It was what Darlene had done with Ronald, but she hadn't fooled Gil MacLean for a second. He knew how it was.

Four years ago his son and Darlene married after exchanging honeyed letters for six months. Ronald never breathed a word to him about any wedding. When Ronald's mother was alive she used to say Ronald was too much under his father's thumb. But the one time he slipped out from beneath it, look at the result.

One morning Ronald had driven off in the pick-up. Twelve hours later he phoned from Regina to announce that he and his bride were bound for Plentywood, Montana, to honeymoon. Ronald was thirty-eight then, had never been married, had never been engaged, had never even had a date that his father could recollect. It was a shock and a mystery. The way Gil figured it, Ronald must have proposed by mail before he ever met face to face with Darlene. Ronald didn't have it in him to offer himself in the flesh to someone with whom he was actually acquainted. He would be too shy, too embarrassed for that.

The old man folded himself into the cab of the truck, joint by joint. "The best work, the worst sleep," he muttered to Ronald's lighted window as he drove under it. In the east there were mares' tails on the horizon, fine as the vapour trails of jets, reddened by the rising sun.

It was Gil MacLean's speculation that his son married only to get his hands on land. Not land of Darlene's, she was a waif and a pauper and had none, but his land, Gil MacLean's land. He never entertained the idea that Ronald might have married out of loneliness, or lust, or any feeling of the remotest kin to either. Just land. That was why he was sometimes troubled, wondering what share of responsibility was his to bear for Ronald's current unhappiness. Maybe he ought to have transferred the title sooner, but he had never trusted the boy's judgment. Events appeared to have confirmed his suspicions. Ronald had his own farm now, a wedding present. A married man needed land, so his father gave him the farm that the MacLeans had always called the "home place." It gave Gil satisfaction to see it pass from father to son and he thought it might bring Ronald luck.

The home place consisted of the original quarter Gil's father had homesteaded, the pre-emption, and another 320 acres picked up cheap from a Finnish immigrant who went to pieces when his wife ran off on him. Over the years the MacLean family acquired other holdings but the home place was special. Situated in a valley, it was a mix of rich bottom land and steep, wooded hills. In the spring, down by the river, blizzards of gulls floated in the wake of tractor and disker, pursuing easy pickings, while hawks rode the air high above the lean hills and, shrieking, fell to plunder these lazy storms of white birds. To Gil it had all been beautiful. It was all he had ever wanted, to possess that place and those sights. A day spent away from the farm made him restless, cranky. Returning to it, even after the briefest absence, he acted oddly, dodging through the wires of a fence in his city clothes to wade about in his crop, hands running back and forth lightly over the bearded heads the way another man might absent-mindedly stroke a cat. Or he might suddenly strike off for the hills with all the energy and purpose of someone hurrying off to keep an appointment, tie flying over his shoulder.

His wife used to say: "Gil's gone off to satisfy himself that nobody so much as shifted a cup of dirt on this place when he was away."

What Gil never confided to his wife was that he felt more present in the land than he did in his own flesh, his own body. Apart from it he had no real existence. When he looked in a mirror he stood at a great distance from what he regarded, but with the land it was different. All that he had emptied of himself into it, he recognized.

The road to the home place ran due east without deviating a hair, rising and falling regularly as a sleeper's breath as it made its way over a succession of bare hills. The emerging sun drew his eyes into a squint when he topped a rise; the blue shadows in the hollows forced them wide again. In the back of the truck the slither and clatter of iron shoes was unremitting. The colt was either highly strung or lacked balance. If it lost its footing and fell it would be a task to get on its feet again; the box was narrow and there was little room for manoeuvring. He'd have to go back and get Ronald out of bed to help him.

Turning Ronald out of bed was not an easy job. Despite his son's difficulties falling asleep, once he was gone he wasn't likely to stir. Often he didn't wake before noon. Gil, on the other hand, roused to the slightest sound. That first night the gritty scraping of the shoes on the stairs had been enough to jerk him out of a dreamless sleep. He'd never been one to lock doors, he had only himself to thank that a night intruder was climbing up to him. It was like the television and its stories of grinning madmen invading houses and arming themselves with drapery cords and butcher knives to strangle and stab. The old man bunched up his pillow and held it out before him, ready to parry the first knife thrust. The footsteps, however, went on past his door. Only when the toilet flushed did he realize it had to be Ronald.

He simply shook in bed for several minutes, too angry and too relieved to ask himself what his son might be up to. Finally he grew calm and curiosity prodded him out into the hallway to investigate. The light was on in Ronald's old bedroom and the door stood ajar.

Ronald was lying flat on his back on the bed, staring up at his model airplanes. As a teenager, even as a young man, he had exhibited little interest in anything other than building models of airplanes from kits, squeezing tubes of glue, pasting on decals, and painting engine cowlings with brushes whose tips he sucked into needle points. The models had never been removed. Forty or more of them hung suspended from the ceiling on fine wires; his room was almost exactly as he had left it when he chose Darlene. Flying Fortresses, Mustangs, Zeros, Spitfires, Messerschmitts, a whole catalogue of war planes dangled there. The light in the bedroom was also as harsh, pitiless, and glaring as it had ever been. When Ronald was fourteen he had unscrewed the bulb in the ceiling fixture and replaced it with a more powerful one. He also dispensed with the shade because he wanted the models hanging beneath the light bulb to cast their shadows on his bedspread and linoleum in the way fighter planes and bombers passing between sun and earth print their images on country lanes and city squares. These shadows were repeated everywhere about the room, and in their midst lay Ronald, gazing up into the strong light, gazing up at undercarriages and silhouettes.

"What's all this, Ronald?" his father said. "This is a hell of a time to pay a visit. It's past two."

Ronald said: "I can't stand it. I can't sleep there no longer." He kept his eyes fixed on the planes as he spoke.

Gil knew there was talk going around town about his son and his daughter-in-law, all of it unfortunate. Darlene had come stamped with the word trouble; he'd seen it from day one. The old man sighed and took a seat on the straight-back chair beside the dresser. Ronald was not exactly the forthcoming type, he was prepared to wait him out.

After a considerable stretch of silence his son said: "I should never have left." Gil knew what he meant. Ronald wasn't saying he ought not to have left Darlene; he was saying he should not have abandoned this room and the comfort and solace of those planes that could not fly.

It was strange that, given all the worrying he had done about Ronald and Darlene, Gil had never seen the real danger. Now he did. The realization of what might lie ahead was like an attack of some kind. Before he could proceed it was necessary to relieve the pressure prodding his breastbone and robbing him of breath. He arched his back and squeezed his eyes tight until it eased and he could speak. And speak he did, urgently, for a solid hour without interruption and with a drying mouth. He said it was the government and the courts. They'd gone and changed the marriage property laws so that the women ended up with half of everything these days. Did Ronald know what that meant? Darlene could lay claim to a half share of the home place. "No divorce, Ronald," he repeated. "No divorce. Don't let that bitch break up the home place. Don't you give her that satisfaction." Only when he had wrung this promise out of Ronald did he cease arguing. For a moment he was overcome by his son's loyalty. He patted the back of his hand and murmured: "Thank you. Thank you."

In a month, however, Ronald came creeping back up the stairs. In baffled rage and fear of the future, Gil shouted through his bedroom door: "Don't expect any sympathy from me if you won't try to adjust!"

Ronald explained that he had a problem going to sleep in the same room, the same house as Darlene. That's the reason he came home every once in a while, to relax and catch up on his sleep. Not that it was easy for him to get to sleep in his old room either, but there he could manage it. What he did was stare up at the glowing bulb and planes until the moment arrived when he could feel the sun hot on his back and suddenly he was winged and soaring, flying into sleep, released, sometimes for twelve hours at a time.

Ronald had been paying his visits to his father's to sleep for a year. About the time they started he commenced on improvements to the home place. This meant pushing bush and clearing land up top, above the valley, in the hills. Gil had pointed out this was nothing but sheer craziness. Marginal land like that was suitable only for pasture, cropping it would never repay the cost of breaking and if the hillsides were stripped of cover they would erode. But Ronald, who was usually willing to be advised, wouldn't listen to his father. A cunning, stubborn look stole over his face when he said: "We'll see. I hired another dozer. Pretty soon the brush piles will be dry and ready to burn."

All spring Ronald fired his huge, gasoline-laced bonfires of scrub oak and poplar. The gusty roar of flames was like constant static in his ears, heat crumpled the air around him and stained it a watery yellow, greasy black clouds mounted indolently into the purity of blue skies. The scars of the dozer blades fresh on the earth made the old man indignant. In places the soil had been cut so deep that streaks of rubbly gravel were exposed.

"You won't grow wheat in that," Gil MacLean shouted. "So what'll it be? Carrots?"

Smiling oddly, Ronald said: "I'm not growing nothing. I'll open a pit and peddle gravel to the Department of Highways by the yard."

"That's not farming," his father returned, disgusted. "That's mining."

It was all Ronald had any interest in at present, pushing bush, clawing up roots, burning. His face appeared hot, scorched. His eyes were forever weepy and red, their lids puffy and swollen, lashes singed away. The ends of his hair had crinkled, crisped, and gone white in the furnace-heat. Everything else Ronald neglected. He hadn't yet done his summer fallow and his cattle were continually straying. This morning Gil was determined to mend Ronald's fences because he was ashamed of what the neighbours would think with his son's cows belly-deep in their crops.

The old man crested the last rise and the valley spread itself out at his feet. There were days when he would pull his truck over to the shoulder of the road and look with deep satisfaction at the slow river and the sombre quilt of green and black fields, look until he had his fill. From such a height the home place looked fatter and richer than with your nose shoved in it. Up close dirt was dirt. There was no time for stopping and admiring this morning though. He was in a hurry.

Gil entered his son's property by a little-used side gate because he didn't want Darlene spying his truck and reporting his doings to Ronald. He parked, unloaded the horse, and slung a duffel bag of tools and a coil of barbed wire on the saddle. Within minutes he was riding down an old trail they had hauled hay on in summer and wood in winter in his father's time. Neither of those things would be possible now, encroaching wild rose and chokecherry bushes had narrowed it so a loaded wagon couldn't pass. The occasional sapling had taken root between the old ruts. Sunlight and sparrows strayed amid the poplar leaves overhead. Ronald's dozers hadn't reached this far yet, hadn't peeled all this back. Maybe his money would run out before they could, that was Gil's fervent hope.

It was eight o'clock before Gil located the first break in the fence. The wires were rotten with rust and would have to be replaced. He set to work. The old man ought not to have been taken by surprise. He knew the very nature of a young horse was unpredictability. It happened when he was playing out sixty yards of wire, lazy-man style, one end of the coil dallied round the horn, the horse walking it out. It could have been the sound the wire made hissing and writhing after them through the grass and weeds. It could have been that a barb nicked the gelding's hocks. Suddenly the colt froze in its tracks, laid back its ears, and trembled all over like a leaf.

Gil had been a horseman all his life, nearly all of his seventy years. He knew what was coming and he fought with all his strength to keep the gelding from pulling its head down between its forelegs. If the colt managed to get its head down it would be able to buck. It managed. An old man's strength was not sufficient. The horse squealed, wriggled, snapped out its hind legs. Gil's lower plate popped out of his mouth. The sky tilted. He fell.

It was bad luck to get snarled in the wire. The colt dragged him several hundred yards, the old man skipping and bounding and tumbling along behind like a downed water-skier without the presence of mind to relinquish his grip on the tow rope.

When it had winded itself the horse came to a halt, stood rolling its eyes and snorting. The old man began to paw himself feebly, searching his pockets for a pair of fencing pliers with which to cut himself out of the jumble of wire. Using the pliers, he had to move cautiously and deliberately so as not to excite the skittish colt. Nevertheless, when the final strand of wire parted with a twang the colt kicked him twice in a convulsion of fear before trotting off a stone's throw away. There it circled about anxiously, stepping on the ends of the dragging reins and bruising its mouth.

The old man lay still, taking stock. There seemed to be a lot of blood, the wire had cut him in many places. He sat up and the blood gushed out of his nose and mouth and spilled down his jacket front. He peered about him, dazed. The colt had dragged him to a desolate place. Ronald's dozers had been at work. Here there was nothing but bare, black earth engraved by caterpillar treads, piles of stones, and the remains of bonfires, charred tree trunks furred in white powdery ash.

While he sat up the blood continued to pour from his mouth and nose. It was better to lie back down. He was feeling weak but he told himself that was because he had taken nothing that morning but a cup of instant coffee. "I'll rest and my strength will come back," he told himself.

Gil closed his eyes and became aware of the powerful scents of sage, milkweed, grass. How was this possible in a place scoured clean? Then he realized they were coming from his clothes, had been ground into them by the dragging.

During the next three hours he tried a number of times to sit himself up, but the blood always ran so freely from his mouth he resigned the attempt. "Not yet," he muttered to himself. "In a while." He had little sense of passing time. There was only thirst and the stiff, scratchy ache of the wounds on his face, hands, legs.

When the sun shone directly down into his face he realized it was noon. The bright light in his eyes and the time of day made him think of Ronald. He would be waking now, looking up at his airplanes.

He had asked Ronald: "What is it with you? Why do you stare up at those planes?" And Ronald had said: "I like to pretend I'm up there, high enough to look down on something or somebody for once in my life."

Gil had laughed as if it were a joke, but it was an uneasy laugh.

Suddenly the old man was seized by a strange panic.

Making a great effort, he sat himself up. It was as if he hoped the force of gravity would pull everything he just now thought and saw down out of his head, drain it away. What he saw was Ronald's lashless eyes, singed hair, red burning face. What he thought was that such a face belonged to a man who wished to look down from a great height on fire, on ruin, on devastation, on dismay.

When the old man collapsed back into the wire he saw that face hovering above, looking down on him.

"You've got no right to look down on me," he said to the burning sky. "I came to fix your fences. I gave you the home place and showed you how to keep it."

His vehement voice filled the clearing and argued away the afternoon. It became harsher and louder when the sun passed out of Gil's vision and he could not raise himself to follow its course. The horse grew so accustomed to this steady shouting and calling out that only when it suddenly stopped did the gelding prick its ears, swing its head, and stare.

Loneliness Has Its Claims

WHEN I WAS ELEVEN, shortly after my mother was diagnosed as tubercular and admitted to the provincial sanatorium for treatment, my dad delivered me for the summer into the care of a virtual stranger, my Grandma Bradley. An only child, mother's darling, and (if I may say so myself) precociously resourceful in the manipulation of adults, I found Grandma Bradley a hard nut to crack, a dangerous customer. None of the tactics so successful with my mother had any effect on her. She scoffed at feigned illness, shed flattery the way a duck sheds water, and made it a policy to assume the worst when it came to children. To be perfectly frank, I don't think she cared for me much.

That she didn't came as no big shock to me – I was not exactly my father's favourite either. I won't say that he actively disliked me because that would be putting the case too strongly. It was just that he was so smitten with my mother, so head over heels in love with her, that she monopolized all his consideration. My father's memory, which never failed him when it came to my mother's birthday and red-letter days such as wedding anniversaries, went all fuzzy when it came to particulars concerning his son and heir.

"Charlie turned eleven, May 7," he'd inform polite inquirers after my age.

"Twelve," I'd correct.

"That's right, twelve," he'd say. "He's going into grade six."

"Seven," I'd say. "They accelerated me last year."

"That's right, grade seven," he'd amend. "He's going into grade seven come September."

After one summer chez Grandma Bradley, I made it clear to my father that the experiment of 1959 had been a failure and that I would prefer hard time in Bible Camp to another June and July passed under her roof. Of course, my father didn't listen then, just like he didn't listen any other time I opened my mouth.

Almost a year later, we got word that Mother was slated soon to be discharged from hospital. Immediately my father concluded that an extended vacation in the bracing, pure, tonic mountain air of Banff would be just what was needed to cap her recovery. Thrilled by the idea of holidays in the blue Canadian Rockies, I encouraged my father in his plans. Don't think I didn't throw a spectacular shit conniption when I discovered I wasn't part of them. However, lacking a mother at home to wheedle and whine at, I didn't have a sniff at getting Pop's mind changed. "You're twelve now, Charlie," he said. "It's about time you learned that the world doesn't revolve around you. Your parents are people with wishes too. After such a long separation your mother and I need to get re-acquainted with one another – in private."

Where was I going? Back to the farm for a rerun of the summer of 1959.

The driver of the STC bus did as my father had requested, he pulled over to the shoulder of the highway and let me off with my bag at the access road to Grandmother's farm. The air brakes gasped wheezily, the tires churned in popping gravel, the roar of the motor faded into the distance and reluctantly I set off, heavy suitcase bucking against my thigh as I lurched toward the farmhouse screened behind the windbreak of evergreens. It was hotter that day than the hubs of hell, and the blowsy, yellowing spruce which lined the road held the air trapped and so deathly still that after fifty yards I was panting like a done dog.

At intervals, whenever my arm threatened to tear loose from my shoulder socket, I would fling the suitcase down in the dust, thump a few kicks into its guts, and curse my father, prompting a drab fireworks of sparrows to explode out of the spruce. For several frantic moments the dizzy, desperate birds would wheel headlong to and fro across the bleached, empty sky and then sweep back into the trees, showering me with plaintive cries and bobbing the spruce boughs as they fussily resettled themselves.

Once I'd exhausted myself victimizing the luggage, I slumped down on it to recover my breath and feel sorry for myself. But in a few minutes that became uncomfortable too, what with the sun drumming up a sick headache behind my eyes and clouds of insects rising out of the ditches to swarm me. Driven to distraction, I'd hoist my bag and stagger forward, telling myself that just around the turn in the road waited a cooling beverage, shade, and, if I was lucky, maybe even an electric fan.

This was the best I could expect up the road. The year before, my father had been able to whip up my enthusiasm, con me with his blather about how I was going to a "real farm." Back then, when I was eleven, innocent and naive, the words "real farm" had conjured up visions of a dog gambolling loyally at my heels, a fishing hole, maybe a pony to ride. Best of all, a gun to shoot and wildlife to massacre. What I discovered on arriving was a dust-bowl-Okie nightmare, junked machinery, unpainted out-buildings patched with flattened tin cans and defunct licence plates, ziggurats of rotten manure, the only farm livestock idiot chickens living an outlaw life, gobbling bugs and flamboyantly strutting about the property. In charge of this god-forsaken garden spot was the most frightening adult I had ever encountered: Matilda Bradley, six feet and 180 pounds of chain-smoking, out-of-the-bottle-auburn-hair, seventy-year-old, hard-ass grandmother.

At last the farmyard hove into view, looking even sorrier than I had remembered it. There was the row of derelict DeSotos Grandpa Bradley had once cannibalized for parts, which were now nesting sites for Grandma's scrawny range chickens, the bright orange of their rusting hoods and roofs decorated with spatters and curlicues of white chicken shit. A number of hens gave me a glassy stare as I trudged toward them, then stretched their necks and scuttled away stiff-legged to seek cover in the weeds which overran the farm, rank plantations of pigweed and ragweed, stinging nettle nearly as tall as I was, buttons of bright yellow dandelion, purple-tipped candelabras of Scotch thistle. Off in the distance I could see that the roof of the nag-backed barn had sunk a little lower in the kidneys and that the sun stared more boldly through chinks in its planking. The house was in slightly better shape – still solid but exhibiting symptoms of senility. Its paint scabby, peeling, and the wooden shingles above the eaves showing a suspicious green stain – maybe lichen. The porch also appeared to be tipping forward, straining to tear itself free from the main building.

Just as I was heaving my suitcase up the worn, splintered steps of the house, Grandma stepped out to greet me, dressed fit to kill in a navy-blue skirt with matching jacket, a jet necklace and jet earrings. Around the house her uniform was a baggy dress and a battered pair of unlaced men's sneakers, but for any public appearance, even grocery shopping, she never failed to deck herself out in all her finery. Naturally I assumed her costume signalled she was off to town.

Taking a ferocious drag on her cigarette she looked me up and down and commented, "So you made it."

I gazed up at her. Her auburn hair was aglow from a fresh retinting and she loomed larger than life and twice as bold, a forbidding billboard of a woman. "Could be I hurt myself carrying this suitcase all that way," I said, clutching my side and grimacing dramatically. "I sort of felt something pop inside me a ways back."

"I'm not your mother," she said coolly. "Don't try any of your cute tricks on me or you just might feel something pop on your outside." She squinted her eyes against the glare of the sun and flapped her hand at a cloud of midges. "So what's the dope on the honeymooners?" she asked. "How long do they intend to gallivant around and leave you parked on my doorstep?"

"Dad took leave," I said. "Five weeks, maybe six."

"What your father took leave of is his senses," said Grandma Bradley. "I haven't got a clue what all this kafuffle is supposed to accomplish."

"He and Mom are getting re-acquainted," I said.

"What he ought to re-acquaint himself with is an honest day's work," she remarked. "Six weeks' leave. I've heard everything now."

I attempted to change the subject – not that I was averse to hearing criticism of my parents – but once Grandma Bradley started lashing out she had a tendency to swing in all directions. I might be the next target. "Were you going out?" I asked hopefully.

"No," she said. "I'm expecting company. So get in the house, wash your face, change your shirt, and keep that famous lip of yours buttoned."

Company was Mr. Cecil Foster, a retired elementary school principal, unknown to anyone in this neck of the woods before he had mysteriously appeared a year before and bought the most modern house in town, a split-level built by the town's former doctor. It was a head-scratcher to everyone why a sixty-eight-year-old bachelor would choose to move to the back of beyond where he had no apparent relations and connections, but there he was.

The moment I laid eyes on him I had no doubts I was face to

face with a former educator. Although retired, he looked every inch the teacher in his drip-dry, short-sleeved white shirt stained with old pen leaks, and his cheap electroplate tie-clip flaking shiny metallic dandruff onto his necktie. He also wore the standard black leather shoes with rubber soles for sneaking up on you.

Right off I identified Mr. Cecil Foster as a disguiser. Buying his clothes too small for his full-figure frame and opting for the camouflage-do – hair swept from a part just above his right ear and plastered in a Brylcreem-soggy grey wing across the steppes of his bald scalp – were proof of that.

Mr. Foster shook my hand, squeezing it between thumb, index and middle fingers like he was testing a peach for ripeness. "So tell me, Charlie," he asked, sending a gale of Sen Sen into my face, "what's your favourite subject in school?"

I sized him up, trying to determine the right answer. The right answer being whatever subject Mr. Foster had himself taught. His pucker-lipped, precise manner of *pro*-nunciating and *e*-nunciating smelled of English teacher. I confessed that English was number one in my books.

This delighted him. "Oh, I'm so glad!" he exclaimed. "And what do you like best – literature or composition?"

I admitted to preferring literature.

"So many boys I've encountered over the years won't admit to an interest in literature – they think it's unmanly to like poetry and stories." He smiled at me. "Always follow your heart, Charlie. It's the first rule of life. If you like poetry – well just like it, despite whatever your friends might say!" He turned to my grandmother. "I believe we have an imaginative young man here. Very imaginative."

"That's the word for him," drawled my grandmother.

It never dawned on me until the tail end of his visit what he was doing at my grandmother's house – you'd have had to have the imagination of an Edgar Allan Poe to even suspect such a thing. So for two boring hours, in ignorance I drooped around the hot living room, pushing dead flies into piles on the window sashes and trying to ignite them into funeral pyres with a book of Grandma's matches. Nothing would burn but the wings. When I got tired of that I'd wander over to where the senior citizens were playing rummy for twenty-five cents a game and Mr. Cecil Foster was riding a winning streak. Every time I paid a visit he'd point to his growing stack of quarters and give me the conspiratorial wink. Grandmother, touchy loser that she was, just kept ordering me in a short-tempered voice to push off.

It was only after Grandma had retired the deck of cards in disgust that the grotesque, unexpected part happened. As he was preparing to leave, Mr. Foster gathered Grandma's hands between his palms and began to stroke them with the tips of his chubby fingers. She offered her cheek for him to smooch, which he did, loudly and wetly.

He was her *boyfriend.* I was gripped by the willies.

My grandmother referred to him as her "gentleman friend," with more stress on the word gentleman than friend. Grandma Bradley, like Mr. Cecil Foster, was an unsuccessful disguiser too. She made a big show of not being taken in by him, but I could see that all six feet and 180 pounds of her was tickled pink by his attentions, despite frequent disclaimers. "The problem with these old bachelors is that when they get to a certain age they start to worry about their health. What's going to happen to me if I get sick? they ask. Who's going to look after me? Remind me to take my medicine, drive me to the doctor? Cook those special diabetes and high blood pressure meals? Men are such big babies. Nothing scares them half as much as the idea of croaking alone. All of a sudden they figure a wife is not such an inconvenience."

"So what's in it for you?" I asked.

"What's in it for me? You think I want to spend what's left of my life watching this dump collapse around my ears?" Grandma Bradley struck a match and sucked the flame into the end of her cigarette, drizzled smoke from her nostrils. "Mr. Foster owns a three-bedroom house, wall-to-wall carpeting throughout, fireplace, developed basement. Hallelujah. Sure, he's not the man your Grandfather was – and thank God for that." Her eyes narrowed. "He's got potential," she said. "Be nice to him. Or else."

Several days later Mr. Foster appeared at the farm and offered to take me on a drive, an outing. Grandma Bradley was overjoyed to get rid of me and my complaints about the quality of the one available television channel, lima beans, and flannel sheets in July. "Don't be in a hurry to get him back," she said, "take your time."

Under normal circumstances I would have considered going for a drive with a man like Mr. Foster a horrible ordeal. But things being relative, it beat the hell out of another afternoon spent watching a cooking show and "Take Thirty" on CBC.

Mr. Foster's car had air-conditioning – a definite plus – and he kept tinkering with the controls until I conceded I was "comfy." What's more, he allowed me to tune the radio to my favourite station and crank it up full bore, something that would have got my wrists broken if I tried it in my grandmother's DeSoto. Nor did he object when I began singing along to the radio to test the limits of his tolerance. In fact, he joined Patti Page and me in a rendition of "How Much Is That Doggie in the Window?" giggling and woof-woofing his way through the song like a maniac. I concluded he was nutty as a fruitcake, but fun.

Radio blaring, we rolled along. Fields, herds of red cattle, clumps of poplars with their leaves blinking green to silver, silver to green in the breeze, sped by. The sky was banked high with mountains of cumulous.

Mr. Foster confided there was something he just had to show me. For the next half hour we jolted over a succession of deteriorating roads, climaxing in a bumpy rutted track that wound its way across the brown face of a vacant pasture.

When the track finally ran itself out amid skimpy grass, sand, and cactus, we got out of the car and walked on until the plateau suddenly dissolved in a dizzying rush of sky and wind and left us hanging perched on a lip of eroding earth, the wind pummelling us and tugging at our clothes like dozens of pairs of children's hands. More interesting, the wind also popped Mr. Foster's hair up and down at his side part like the lid on a jack-in-the-box. I was studying this intriguing phenomenon with close attention when my companion suddenly made a lofty sweep of the arm and cried, "Isn't it grand!"

The quick movement, the abrupt exclamation startled me. A small avalanche of dirt trickled out from under my sneakers and spilled down the sheer slope.

"Do you know what this reminds me of?" he asked, putting his hand on my shoulder, steadying me.

It reminded me of a valley. Far below my feet was a sleepy river winking a semaphore of sun, a concrete bridge which looked like part of a model railroad set, a yellow road that switchbacked up blue and distant hills, a red Tinker Toy tractor raising smoky dust in a black field.

I told Mr. Foster I had no idea what this reminded him of.

"Scotland," said Mr. Foster.

As far as I was concerned this was stretching it. What I was looking at didn't resemble any pictures of Scotland I'd seen. When I asked him why what we were looking at was like Scotland, he ignored me. Likewise, when I asked him if he'd ever been there.

"Oh Scotland!" he murmured. "When I was your age, Charlie, how I was in love with Scotland!" He turned to me eagerly. "Have you read Robert Louis Stevenson?"

I shook my head.

"Long John Silver and Jim," he said. "The man wrote the most beautiful books. *Kidnapped.* I adored that book. When I was a boy there was nothing I wanted more than a friend like Alan Breck, someone older to look up to. I thought David Balfour the luckiest boy in the world because he had Alan Breck to share his adventures with. Have you ever wanted an older friend the way I did, Charlie?"

I shrugged. I hadn't thought much about it. But on consideration I wouldn't have minded having Ernie Tastin for a best buddy. Nobody would fuck with me then. Ernie was in grade nine and older than a lot of high-school seniors. "I wouldn't mind," I said.

Mr. Foster smiled. "I would like to be your older friend," he said. "I'm sure you and I could be great friends. Shall we be friends?"

I didn't see what I had to lose. "Okay," I said.

On the way back to the car my new friend tried to teach me a song about taking the high road or the low road. It was a Scottish song, he said.

Uncle Cecil (it was his idea for me to call him that) proved to have the schoolteacher's habit of wanting to improve you. Some attempts at improvement were interesting and some were not. For instance, I wasn't too nuts about him pressing his own personal copies of *Treasure Island* and *Kidnapped* on me to read. But I did like learning chess, a version of war that suited crafty runts like me. Now when he came to visit, Uncle Cecil brought his chess set and we battled it out on the dining-room table under Grandma's disapproving eye. She believed she had first call on Mr. Foster and *she* wanted to play cards, prompting her to make sarcastic comments like: "If chess is supposed to be such a brainy game, how do you expect to teach it to someone who can't learn to count a cribbage hand?"

As far as I was concerned, what was really aces about older friends was the money they had. Just let me mention that the glare of the sun gave me a headache – he bought me sunglasses. I got a hula hoop, yo-yo, chocolate bars, comic books, a straw cowboy hat simply by strategically dropping hints. All I needed to do was suggest I was hungry or thirsty and we'd be wheeling up to the nearest cafe for a burger and Coke float. What's more, I talked him into letting me drive his Buick on deserted stretches of country roads – you wouldn't have caught my old man doing anything along those lines. Just worrying about the insurance would have given him a haemorrhage.

I felt a little guilty about Uncle Cecil being so nice to me, so generous. I assumed he thought that being peachy to me would get him into Grandma's good books. Nothing was further from the truth – the more stuff he bought me, the more time he spent with me, the more resentful she got. It was obvious, the old girl was jealous. Somehow Uncle Cecil didn't seem to realize this. He didn't get it that maybe it was more important to tell her how wonderful she was than sing my praises to the sky.

At first I enjoyed it, seeing her nose twisted out of joint. But after three weeks of Cecil's Be Nice to Charlie Campaign the atmosphere in my grandmother's house was a little too sour for my taste. The old girl was a wounded grizzly. I would have warned Uncle Cecil that an ill wind was getting ready to blow except for one reason and one reason alone. Before I sat him down and clued him in that being sweet to me was not such a wonderful policy, there was something I wanted to get from him. And this thing I wanted to get was the one thing he hesitated to buy me.

I wanted a gun.

Uncle Cecil was not enthusiastic about this idea. "I don't know, Charlie," he said doubtfully whenever I dredged up the topic. "I don't know. What do you want with a gun?"

"It's for Grandma's sake," I said, hoping that such a claim might sway him. "You know how she's always complaining about the birds in her garden. If I had a gun I'd be able to put the run on them for her. Believe you me, she'd thank us both."

"I'm not sure," reflected Uncle Cecil. "Maybe the two of us

could put up a scarecrow for her. Don't you think it might be more fun to make a scarecrow and dress it up?"

No I did not. I was not some half-witted six year old. Blazing away with my own firearm was my idea of fun. In my books, the opportunity to shoot a gun was the only recommendation for life in the country. Give me a gun or give me nothing.

"And another thing," I said. "Let's say some escaped convicts were to come to the farm in the middle of the night. We're awful isolated, and yelling for help wouldn't do much good way out there. But if I had a gun I could protect Grandma." I paused. "In case they tried to rape her or something."

That was a mistake, mention of turning a gun on anybody. He looked even more doubtful. "A gun is a great responsibility," he said. "And you're very young, Charlie."

"Yeah, right," I said desperately. "But that's the great thing about a gun. Don't you see? It'll teach me responsibility. I'll get more mature with a gun around. And also – also," I was flailing around madly in my mind for a clincher. "Also it doesn't matter that I'm young because I've got an older friend to supervise me and everything."

"I don't know very much about guns," said Uncle Cecil. "In fact, I don't know anything at all about guns."

"No problem," I assured him. "Just leave all the *technical* stuff, the loading it with bullets and all that crap to me. I can read up on it." I gave him a look of great frankness and sincerity. "But how can you learn responsibility and maturity from a book? That's where an older friend is so important."

Uncle Cecil was showing signs of acute discomfort. "But, Charlie," he blurted out, "I don't *like* guns!"

Right, I almost said. So what? Do I *like* the world's most deadly book, that *Kidnapped* you gave me to read? No, but I'm reading it, aren't I? I'm ploughing through it a couple of pages a night, all those Scottish words I don't understand. Muckle this and muckle that.

But I knew better than to let fly on that topic. When it came to the care and maintenance of grownups, I kind of prided myself on being a first-class operator. The last thing you ever wanted to do was show up an adult in delicate negotiations, or poop on something they thought was top notch. From the time I was six years old and used to plead with my mother to play me her Frank Sinatra records to get on her good side, I knew that much.

"It'd probably save Grandma's garden," I said. "And I'd learn a lot from owning a gun."

"Well, let me think about it," said Uncle Cecil.

If it would help overcome his hesitation, I was willing to go cheap. "You can get a Cooey single shot bolt action twenty-two for around twenty dollars," I informed him. "A real bargain."

"I'll think about it," he promised.

Uncle Cecil and I were seeing each other every day now. Sometimes we didn't bother to go on the drives we told Grandma we were going on, we just went to Uncle Cecil's house and hung out. He had a huge, varnished piano, the surface of which I could watch myself in when I fooled around on it. It was a big hoot to do imitations of the concert pianists I'd seen on CBC, scrunching down so that my face almost touched the keys like Glenn Gould while playing by ear ecstatic renditions of the themes of "Bonanza" and "Have Gun Will Travel." As I tickled the ivories, Uncle Cecil sat in his easy-chair, sipping scotch, and flashing his finger in the air like he was conducting. Grandma didn't know about Uncle Cecil and the scotch, whisky was something he tried to keep private the way he did his baldness. He wasn't a big drinker, never indulged in more than a couple of drinks, but a couple were enough to bring about a sea change; he talked peculiar, he talked to me as if I was an adult. I didn't like it. It wasn't that I was learning anything shocking, I'd heard lots more interesting and shocking things just by keeping myself as quiet and still as a mouse in a corner and letting adults forget I was there to eavesdrop. They didn't know the half of what they had given away to me. But this was different. To be told things straight out like I was grown up broke hallowed conventions, was somehow plain wrong.

What did he talk about? Mostly friendship. And loneliness. He said he'd never had many friends. It was his one regret. Only when you were older did you realize what you had missed in life – and he had missed out on the joys of friendship. He wondered if perhaps his difficulties weren't a result of having been a person in authority. It wasn't easy to be intimate with a member of your teaching staff and still observe professional standards of conduct. Besides, so many elementary teachers were women, and friendships with women were risky because they were so easily misrepresented and misunderstood. Also, it was his belief that women's friendships lacked the idealism which was such an important element in male relationships. No one could ever imagine a woman dying for a friend.

He would tell me how he had always thought of himself as a friend to all the boys and girls in his school, yet doubted if they had seen him in that light. It wrung his heart to know that many students had been actually terrified of him – just because he was a principal. It wasn't fair. Each year on the first day of school he had made a speech in which he urged all the boys and girls to think of him as their friend, encouraging them to come to him if they needed advice, or a sympathetic and understanding ear. Yet in all his years of teaching no one ever came to him with a problem. There had been days when this distrust was so upsetting that he had closed the door of his office to conceal his tears.

When he started going on in this vein there wasn't anything I wouldn't do to sidetrack him – for instance, right in the middle of a sentence commence hammering out the theme from "Bonanza" on the piano so hard I thought my fingers would snap. Once, before I could stall him, he said, "You know, Charlie, there was a time when I used to look around me and say, 'How is it possible? How is it possible that a little town like this, a town with a population of a mere thousand could contain two people fated to love one another? The odds are against it. And yet it happens. All around us people fall in love with people they've known since they were children. Time and time again it happens. Except to me.' " He hesitated, smiled. "But perhaps my luck is changing."

"You mean Grandma?"

"That's for me to know and you to find out," he said coyly.

Uncle Cecil was hard to figure. One minute he was talking to you like you were on his side of the fence, age-wise, the next minute he was acting as if he was the kid. Sometimes when we were playing chess at his house he'd pretend to slip out to the kitchen for a drink, then sneak back on his squeak-proof schoolteacher shoes while I was absorbed studying the board, clap his hands over my eyes and yell, "Guess who!"

Such goofball behaviour would have been embarrassing in a ten year old, let alone in someone as mature as Uncle Cecil. Worse, he wouldn't lay off until I'd said his name. He wanted to hear me *say* it. Digging in my heels and trying to out-stubborn him didn't work because I couldn't stomach the cold, clammy, icky feel of his hands over my eyes. I'd bellow, "I'm warning you, lemme go!" a couple of times at the top of my lungs to scare him off but it never did. Every time I hollered, he just giggled and purred, "Come on, guess who. Guess." So finally I had no choice but to yell "Uncle Cecil!" When I opened my eyes he'd be grinning like a maniac, running his sticky palms up and down the fronts of his trouser legs, and dancing about on the spot from one foot to another like a little boy needing to go wee.

Worse than any of this, however, was the time he came out in a kilt and pranced and jigged around the house, showing off his fat, lardy white legs, and asking me did he remind me of anybody? After reading about a quarter of *Kidnapped* I had some idea of what I was supposed to say. Alan Breck. So I said it. Even though I thought he looked a dead ringer for Little Lulu.

But he didn't behave this way often, only when he got a few scotches under his skin. That is, with one exception, which was partly my doing. It happened one day when we were down in his basement playing table tennis, which Uncle Cecil advocated as a way of keeping fit and gently encouraging sluggish circulation. Not that he, with his watermelon shape, was exactly a walking advertisement for its benefits. Still, despite his weight problem and the fifty-five-year age difference between us, Uncle Cecil never failed to wax me at ping pong. It's true I was not what you would call coordinated, or an athlete, but it was still shaming for a twelve year old to get pulverized by the likes of him. Inevitably, the more I lost to Uncle Cecil the more frustrated and infuriated I got, swinging out wildly to spray the ball into the rafters overhead, or send it ricochetting off the walls, skittering and skipping frantically across the floor. Meanwhile Uncle Cecil filled the other end of the table like the Berlin Wall, intimidating, impassable. If one of my shots did manage to land on the table, Uncle Cecil would deftly flick it back, his feet never shuffling more than an inch or two to the right or left. This imperturbable, unswerving grace under pressure reduced me to frothing at the mouth.

The day under discussion I was following him up the basement stairs after yet another severe shellacking (eight games to two). Here we were, plodding up the steps, Uncle Cecil droning his maddening, patronizing advice about how I might improve my table-tennis game, while a foot from my face his big fat ass was walloping around in the seat of his pants like two bulldogs fighting in a flannel sack.

All my life I've been prone to weird impulses that unexpectedly take possession of me. Suddenly I realized I hadn't left my ping-pong paddle on the table, I had it in my hand. And then, before I knew what I was doing, I gave one of the bulldogs a terrific smack with it. Uncle Cecil let out a piercing squeak, clutched his derrière with both hands, and whirled around on the stairs.

His reaction was not quite what I expected. I saw his face light up like a lantern in the gloom of the stairs. "Spank my bum, will you! Look out now, Master Charlie!" he squealed.

That was enough for me, I hurtled back down the stairs.

"We'll see how you like some of your own medicine! I'm going to warm your sit-upon for you, young man! Warm it but good!" Uncle Cecil cried in a mock-menacing voice, thundering down the steps after me like an avalanche in a canyon. A couple of circuits around the ping-pong table didn't lose him – with his blood up Uncle Cecil had a surprising turn of speed. Around and around the basement the two of us scampered, Uncle Cecil shrieking playful threats as I hurdled storage boxes, feinted my way out of corners, dodged outstretched arms, veered and deked and doubled my way here, there, everywhere. And still he kept coming, a sound like a handsaw cutting wet wood beginning to whine deep in his chest, crazed, merrily determined eyes shining in a hot, red face.

Embarrassed and worried described me. Playing tag with a senior citizen was even more humiliating than Uncle Cecil's other favourite game, Guess Who. Besides, I was starting to get alarmed he was going to have a coronary. Let him catch me. Big deal. I halted dead in my tracks. Uncle Cecil crashed into me.

The next thing I knew, I was swept up in his arms. Suddenly my nose was mashed into flab and a damp shirt front. I was suffocating. From overhead I heard words trickling down, a slurred, monotonous, sing-song waterfall. "I got you now. I got you now. What are we going to do with you now that I got you now?" All the while his arms, which pinned mine to my ribs, were slowly tightening, slowly squeezing the breath out of me. Panicking, I writhed and twisted, fighting to break his hold. But Uncle Cecil was stronger than I could have imagined and all my struggles only caused him to totter unsteadily back and forth on his feet as if he was rocking an infant. "I got you now. What are we going to do with you now?" he crooned, the breath from his lips ruffling my hair.

The more I resisted, the deeper I seemed to sink into the soft mattress of his torso. It was like trying to breathe with a hot, steamy towel stuck to your face, a used towel smelling unpleasantly of a stranger's body. Nerves, the distasteful smell, the lack of air made me feel faint, my ears buzzed, my head whirled, and – more ominous – a hard bud of queasiness popped up at the root of my tongue. I tried to give a last choked warning but it was lost in the mutter, "I got you now. I got you now. What are we going to do with you now?"

I heaved several times before Uncle Cecil realized hot barf was streaming down his shirt and trousers. He cut me loose then, believe you me, and I staggered off, doubled-up, circling like a crab, upchucking right, left, and centre while Uncle Cecil, horrified, tiptoed after me, crying plaintively, "Oh dear, oh dear, Charlie! Are you all right, my boy? Oh dear!"

I wasn't all right. I was wild at having the bejabbers scared out of me, wild with shame at puking up like a baby, wild with the indignity of being *handled*. At that moment I would gladly have murdered him. But homicide not being an option, I did whatever I could. I refused to speak to him and stomped up the stairs. Uncle Cecil followed at my heels, anxiously inquiring, "What's the matter, Charlie? Charlie, don't be like this. Speak to me. Say something. Where are you going?"

"Home."

"Wait a minute," he said. "I'll get my car keys."

"I'm walking." This idea had just presented itself.

"No, no, Charlie," he said. "You're not feeling well. You can't walk. It's five miles to the farm."

"You think I'd get in a car with you! You fucking tried to strangle me!"

Uncle Cecil shook his head, clucked: "Nonsense, Charlie. Nonsense. And language. Careful with the language."

"*Fucking tried to strangle me!*" I screeched again.

"A game, Charlie," he said nervously, self-consciously.

"Maybe next time we can play Jack the Ripper." I jerked open the screen door.

"I forbid you to walk home!" he shouted at me.

I didn't take this assertion of authority seriously. Poised dramatically in the doorway I gave him a hostile, defiant stare. It was only then it struck me his face was white, gone white with deathly fear.

"You must let me drive you. Your grandmother would never forgive me if I didn't bring you...." He let the sentence die.

"No way." I turned calculating, clinical. I wanted to test his response to this.

"Please, Charlie," he said. "Don't be like this. You mustn't be like this. Please, you're not being fair. Please let me drive you. You got over-excited. It wasn't my fault. Please."

He was begging now, lowering his voice, making soothing, coaxing gestures with his hands, patting and stroking the air between us as he talked. "All a misunderstanding," he kept repeating. "No harm done. Where's the harm, Charlie? No harm at all. All forgotten, all forgiven?"

He smiled weakly, waited apprehensively for a reply. All forgotten, all forgiven? It was some time before I answered. I watched him crumble and flake a little more while I remained silent.

"The gun, Uncle Cecil," I said. "I better get that fucking gun."

I took the ride and I took the gun. Grandma Bradley being present when he handed it over, I mimicked utter surprise and amazement at the unexpected gift. The .22 was a beauty, a pump action Remington that surpassed my greediest dreams. Grandma was clearly not enthusiastic about the idea of me armed, but the only thing she said was, "If he blows his brains out with that thing – or anybody else's – I'm not the one who'll be responsible. I want to go on record that I don't approve."

Once I got my hands on the rifle my interest in chess, car rides, and Glenn Gould impersonations evaporated. To my twelve-year-old nose nothing smelled as sweet as gun oil, although I was careful to make sure that Grandma Bradley didn't find out I slept with the Remington lying beside my bed, loaded, within sniffing distance. I developed a nightly ritual, easing myself down on my mattress, shaking out my arms, closing my eyes. Of course, this was only a ruse to draw the Night Stalker into showing his hand. When Stalker made his play and burst through my door, I rolled to the right, snatched my gun from the floor, and blasted him back to the very doorstep of Hell. This move and variations on it was practised dozens of times until I could settle down to sleep in full confidence that despite having a weak chin and being a shrimp for my age, I was still a damn dangerous hombre.

Daylight hours were spent expending real ammunition. Nothing on the farm was off limits or out of season except Grandma and her chickens. Hour after hour I tramped the property dazed by blood-lust and heat, blazing away at rats in the tumble-down barn, discharging salvos into the bird-infested windbreak, and lying in wait in the brome grass at the edge of the garden for the sparrows to flutter to earth. Strange, novel sensations linked to the gun kept me prowling from sunup to sundown. Only a silhouette of Grandma in the matte grey of late dusk bellowing, "Charlie, get in here now! And I mean right now, goddamn it!" could override these feelings.

She wasn't the only one calling me. So was Uncle Cecil. The very day after he conferred the Remington upon me I watched him park his car and laboriously mount the steps to the house. Five minutes later he was in the yard again, shading his eyes and turning on his heels slowly and deliberately through the four points of the compass. Noting that, I hastily retreated to the barn and scrambled into the hayloft from where I watched him clamber over fences, poke his head into abandoned sheds, peek around the fenders of junked automobiles, all the while mournfully imploring "Charlieeee! Oh, Charlieee!" at the top of his lungs. Finally after forty-five minutes of searching he gave up with a sad, resigned shrug of the shoulders, got into his car, and drove off.

But he was back the next day and the day after that and the day after that and every day following for a week and a half. And each day I hid. I found his confusion comical; it was a laugh to see him fuss-budgeting around the property, clumsily snagging his trousers on barbed wire, desperately squinting into collapsing sheds and derelict autos, cupping his hands to his mouth to halloo dramatically like a sea captain hallooing into the fog for a man lost overboard, smiling to the windbreak, the outbuildings, on the remote chance I might be lured out of them by his shit-eating, apologetic grin. Looking down at Uncle Cecil from the height of the hayloft gave me a feeling of control similar to the one I got with a gun in my hand. I did my best to persuade myself he had this coming to him for the way he had behaved in the basement. Maybe this would teach him to forget the stupid kids' games and act his age. Yet another voice quietly argued that loneliness, too, has its claims.

This behaviour of Uncle Cecil's definitely put him in Grandma Bradley's bad books. It didn't sit well with her that he should spend an hour each day sweating after me and then refuse to stop in her parlour for a cup of tea, or a game of rummy. At night when I dragged my gun and exhausted self into the house I could be sure to get a sprinkling of her spleen. "Charlie Bradley's social secretary reporting. Mr. Cecil Foster requests – as he did yesterday and the day before yesterday – that you phone him this evening. I believe it's urgent boy business, a date for a ride in the country."

I walked past her without acknowledging the message.

"Well, are you going to phone him or not?" she snarled at my back.

"No, I'm not," I said. I had a couple of more weeks of rural purgatory before my sentence expired. Given Uncle Cecil's present low standing with Grandma, any friendliness directed towards him might see me promoted to hell.

My shunning Uncle Cecil may have cheered Grandma but

it didn't really satisfy. I was left with the strong impression that she really wanted his head decorating a stake. Grandma began to ask lots of questions and ask them in an untypically affable way. I had no idea what she was after but I did know that the less I said the better.

"Did Mr. Foster and you have some kind of a fight?"

"No."

"Then why are you hiding from him?"

"I don't want to do what he wants to do."

"So what is it that Mr. Foster wants to do that you don't want to do?"

I seemed to have painted myself into a corner on that one. I shrugged.

Grandma rolled her cigarette around between her thumb and index finger and bored in like a drill bit. "What is it that Mr. Foster wants to do that you don't like to do?"

Evasive action was clearly in order. I didn't quite answer the question posed. "I want to hunt," I said. "Mr. Foster doesn't like hunting."

Grandma pursed her lips, looked as if she might restate the original question, then decided against it. "Why would Mr. Foster buy you such an expensive gun, Charlie? What's in it for him?"

Had she surmised Uncle Cecil was a victim of a shakedown? I turned nervous. Extremely so. I didn't answer.

"Uh-huh, so that's how it is," said Grandma, slowly nodding her head. She lit a fresh cigarette off the butt of the last. "Keeping secrets from our old grandma, are we? You ask Grandma, something smells in Denmark."

My experience of a year ago with my grandmother had taught me that you didn't cross swords with her unless you wanted a blade through the gizzard. What surprised me was that she hadn't put the run on Uncle Cecil, was still allowing him to show up every day and mooch around the property, and, as far as I could make out from my distant perch, she remained polite and pleasant to him. But there was something else I noticed. Now she was spying on him too, watching from a second-storey window as he shuffled up the lane, probed the underbrush of the windbreak with a stick, got down on all fours in the dust of the road to peer under the branches of the spruce trees and rise, disconsolate, to wipe his palms on his pant legs and carry on his fruitless search.

Uncle Cecil didn't overlook the barn. Below me I would hear shrill bird cries, the flutter of disturbed air, the shock of silence following flight. Then the slow scrape of shoes on the remains of the frost-heaved and pitted concrete floor, the muted bumps and knocks of a large soft body colliding with things in the dark. Once he tried to climb the rotten ladder which led to the loft. There was a sudden crack, the squeal of a rusty nail pulling loose, the sound of splintering wood. The bottom rung had given way under his weight. On subsequent visits he just snooped half-heartedly in corners, stalls, and mangers before leaving. Another time, standing in the dark below, he addressed a few quiet words to the possibility I was there. He said, "I am sorry. Please come out." When I didn't, he left.

Grandma Bradley's inquisition resumed a day later.

"What do you like doing best with Mr. Cecil Foster?"

What I liked doing best was driving the car. But there was no way I was going to say that. I tried to think of the most blameless activity I had engaged in with Uncle Cecil. Piano playing. What was more innocent and commendable than piano playing?

"Playing the piano."

Big mistake.

"Where were you playing a piano?"

Where did she think I was playing a piano? Carnegie Hall?

"At his house."

Her eyebrows arched spectacularly. "You were in the great man's house? Well, well, isn't that something. How is that, I wonder? Here I've known Mr. Cecil Foster much longer than you have and yet never once has he invited me to his house. Yet in no time at all you get free run of the place, messing around on his piano and getting into God knows what else. How is that, Charlie?"

I mumbled I didn't know how that was. We just went there sometimes when we were tired of driving around.

"If you were tired of driving around, why didn't you come home?" she snapped.

I knew better than to state the obvious so I kept quiet.

"What else did the two of you get up to in his house when you weren't playing the piano? Anything else you'd like to tell Grandma about?"

"We talked."

"Oh yes," said Grandma Bradley, "talking's nice. What did you talk about?"

"Friendship."

"Friendship?" said Grandma. "Hoity-toity. My, my, but the two of you were having a high old time of it, weren't you? Friendship, eh. Sounds like a topic for a C.G.I.T. Discussion. So, as concerning friendship, what did you two masterminds conclude?"

Before I got my own back, I wanted to establish some distance between me and the sentiments I was about to express. "I didn't conclude nothing," I said innocently. "But Mr. Foster did. He said that friendship with women wasn't as good as friendship with men. Women were always too busy looking out for themselves." Although a loose rendering of Uncle Cecil's position, I didn't think I had mangled it. At any rate, it produced the results I was looking for. Grandma's face coloured a deep red while her thin lips blanched white.

"Well," she said, "maybe Mr. Fancy Foster didn't think of something. Maybe he didn't think women are busy looking out for themselves because they have to." She paused. "And maybe not just themselves but other people as well. Ever think of that?"

I had pinched raw hamburger from Grandma's fridge. Raw hamburger was great bait for magpies. All you had to do was put a little of it on top of a fence post, hide yourself behind an abandoned watering trough or piece of broken-down machinery and wait for the scavengers to land. Then you let them have it.

So here I was whistling to myself, making up eensie-weensie hamburger patties and dabbing them down on a line of fence posts, one after another, when what should I do but look up and see Grandma Bradley a couple of hundred yards off, head thrust forward, arms pumping wildly, bearing down on me hell bent for leather across an expanse of wolf willow, buck brush, weeds, and knee-high couch grass that had reclaimed what was once a field. As soon as I saw her high-stepping it along in her men's sneakers, house dress flapping and tucking itself between her legs in the wind, I figured that she had discovered ground meat gone missing, and nothing but divine intervention could stand between me and an unspeakable death. In despair, I began frantically pulling up bunches of grass to wipe the grease and bits of meat from my hands, hoping like hell Grandma wouldn't spot the magpie hors-d'oeuvres pasted to the tops of the poplar pickets.

The closer she got, the more dire the situation looked for me. There was a blood-curdling gleam in her eye and the determined set of her mouth reminded me of the jaws of a trap locked down on the leg of a cute, furry animal. And then Grandma Bradley was on me, all six feet and 180 pounds of her *there*, blocking out the horizon and the majority of the sky, invading my private space with her big powerful hips and mountainous bosom and flushed angry face and fiery auburn hair. A book was suddenly thrust under my nose, making my eyes cross as I attempted to focus on it.

"I got my evidence now," she said, slapping the cover of the book with her big chapped hand. "In black and white. In print."

What the hell was she raving about now? Evidently not missing hamburger.

"What I want to know," she said, squinting her eyes menacingly, "is which one of you is responsible for underlining in this book. You, or Fancy Foster?"

This was the last thing I expected, Grandma Bradley livid because somebody had marked up a book. "What underlining?" I chirped brightly, a picture of guiltlessness. And guiltless I was. I had no idea what she was fuming about.

"This!" she exclaimed, flipping open the book. Finally, I recognized it. Grandma Bradley had been going through my personal effects; it was Uncle Cecil's copy of *Kidnapped.* There, underlined in a watery ink, faded with time, I read: *He came up to me with open arms. "Come to my arms!" he cried, and embraced and kissed me hard upon both cheeks. "David," said he, "I love you like a brother. And O, man," he cried in a kind of ecstasy, "am I no a bonny fighter?"* At the end of this passage, in the same ink, someone had added several exclamation marks. I hadn't seen this before for the simple reason I hadn't got this far in the book. Whatever significance it had for Grandma was lost on me. The words and expressions were just weird, the way a lot of old books were weird. I looked up at her puzzled.

"Was it you?" she asked.

I shook my head.

"Then it was him," she said, clearly pleased that Uncle Cecil was the vandal.

"Well, it's his book," I pointed out. "I guess he can write in it if he wants."

"Imagine," said Grandma, "giving a book like that to a boy your age."

Directly Grandma went on the march. Uncle Cecil's appearances at the farm ceased. I was instructed to keep indoors and told I must never, under any circumstances, speak to him again. The telephone rang six and seven times a day but I was ordered not to answer it. While it jangled in the kitchen, the two of us sat staring off into space, Grandma mumbling under her breath. When I whined about being kept indoors, arguing it was unhealthy for a growing boy like me to be deprived of fresh air and sunshine, she gave me a cold look and said, "As long as I don't know what's lurking in the bushes outside, you can do without fresh air and sunshine."

I wanted to be hunting. House arrest was driving me crazy. I couldn't see why I had to suffer because Grandma Bradley was on the outs with her gentleman friend. We'd be sitting watching television and out of the blue she'd say, "I'm no Marilyn Monroe, but I'm not a bad-looking woman for my age. I always wondered why he was backward in that respect. Now I know." Or, "You can lead a horse to water but you can't make him drink." After a couple of days her mood grew darker and became fixated on revenge. More and more often I heard things like, "Stringing up from a lamp post is too good for the likes of him."

Quite frankly I didn't care how she fixed Uncle Cecil's wagon as long as it got done soon, allowing things to return to normal and me to go hunting again. I changed my tune when I learned what she had in mind.

"I called Mr. Fancy Foster after you went to bed last night," she volunteered.

"So?" I said.

"I told him that you wanted to see him."

This was news to me.

"He seemed real pleased," mused Grandma. "Real pleased. He's coming by tomorrow afternoon three o'clock." She indulged in a suspense-building pause.

"And?" I said irritably.

"And when he comes three o'clock tomorrow you're going to give him back that gun."

"Not likely!" It popped out before I even knew it.

"*Likely,*" said Grandma. "And then you're going to tell Mr. Fancy Foster exactly what you think of him and his tricks."

"Not the gun, Grandma," I pleaded. "Not the gun!"

"The gun," she said definitely. "Believe you me, you'll thank me for it in years to come. When you're older you won't want any souvenirs and keepsakes of him hanging around, reminding you of anybody's bad behaviour. Trust me, clean break is always the best."

I knew it was a lost cause, but I begged and bargained. Anything she wanted. I'd turn myself into the model grandchild. But don't make me surrender the gun. Grandma was unyielding. At one point, I even faked hysterical tears.

"What's this now?" she snapped.

"You're giving me a case of nerves," I accused, swabbing my eyes with a shirt cuff.

"Nonsense. Children don't have nerves. Nobody has nerves until they're twenty-one. Pull yourself together and quit angling for sympathy," she said.

It was one of those fresh, late summer mornings when the air has an autumn-like snap to it and the sun is a flood of pure, chill light that lends everything an air of stark, arrested tranquillity. I was sitting in a chair by my open bedroom window and Grandma Bradley was in the garden below, picking corn for dinner. I watched her for several minutes before I picked up my .22 and slid the barrel over the window sash. Each time she reached up to break off an ear of corn her skirt lifted in back and sank again when she dropped the corn in the bucket beside her feet. I sighted in on the backs of her knees where the hem went up and down like a curtain on a theatre stage. I fantasized squeezing off a shot just as the curtain went up, dropping the old buffalo in the dirt. I continued sighting in on Grandma's rickety knee joints until she worked herself far enough down the row so that only her shoulders and head of hair showed. I drew a bead on the nape of her neck. I was toying with her, the way she toyed with me. I slipped my finger inside the trigger guard and laid it lightly on the trigger. The gun was loaded. I always kept it loaded.

Neither Grandma Bradley nor I really believed there was a chance that Uncle Cecil would fail to arrive that afternoon, yet as three o'clock approached we sat in the living room on tenterhooks. Every few minutes or so Grandma would grunt her bulk off the chesterfield to part the curtains and stare up the approach for a glimpse of Uncle Cecil's automobile, spider waiting for the fly. I, on the other hand, sat with crossed fingers tucked under my thighs, hoping against hope that he wouldn't show and fate would decree I keep the gun.

Then, just as the arms of the clock on the china cabinet indicated five minutes to the hour, the sound of a car motor reached our ears. Grandma, who had decked herself out in her finest duds and costume jewellery, smoothed her dress down over her thighs, gave me a significant look, and said, "Like I told you earlier, I won't be going out with you. Me he just gets a look at through the window. But I'll be able to see whatever goes on out there, so you'd better do as you're told. We been through it plenty of times, so don't pretend you forgot what you are supposed to do. One more time now. You hand him the gun and then what?"

"I say, 'The last thing in the world I want is anything that you ever touched or would remind me of you, Mr. Fancy Foster,'" I mumbled reluctantly.

"You bet," said Grandma. "That'll tighten his tourniquet for him. He won't be expecting that welcome. He thinks this is some kind of kiss-and-make-up party. Kiss my ass and make up a face after, Mr. Fancy Foster," said Grandma. Out in the yard we heard the car stop. "Out you go!" barked Grandma. "Now!"

Uncle Cecil was combing his hair in the rear-view mirror when he saw me crossing the yard to his automobile, pump gun in my hands. He sort of spilled himself out of the car and rushed at me in an eager, stumbling trot. "Oh, Charlie," he said, "how good it is to see you after all this time! How good it is to have this terrible misunderstanding cleared up at last!"

He broke off as I shoved the gun at him with both hands. "Here!" I shouted. "Take it!"

"Whatever does this mean, Charlie...." Dazed, he limply accepted the rifle I pressed on him. In the last nine or ten days he had grown worn, haggard, and shaky-looking. His eyes had the fogged, bleary quality of a very old man's, the misted look of a bathroom mirror after someone has taken a hot shower. He needed a shave and his beard appeared to be sprouting out of damp chalk dust. Encountered at close range he was different from the funny little man I had looked down on from the heights of a barn loft.

"I'm giving it back," I said. "I don't want nothing from you."

"It's her, isn't it?" he said.

Trying to evade his eyes, I lifted mine to the sky. A mob of crows was in a slow boil above the windbreak, disturbing the sky with a ragged, awkward, black quarrel.

All at once Uncle Cecil began a broken, urgent, disconnected ramble. I must never believe her, believe the things she had accused him of. I knew better. I did know better, didn't I? Of course. There was nothing to reproach himself with. We both knew that. He knew in his own mind there was nothing to what she had said. Ugly talk. Rumours. Unfounded suppositions. To think he would hurt a child in any way. There wasn't an ounce of harm in him. If he had even the smallest doubt that there was, he'd take steps...but there wasn't. People didn't understand there were no boundaries to friendship. They didn't believe young and old could be best of friends. But they could. Like Alan Breck and David Balfour. We had been the best of friends, hadn't we? Yes. Yes. Yes.

On the final yes the gun slipped from his fingers and dropped to the ground beside him. Covering his face with his palms, he stood mute under the bright, hot light. Moments passed and still he said nothing, did nothing, except stand at attention with his face in his hands like a prisoner awaiting pronouncement of sentence. I glanced back over my shoulder to the window where my grandmother was posed in her black dress, scrutinizing us. She made no sign as to what I should do.

And then I thought I heard Uncle Cecil say something. I turned back to him, straining to catch the soft voice muffled by the soft hands. "Charlie," he said, "tell me that you only hid from me because she made you. Tell me that, Charlie."

I couldn't answer.

"Say you didn't hide from me."

I didn't cry much as a kid. I cried so little my mother actually worried about me. But I was so near crying that day that I moved alongside Uncle Cecil and placed my arm loosely around his waist. For a time he stood stock still, blind, then his body relaxed and a hand came down to rest lightly on the nape of my neck.

I heard the screen door slap behind her when Grandma Bradley stepped out of the house.

Things As They Are?

A MONASTERY SURROUNDED by fields of lush grain, girdled by dark pines. Iron bells ringing the morning stars out of the skies and the black crows into them. A dusty road at noon, butterflies in the ditches folding brown and yellow wings on purple-headed thistles, stooped monks pulling weeds in a distant garden. A young man greatly afflicted in body but ardent to serve God. A setting and a character for a nineteenth-century story, most probably Russian. Last of all, a writer.

The monastery, like nearly all ecclesiastical establishments in the latter half of the twentieth century, had fallen on hard times. Each year the number of postulants dwindled and the surviving monks grew older, feebler, greyer. The boys' boarding school attached to the abbey was forced to close and farming operations were curtailed. But as the abbot was fond of saying, "New circumstances create new challenges." The monastery welcomed busy Catholic laity seeking to examine and test their souls in solitude, some of whom left substantial testimonials of appreciation upon departing. In time, reports of the monastery's natural beauty and isolation reached the ears of other, more secular-minded individuals eager to make a temporary withdrawal from the world, sort through their lives – "find themselves," as so many of them passionately put it. These, too, the abbey was willing to accept, charging ridiculously small sums for the provision of room and board, unlimited fresh air, and restorative quiet. All that was asked of these guests was that they behave modestly and decently, and permit the monks to go about their business undisturbed.

It was an old friend, a poet concerned that Jack Greer seemed to do nothing whole-heartedly any more but booze, who suggested a retreat to the Alberta monastery might lend Jack's infamously stalled book the push it needed to get moving again. For the first time in living memory, Greer acted on someone's advice, applied to the monastery, and was accepted.

The monk who greeted him upon his arrival at the abbey inspected a tall, bony, angular, sad-faced man, at least forty but probably older, whose hair was cropped so short it was difficult to detect the grey in it. He reminded Brother Ambrose a little of the convict Magwitch in the David Lean film of *Great Expectations* which Brother Lawrence had used to show in English classes in those long ago days when the boys' school was still in operation and he was still a teacher. Of course, Brother Ambrose couldn't know that Greer's hair had been cut only two days earlier to foster a certain disposition. What Greer was aiming at was simplicity, discipline, control. A monastery seemed the place to achieve these things. He was travelling light all around, a pair of Adidas on his feet, six shirts still in cellophane, and an equal number of tan workpants bearing sale tags packed in his large knapsack. The only things that weren't new were his socks and underwear, a portable typewriter, and a dog-eared manuscript, five and a half years old. For reading he had Chekhov's *Selected Letters*, the Viking *Portable Chekhov*, and a copy of Goethe's *Faust*, nothing more. These were books to clear the head, lift the fog, correct the drift.

Greer was giving himself three months to finish the book and get his life in order. Almost six years ago he had published a first novel that went beyond being a modest success and stopped just short of being truly celebrated. Suddenly agent and publisher began to talk to him about his "career," making him feel like one of those young men who have passed bar exams or been accepted into medical school. But six years was a long time between books and nobody talked to him like that any more. He was a fucking walking disaster and knew it.

But maybe here it would be possible to make himself fit to write again. He would read Chekhov and Goethe, hike hard in the countryside, eat well, sleep better, cut back his drinking. The bottles of brandy clinking in his knapsack were to be strictly rationed, no more than three drinks a day no matter how badly the work went. There was a shot glass for measuring so he couldn't cheat.

Brother Ambrose led him down a seemingly endless corridor, unlocked the door to a room so bare it nearly made Greer shiver, and then carefully pointed out where everything was, desk, closet, chair, bed. It was all obvious but Greer supposed the monk considered the room tour part of his job. In the doorway, before leaving, Brother Ambrose said: "There's only the two of you."

For a second Greer had no inkling what he was talking about.

"There'll be more arriving throughout the summer," Brother Ambrose continued, "but for the time being there's only you and one other gentleman in this wing." Having said that, he departed, leaving Jack to turn his attention to his new home.

There wasn't much to hold it. The walls were painted white. There were no pictures. The bathroom was the sort found in a hospital. On the wall directly above the desk there was a crucifix.

Greer opened a window and lay down on his bed. The scent of damp hay lying in windrows came drifting in, smelling yeasty and sweet. The silence of the building was absolute except when a door closed somewhere at the ends of the earth. Through the open window he heard insects sizzling and thrumming in the hot grass, the ripple of a meadow lark, a hawk's rusty shriek, the dry clattering of a woodpecker, sounds that he had presumed were extinct. He thought of Chekhov and his love for his six hundred acres at Melikhovo. Spring in the countryside had given his favourite Russian hope there would be spring in paradise.

Clean slate, Greer promised himself. New start.

The next morning the tolling of the bells shook him out of sleep, chapel bells summoning the monks to some service. Greer turned on his side and looked out the window while the bells rang relentlessly. A skim of spreading light, a milky flush in the eastern sky told him how very early it was. Abruptly, the bells broke off and in the sudden silence he heard muffled grunts and groans, a dull thumping and scraping outside his door as if something very awkward and very heavy was being lugged down the corridor. Curious, Greer climbed out of bed, eased open his door, and peered out. Except for red exit lights shining at either end, the corridor was in darkness. In the bloody light of the furthest of these exit lights, Greer could see a man starkly silhouetted.

The man hauled nothing down the passageway but himself.

Propped on crutches, he dragged legs encumbered by heavy braces, propelling them forward with violent spasms of effort, groaning as he swung on his crutches and his lifeless legs struck the floor rhythmically, again and again, with a dull, metallic clunk. Throwing himself at the swinging door, he drove it recklessly open with his braced legs, rattled through, and disappeared from sight. Behind the door lay chapel and monastery proper. Was he answering the call of the bells?

Greer hurried back to bed. Although it was June, what he had just seen left him feeling cold.

In the mornings following, Greer found himself waking earlier and earlier in anticipation of the unholy racket in the hallway.

It was deeply unsettling, but he could hardly complain about what the unfortunate man couldn't help. Still, Greer was losing sleep and, worse, the whispered mutterings and groans got his working day off to a bad start, lent it a troubling, slightly surreal air.

I came to write a book and instead I find myself starring in a Bergman film, Greer told himself, trying to laugh it off.

But the Bergman film continued, even out of doors. Strolling in the monastery grounds Greer was astounded by the number of elderly, disabled monks he encountered: hunchbacks and clubfoots, the mildly retarded and profoundly disfigured. Meeting handicapped brothers on the gravelled paths, he hurried by them with nothing more than a curt nod of the head. He couldn't help himself. The sight of them, infirmities cloaked in medieval-looking habits, increased his free-floating anxiety. For Greer, the whole place was taking on a gothic air.

He discreetly questioned Diane, one of the women who served in the dining hall reserved for the abbey's guests, about the handicapped monks and she explained. Fifty years ago, Catholic parents concerned about what might happen to a disabled son after they died would encourage him to seek to become a brother in the monastery. If he were accepted, his parents were assured they need never worry about his future; he had a home for the rest of his life and would be taken care of. What Greer was seeing, she said, was the last generation, now old men, left in the care of the Church.

Then one evening when Greer was sitting in the empty visitors' lounge playing a game of solitaire before supper, someone entered the room and dropped himself into a chair. When Greer looked up and saw the crutches and braces, he knew this was the disturber of his sleep, the cripple who groaned his way down the hallway every morning. The surprise was his face.

Greer bobbed his head politely, said hello, and immediately turned his attention back to the cards to avoid staring. The man in the armchair had at one time been horribly burned, so hideously burned that his features had been reduced to an expressionless mask of livid scar tissue that resembled the scales of a reptile. His mouth was a lipless slit, his nose a snake-snout, his blue eyes puckered in flesh as lifeless as plasticine. He had neither eyebrows, eyelashes, nor whiskers, and the bald dome of his skull was stippled with slick, shiny scars that looked like drippings from a wax candle.

Greer's distaste shamed him, but that didn't make it any less real. He kept thinking how much the man looked like a lizard. No matter how hard he tried to concentrate on the game of solitaire, Greer could sense the stranger watching him, sense the man's rigidity; his blank, fixed face, his legs thrust stiffly out from the chair as if they were planks nailed to his body and not really limbs at all. And Greer began to feel his own body going rigid too, brittle with tension, unease, anticipation.

When the man suddenly spoke to him, Greer started violently. "Pardon me?" he said, confused.

"You're one pitiful solitaire player," the man repeated. Greer looked hard and recognized an ironic, challenging intelligence gleaming in the eyes of the frozen face. The slash of mouth widened and Greer assumed it was a smile.

"Says who?"

"Five of hearts on six of spades! There!" the stranger said pecking at the cards with his fingers. They were hooked like the talons of a bird of prey, several of them lacking nails.

Jack moved the card. "Maybe I ought to surrender the deck to the expert," he said, "and learn something."

The young man held up his hands. "I'm a clumsy shuffler and dealer. It takes me a long time to play a game."

"Well, my head obviously isn't in it," said Greer. "Let me lay a game out and you can shift the cards. How does that strike you?"

The fellow extended a claw. "Roland Madox."

Jack reached for it. "Jack Greer," he said.

That night the two men ate supper together in the separate guest dining room. Madox explained he was not a monk yet and was only at the abbey on trial, working in the library until the abbot arrived at a decision as to whether he truly had a vocation. For the present, said Madox, he was free to choose where and with whom he ate. Over the abbey's famous fare – farmer's sausage, sauerkraut, boiled beet tops, and new potatoes, followed by apple crisp and ice cream – Roland Madox told his story. When he was five, he and his grandfather had been involved in a car accident. The old man had been instantly killed when he pulled out into the path of an oncoming fuel truck. His grandson, however, had survived the wreck and conflagration with disabling spinal injuries and third-degree burns over eighty per cent of his body. With a kind of perverse defiance Madox mockingly referred to himself as a "fry." According to his self-portrait, perversity seemed second nature to him. The night of the accident, the doctors said he wouldn't see morning. When morning came they didn't give him a week. When a week passed, not another month. On the burn ward everyone expected him to succumb to infection. Nothing doing. He had survived the burn ward, years of hospitalization and rehabilitation. Here he was, twenty-five years old, still defying the odds. He had battled his way through elementary school, endured the adolescent hell of high school, earned a university degree in history. Implausibly, it was in a university philosophy class that he had discovered the existence of God, a startling reversal of what Greer took to be the customary outcome of acquaintance with academic philosphers. Now he was determined to become a monk.

When Greer inquired as to why he had this particular ambition, the answer was simple. "I love God," he said. Adding, "There's not many things I can do as well as the next guy – but praying is one of them."

At last the two men rose and went out into the calm sunshine, the blue shadows, the summer stillness which descends on the prairie only after the day's wind has blown itself out in the grass, or the sky, or has lost itself beyond the brackets of earth and horizon. Greer, at that moment, had no inkling of what he had embarked upon.

After ten days, Greer had still to write a word worth keeping. This place, this monastery, didn't seem to be the solution either. All day he exhausted himself with the struggle and when evening came he lay on his bed watching the sky through his window, a sky as pale as a bowl of cream. At such times he often thought of Miriam, where she was, how she was, and especially of the night in that quiet street, the Herengracht, outside their hotel in Amsterdam. Miriam, who had stood by him for the four years he was writing the book that was supposed to change his life, and who had remained steadfastly loyal for the three more difficult ones which followed it.

Gazing over the canal, she had asked him exactly what it was he wanted. Because on how many occasions past had she heard him claim that all he wanted was a *book*, one book to prove to himself he was a writer. Well, he had got his book but it hadn't made him happy. Now he claimed it was a disappointment to him. And the new book he was writing disappointed him even more. When was it going to stop? When was he going to get this bad taste out of his mouth?

Miriam told him these things in a calm, agreeable voice, without a trace of the anger she was so richly entitled to. While she did, Greer kept his eyes fixed on the oily, yellow blur of light on the canal, reflections of the windows of the tall, narrow houses that hedged it in, afraid to tell her how afraid he was of failure. A fine, misty rain hung quivering in the air between them like a veil.

He was always complaining that what he wrote didn't measure up. She didn't understand what he meant. Measure up to what? To whom?

He swung round on her, eyes burning. "To me, goddamn it! It doesn't measure up to me!" he shouted. Embarrassed by this outburst, he turned back to his contemplation of the canal, forearms propped on the railing.

"If that's really the case, Jack," he heard her say, "it seems to me there are only two possibilities. Either you underestimate the quality of your writing, or overestimate your talent. If you want a life, you'd better make up your mind which it is."

The next morning they divided up the currency and travellers' cheques in a cafe near the Concertgebouw and separated.

It wasn't long before Greer and Madox fell into a routine. By ones and twos more guests began to take up residence in the monastery, but Roland ignored their existence; he clung exclusively to Jack. The two men ate all their meals together, Greer helping Roland load his plate and manage his tray in the cafeteria-style line. In the evenings they played Trivial Pursuit, which Roland always won, earning him the nickname Mr. S.O. Teric from Jack. But it was the hour before supper that was sacrosanct, the hour devoted to solitaire – which Roland happened to be addicted to. As a boy it had been his substitute for Little League and Minor Hockey, later for the Teen Dance, rec-room parties, other excitements.

There were times, however, when Greer grew short-tempered with his new friend. Of course, Greer blamed his frustration with his own work for making him impatient and peevish. He regretted the way he sometimes behaved, comparing the stubborn stoicism with which Roland, in public, silently bore pain, to his own outbursts of irritability. Although each morning Jack lay awake listening to the gut-wrenching noises from the hallway, he couldn't recall a single occasion when Roland had allowed so much as a murmur to escape his lips when they walked together. And the effort to suppress his pain was often evident in his face, the waxy scars taking on a sullen, leaden cast, a shine like the tip of a bullet.

Yet Jack couldn't deny there were things about his new friend that drove him crazy, exasperated him beyond belief. With Chekhov's example before him, Greer was attempting to cultivate the ability to see things lucidly, with nothing more than a pane of the clearest glass to put distance between himself and what he looked at, without even so much as the breath of a lie to mist and cloud the glass for his or anyone else's benefit. The famous objectivity, the pitiless refusal to delude oneself, to see clearly and not lose heart was, for Jack, the mystery of Chekhov's conscience as a writer and a man. The acceptance of things as they are. It was the gift Jack wanted most.

So, naturally, Greer found Roland Madox annoying. It annoyed him the way he gushed about his life to come as a monk, sounding like some bride-to-be burbling about the prospect of a totally fabulously unique June wedding. He talked as if he were on the point of crossing the threshold of some never-never land of unfading, unfailing happiness. Was that likely? Because it was clear to Greer that Roland had not been accepted by the happy band of monks he was so determined to join. They obviously had as little to do with him as possible, grateful to leave him in Greer's company and care. Wasn't it Jack Greer who shuffled his cards, ate with him, listened to his stories, nodded over his plans for the future? Meanwhile his brothers in Christ didn't pay the least attention to him.

Jack resented that. He had come to this place to write a book, not to get saddled with responsibility for another human being. Besides, anyone who had fucked up his own life as badly as he had, had no business letting anybody get in the habit of depending on him. He owed it to Madox to keep him at arm's length.

When the situation became too much for him, Jack Greer took the coward's way out and fled; struck out across country, knowing Roland couldn't pursue him over rough, broken ground. Madox had tried once and taken some bad tumbles over ridges in a freshly cultivated field. Greer, returning to the monastery in the twilight, had found him collapsed in a furrow, panting, dishevelled, dirty, utterly done in. He had had to half carry him back to the abbey.

But if he turned his back on the disappointed man watching

reproachfully from the window and strode off in the direction of the shelterbelts and fields, he won a temporary freedom. Two things never altered on these expeditions. There was always brandy in his knapsack and he was always angry; angry about the guilt the figure at the window made him feel, angry at Roland for banking so much on becoming a monk. It wouldn't heal his body, turn back the clock to the time he owned a face. Couldn't he see that?

Past the hot stench of the pig sties, past the black and white cows sedately lowing their way to the dairy barns for milking, past the market gardens, past the rippling fields of wheat and oats, he marched, trying to tramp the fury and frustration out of himself, slashing weeds with a stick, sweating until his shirt clung to his back like a leech. A couple of miles bled the anger out of him. By the time he reached the railway embankment and stood in the cinders looking down at the slough and the ducks, it was spent. In early evening light the flat sheet of water was a mirror. And what does it reflect? Greer asked himself. Bullrushes, sky, cloud, streaks of sun, the wind brushing and wrinkling the surface. Things as they are. Nothing else. The last light of day is the truest light.

When he had had enough of ducks and water, he headed for the tennis courts. Some of the visitors on retreat passed the evenings there, playing a set or two. They weren't aware he watched. The stand of evergreens planted forty years ago as a windbreak to ring the courts now towered over them, providing cover for a stealthy approach. Slipping from tree to tree, he reached his customary spot. Here the ground was thickly carpeted with dry needles, the resinous air was pleasantly sharp in his nostrils and he could comfortably prop his back against a trunk and view the court through the dark shelter of a screen of boughs. It was in bad shape, the asphalt surface heaved and split by frost, weeds bursting through its cracks, the lines practically obliterated by weather and wear, the net drooping and in need of mending.

Tonight, as they did every evening, middle-aged men and

women politely patted a tennis ball back and forth across the net. Greer quietly unzipped his knapsack, took out his bottle and glass, and poured his first drink of the day.

There was nothing preventing him leaving the trees and standing at the fence. Nothing except that on his first visit, entirely by chance, he had overheard some of the other guests discussing him. One of them said: "Brother Ambrose mentioned he's a writer – but not a *Catholic* writer. He's certainly stuck-up. I have a feeling he's keeping that poor boy from associating with the rest of us. What do you think could be the reason?"

They played on late, until the edges of their shadows on the asphalt began to blur and flocks of sparrows whirled erratically from evergreen to evergreen, preparing to settle for the night. When the players did eventually go, their voices fading off into the darkening distance, Greer realized his hands were sticky with the resin he had nervously picked from the tree bark with his nails.

Then the moon came up as it did in a Chekhov story and shone on the deserted, crumbling court and sagging net while he drank his second and third brandies. As Greer looked at this scene from behind the trees, a moon of loneliness rose in him too, a staring moon, as cold and bright and hard and huge as the one in the sky above.

Knowing first hand the effect disappointment could have on a man, Jack Greer feared for Roland Madox. Wanting to spare him that, he did his best to interject an element of reality into Roland's speculations about his future in the Order. It didn't work. Some days Greer would have sworn Madox was already a bishop.

"The abbot will probably want to make use of my degree," Roland said one afternoon. "I wouldn't be surprised if he assigned me to teaching."

Jack knew he ought to let it pass but didn't. "Teaching

where? The school's been closed for five years. Maybe you haven't noticed, but this place is evolving into Palm Springs for the pious Catholic and the budget-conscious bohemian. That's the only growth industry in this place."

"There's the library. He could make me head librarian."

Greer had surveyed the card catalogue one afternoon when he dropped in on Roland. It comprised devotional works, biographies of saints, apologetics, and old high-school texts, the intellectual equivalents of Father Bing Crosby movies. Jack considered it an act of extreme charity to call it a library at all. He raised his eyebrows.

Roland tried again. "Few of the monks have any education. He won't want to let me go to waste. The Order is short of priests. I could be sent to a seminary. I could be ordained."

Greer made no comment on the likelihood of that. The two men sat silently, pretending to be absorbed in a study of the cards spread on the table.

After a bit Roland said, "Why do you have to pick holes in everything? Can't you just be happy for me?"

Greer reached for the deck. "It's not up to me to be happy for you. Be happy for yourself."

"What's that supposed to mean?"

"Look," said Greer, "who's fooling who? If you're so crazy about the monastic life, why don't you show any sign of it? Why is it that you eat every meal with me instead of the brothers? Do you think by avoiding them at all costs you're making a favourable impression on the abbot? If you're their kind, why don't you stick with them?"

"I thought we were friends," said Roland. "I eat with you because we're friends."

"Yes," said Jack, "we're friends." He had been on the point of saying something else, something cruel. He had almost said: The reason you choose to eat with me, cling to me, is that one misfit recognizes another. We're both misfits and there's no point pretending otherwise. Things as they are.

Yet he let it drop. At the last moment, Greer had recalled

Faust, and Mephistopheles' claim to be part of that power which always wills evil and always works good. Was it also possible that there might be uncalculated danger in willing good?

For nearly two days the sky wept grey rain, trapping Greer indoors, further dampening his spirits, deepening his melancholy. Hours at a time he stood at his window, one palm pressed to the glass, watching the dismal curtain of rain sweep the landscape on gusts of wind. Or he lay on his bed, forearm across his eyes; paced up and down the room until his knees ached; rehearsed sentences in his mind that he knew would never find their way to paper. After getting soaked to the skin on his way to lunch the first day of the downpour, he didn't bother to cross the courtyard for meals, it seemed too much trouble.

During the night, the sound of falling rain was magnified in the darkness. He slept in brief snatches, drowsing off to disconnected words, images, thoughts that were not his own but were provided by his reading of the past few weeks. He relived Chekhov's description of Venice, the strangeness which invited a longing for death. Warmth, calm, gleaming stars. The movement of the gondola. The silence of the countryside in a city without horses. This was the silence which surrounded Greer until morning arrived, the bells rang, and Roland struggled his way down the corridor. Suddenly fearful of crying out himself, Greer bit his lips. All morning he did nothing but watch the hypnotic rain. His hands trembled uncontrollably – he hadn't eaten in twenty hours and had no more than a couple of hours' sleep the night before. Between eleven o'clock and noon he drank the day's ration of brandy, emptying three shot glasses in rapid succession while standing at the streaming window. For the first time in several weeks he was on the point of losing it, was prepared to dive down the neck of the bottle and hit bottom. Then, suddenly, the rain stopped.

Greer threw on a jacket and rushed outside, as desperate to flee that room as he often was to flee Roland. The problem was where to run. Striking across country was out of the question. The downpour of the past thirty-six hours had flooded the fallow fields, turned them into quagmires, soaked the tall grasses of the pastures. The road he found himself standing in might as well have led nowhere; the nearest town was twelve miles away.

Then he thought of the church. He remembered overhearing Diane talk about it in the dining room, some story about a self-taught artist who fifty years ago had gone from prairie town to prairie town, decorating churches in return for room and board, a kind of Johnny Appleseed of religious art, very likely half-mad. One of his churches was hard by, just two miles up the road. Greer decided to check it out.

The road he tramped through the flat landscape was a grid road, a pencil line on a sheet of paper. The clouds overhead reminded him of ones Miriam and he had seen in Holland, mottled grey and white, so oppressively low and heavy that they left him with the impression he could reach up and stroke their bellies with his hand. Despite there being no wind Greer could detect, the clouds kept rolling and churning, permitting a surprising amount of light to filter through, an odd opalescent light which turned the wet, yellow gravel crunching under his shoes to brass and lent the green of the crops of new oats and wheat an intense, smoky cast.

After Greer had walked for twenty minutes, he saw the church appear on the horizon, a white structure set upon an unexpected knoll rising out of level fields vacant of any other buildings. As he drew near, as the ground rose, tilting his angle of vision upward, the church grew brighter in the strange, beguiling light, more and more luminous against the setting of dark, restless, changeable sky.

Crossing the deserted parking lot, Greer realized he hadn't thought out this visit very well. Surely the church would be locked on a weekday. Yet when he tried the big double doors, one pulled open in his hand. Apparently rural churches could still stand open and unattended. He went in.

The first thing Greer noticed was a peculiar odour suspended in the motionless air, a blurred, sweet scent that struggled to mask a more insistent chemical smell which he associated with science laboratories of his high school days. Stale incense, he supposed.

Greer entered the nave, footsteps echoing hollowly in the empty church. To his right, a depiction of Christ's resurrection was painted directly on the plaster of the wall. To Greer it looked crude, Jesus rising before an incongruous backdrop – a fiery orange sun which improbably shared a night sky of incredible blackness with a moon and a multitude of blazing stars. The limbs of this God were too white, his hair too blond, his lips too caressingly pink and full. Smiling shyly, he held out to the viewer the red wounds on his palms.

Greer cleared his throat. The strange, nasty, candied odour was stronger than at first. So strong, it was now a taste on his tongue. He began to move down the right-hand aisle from one picture to the next, forcing himself to halt and look. It was some of the most unpleasant, unsettling art he had ever seen. An oyster Saint Sebastian dripped gravy instead of blood; a dead-white Virgin suckled a blue-baby infant.

The emptiness of the church, the hallucinatory pictures, the sickly odour was tightening his breathing, constricting his chest. The smell was everywhere. Linked in his mind to the unnatural complexions of the saints, it was as if he could taste the repulsive-looking flesh itself.

Jack paused to catch his breath. Goddamn it, it wasn't his imagination. The taste *was* in his mouth. Without thinking, he pulled a handkerchief from his pocket, cleared his throat, and spat into it. Then, realizing what he had done, gobbed in a holy place, he swept the bare church with a furtive look.

It was then he saw the open coffin before the altar, small and white, resting on a mortician's portable aluminum bier. In a moment of blind shock his mind staggered, then the corpse of the little girl sprang sharply into focus. She had curls. Her upper lip had relaxed, baring tiny front teeth.

The next thing Greer knew he was outside, taking the steps of the church two at a time, plunging across the parking lot, turning into the road in a panicky lope. Clear of the churchyard he tried to curb himself to a walk, but could only manage an undignified, stilted trot. Nor could he stop himself from darting a glance over his shoulder and, when he did, he blundered through a puddle, stumbling and nearly falling.

Looking up, he discovered himself face to face with a huge, coal-black dog. There was no explaining its bewildering appearance; the surrounding fields of grain were still too short in the stalk at this time of year to have hidden the approach of such a big dog, and there were no farmhouses or outbuildings from where it could have come. The two stood staring at each other. The dog did not pad up to make friends, nor slink away. Hollow flanks, matted, muddy coat and sore-looking, crusted eyes, it simply waited, motionless.

A minute, two minutes crawled by and still neither moved a muscle. The blood surged in Greer's temples, he could feel it throbbing in the ends of his fingers. A single thought was running round and round his mind like a toy locomotive on a circular track. *The dog belongs to the little girl. Belongs to the girl. Belongs to the girl. Belongs to the girl.*

And then these words were replaced by others. He heard himself speaking aloud in a wheedling voice. "Go away," he said. "Leave me be. I didn't do anything."

His voice acted as a trigger for the dog. Suddenly it bristled, the hair on its neck rose in a ruff and its head began to weave from side to side with a supple, snake-like menace while it snapped its jaws. The clicking of teeth was the only sound the dog made.

Rabies, thought Greer. *The son of a bitch has rabies.* Frantically seeking something with which to defend himself, his eyes fell on a large stone lying on the shoulder of the road. He bent to snatch it up and a roaring wind filled his ears, the stone turned unimaginably heavy in his hands, dragged him to his knees, and for the briefest of moments everything went black. Then his surroundings woozily squeezed back in upon him and he felt the stain of wetness working its way up out of the damp ground and through the cloth of his pants, the gravel biting his kneecaps. Sparking lights, swimming in a cloud, gradually extinguished themselves one by one, and his eyes fastened on the rock, lying where he had dropped it.

The dog. He snatched up the stone and swung it threateningly above his head.

But the dog was gone.

Greer climbed to his feet, hugging the muddy stone to his shirt, and turned slowly around in a circle. The clouds were twisting sluggishly, the green fields running smoothly out to merge with the sky, the church commanding the height. But there was no trace of a dog. Anywhere.

Although he had not been drinking nearly as much as was usual for him, Greer recalled his doctor's warnings about alcoholic psychosis and wondered whether any of this had actually happened. He drew up categories in his mind – this he would accept as real and this he wouldn't. The corpse was probably real because he could not recall a dead child in Chekhov. The black dog was probably *not* real because of the *schwarzen Hund* in *Faust*. Terrified, he went no further, left it at that.

Roland was innocent of modesty. Greer relished the way he was never shy of making himself the hero of his own stories. Greer's favourite was the one about the bicycle. Madox claimed he could ride a bicycle. Before the accident he had been the youngest kid on his street to ride a two-wheeler and after he got out of hospital he had a goal – to ride again. For six years his mother helped him, outfitted him in elbow pads and a hockey helmet and spent summers running up and down their suburban street, holding his bicycle upright while he fought to achieve a precarious balance.

It was a scandal on the block. Neighbours complained to his father. "Ted, it was ninety-two degrees today and humid. *Humid.* You've got to tell her to quit or she's going to have a heart attack out there on the street. The wife says she can't stand to look out the window any more. And the kid falls. Lots of times he falls. He's going to get himself hurt."

So far, so good. The writer part of Greer approved of the telling details, the hockey helmet, elbow pads, concerned neighbours, humidity. Where Greer believed Roland went wrong was in his failure to explain how he could pedal a bike with his legs in braces. Still, that was the critic speaking. Greer, the friend, still loved to hear him tell it. He would say, "Give us the one about the bicycle again, Easy Rider," and Roland would willingly oblige, always climaxing the story with the unassisted, joyous sweep down a twilit street, bicycle flying through an autumn evening, scattering fallen leaves while Roland whooped his delight and his mother did an impromptu jig on the sidewalk in honour of his recovery of solo flight.

By now, Jack, realizing it was hopeless, had given up even the pretence of trying to write. As a result, he found himself spending more and more time in Roland's company, often filling the long hours of the day by assisting him in the library. While they sorted and shelved books, Roland talked excitedly about his plans. There was nothing new in this. But the insistent, urgent way he spoke was new, as if he was trying to reassure himself, as well as convince Greer.

Something else was new. Greer started to drop hints about himself and his past. On several occasions he even casually mentioned her name: Miriam. With Roland, who was a stranger to their history, he could do this because her name signalled nothing, set off no warning bells. To speak of her in this off-hand fashion helped Greer feel she was somehow a normal, everyday feature of his life, simply there. And that released in him a quiet, calm affection for her memory that had been impossible to experience whenever he spoke of her with anyone who had known them together, in the old days, and knew the score.

Mostly, though, it was Roland who talked, more and more often going obsessively over old ground. The doctors had thought he wouldn't last the night – but look at him now. Nobody had thought he could come so far. He had a degree in history, he could ride a bike, he had learned Latin. The rest went unsaid – that he would become a monk. Even though the decision wasn't his to make but the abbot's.

It was obvious the uncertainty was playing on his nerves.

"I'm not going to give him much longer," he said one afternoon over solitaire.

"Who?" said Greer.

"The abbot."

"You ask me," Jack said, "no news is good news."

"How long does he think he can keep me dangling?" Roland pleaded. Greer avoided his eyes and shrugged.

Two days after this, Greer missed Roland at breakfast. He didn't think anything of it, but later that morning when he dropped by to give his friend a hand he was surprised to find the door of the library locked. Assuming that Roland must be ill, Greer didn't look in on him so he wouldn't disturb him if he were resting. Instead, he returned to his own room and found Brother Ambrose waiting there with a request that he accompany him to the office of the abbot.

The abbot turned out to be a wisp of a man with greying sandy-coloured hair like a shock of November grass, and a parchment complexion. Inviting Greer to take a seat, the abbot settled himself fussily, chair creaking.

"How's the writing going, Mr. Greer?" he asked as a conversation-opener.

"It's going," said Greer.

"You understand – I get so little time to read – it's difficult to keep up." An apology for being unfamiliar with Greer's work.

"Of course," said Greer.

"But Trollope," said the abbot. "I have a weakness for Trollope. The clerical novels," he qualified.

Greer nodded.

"And you, Mr. Greer," he inquired politely, "you have a favourite writer?"

"Chekhov."

"Ah," said the abbot and stared off into space, palms pressed together in a prayerful attitude. "I have the greatest respect for your profession, Mr. Greer. Writing. You can touch so many people, do so much good."

Not bloody likely, thought Greer.

"But, as you have probably guessed, I didn't ask you here to discuss writing – no, something else entirely," said the abbot, abruptly becoming business-like.

"Yes?"

"Several of the brothers have noted that you are a special friend of Roland Madox." He waited for confirmation.

Greer didn't care for the adjective "special." It sounded like an accusation of immorality. "A friend, yes," he said.

"Then I would like to ask you a favour," said the abbot.

"What kind of favour?"

"I understand you have a car?"

"Yes."

"As you may imagine, none of us here owns a car. If you could drive Roland to the city tomorrow to catch his flight, it would be most appreciated. Of course, the abbey would be glad to recompense you for gas and incidentals." He hesitated delicately. "And having a friend see him safely off – it would ease our minds."

"Roland didn't say anything to me about going anywhere," said Greer, mildly alarmed.

"We felt it best that he leave immediately. I have been in touch with his father and he has purchased Roland a ticket home to Winnipeg. It will be waiting for him at the airport."

"I don't understand why you're banishing him," said Greer. "Don't you have any idea what this means to him?"

"You may not be aware of it, Mr. Greer, but in the last five years Roland has made at least six attempts to be admitted to monasteries across the country. None would accept him." The abbot shook his head sadly. "He is a troubled young man."

"More remarkable than troubled," said Greer.

The abbot scrutinized Greer shrewdly for a moment. "You're angry with me, Mr. Greer," he said. "But perhaps you don't know all the facts of the case."

"I didn't realize it was being treated as a case," snapped Greer.

Overlooking this, the abbot continued in a patient voice. "This is the second time Roland has been with us. The first time was two years ago when the old abbot was still alive. It was not a happy experience for all concerned. I do not know what he has said to you, but I allowed him to return only on the understanding that he would not be considered for admission to the Order. That was made unequivocally clear. It was done as a favour to his father. He hoped that if Roland was provided with some small job he could manage, it might prove helpful to him. Mr. Madox is a layman of some standing in the Church, well respected. However, I may have made an error of judgment in obliging him."

Greer was confused. "But Roland's father isn't a Catholic," he protested. "Roland told me himself he converted to Roman Catholicism against his parents' wishes when he was at university."

"You see what I mean?" said the abbot. "Roland was born a Catholic. But that does not suggest the spirit of independence he likes to project. So he altered the facts to conform to his picture of himself. Mr. Greer, not everything is quite as Roland portrays it. Yesterday he was in my office, demanding

I come to a decision about admitting him to the Order." The abbot paused. "It was in the nature of an ultimatum. Now he knew when he came here there was no possibility of my accepting him. Yet when I reminded him of this he seemed astonished, as if I had gone back on my word. He made threats."

"Threats?"

"Threats," repeated the abbot enigmatically. He took a deep breath. "At present he is very angry and wants nothing to do with any of us – the religious, I mean. It would be difficult for any of us to accompany him. You see our problem. But if someone he likes and trusts could take him to the airport, it would be most helpful. Would you be so kind as to do us this favour, Mr. Greer?"

"When's his flight?"

"Tomorrow afternoon, five-thirty. Air Canada Flight 183," said the abbot.

Greer got to his feet. "All right," he said. At that moment, he felt sad and injured and angry, a little like the father asked to remove from school the boy of whom he is so proud.

As Greer drove, he glimpsed, out of the corner of his eye, metal machinery sheds, dull-red granaries, farmhouses with big satellite dishes in their front yards stuttering by. Meanwhile Roland was in a passion, body jerking and twitching in the seatbelt. "Justice is all I asked," he said bitterly, for what seemed to Greer the thousandth time. "Justice. Who did Christ hold his arms out to if not the crippled and the blind? And now the Church turns its back on us."

Greer felt sorry for him, sorrier than he could say. He had tried to take the line with Roland that he was well out of it, look what he had been saved from – chastity, poverty, obedience. Who needed it? But Roland wasn't buying it, nor was Greer exactly surprised. In his experience, of all slighted parties, the refused were the least responsive to reason. Maybe because refusal so intimately connected injury with humiliation. It isn't an easy thing to swallow, the news that someone doesn't want you. Greer had found that out with Miriam.

They arrived in the city with nearly three and a half hours to spare before Roland's flight was scheduled to leave. It was Jack's plan to mark his friend's departure by treating him to a farewell lunch. Greer wasn't certain of the ins and outs, the rights and wrongs of it, but he knew Roland felt genuinely betrayed at being given the push by the abbot. The least somebody could do in this situation was to give him a proper send-off. The restaurant Greer chose for this was the Golden Wok – on the recommendation of Diane – who provided him with directions to find it. The Golden Wok turned out to be an establishment more upscale than the type Greer usually frequented, the decor insistently bellowing "Chinese Experience" – brass gongs, plaster lions, kites, ornamental screens, a multitude of fire-breathing dragons. *Early Shanghai Whorehouse,* Greer thought, surveying the scene.

They had arrived late for lunch and the dining room was almost empty. As Jack and Roland were escorted to a table, they passed the only other diners, a large party of what appeared to be office workers marking some festivity, perhaps the birthday or retirement of a co-worker. Each of the ladies had a pastel-coloured cocktail – a grasshopper, brown cow, or daiquiri – set in front of them and were having a high old time noisily joking and cutting-up in front of their indulgently smiling male bosses. But as he and Roland went by, the noise of clattering cutlery nervously subsided and the shrill, high-pitched laughter died.

Roland paused, shifted his crutches as if to move on, reconsidered, swept the uneasy gathering with a long cool stare and said, "You're all wondering, no doubt. I'm Jim Morrison – the Lizard King."

If there was anything Jack Greer hated, it was public

embarrassments. "Jesus Christ," he said angrily, trailing after Roland as he lurched haughtily to their table on his crutches. "What was the point of that?"

"I detected a certain morbid curiosity," said Roland. "I tried to satisfy it."

Greer was at a loss how to respond. All he managed to do was mumble, "Jesus Christ."

"Any guesses as to why I prefer a monastery?" asked Roland.

Behind him Greer could feel a distinct chill of disapproval, hostile whispers. Someone said, "A person expects to be able to go out and have a nice time and enjoy yourself. We're supposed to accommodate those people – but what effort do they make to accommodate us?"

Greer partly blamed himself for the incident. Christ, how could he have been so stupid, bringing Madox into a place like this! That's all Roland needed, another humiliation. Why hadn't he taken him to a drive-in where they could have eaten in the privacy of the car, rather than this hang out for the blue-suit crowd?

Perhaps his discomfort made him try too hard. He insisted on ordering too many dishes, dismissing Roland's protests with, "A taste from each then. We'll have a taste from each. And besides, what do you care? I'm paying." He called for a pitcher of beer and proposed a toast. "To your future," he said, lifting his glass. It was, on reflection, ill-advised because once they drank, the unspoken question hung between them. What was Roland's future?

Roland tried to answer. "There are monasteries all over the States," he said. "Dominicans in Vermont, Cistercians in Kentucky, lots more. I'll keep knocking on doors. I'll keep trying. You've got to keep trying."

"But not right away," cautioned Greer. "You'll have a rest, catch your breath, won't you, before you start this all over again?"

"A couple of days maybe," said Roland. "Then the old

man can buy me another plane ticket, or bus ticket, and see I get wherever I'm going. He owes me after this."

"And where will you be going?" asked Greer.

"Wherever there's a chance. I still have a long list of possibles to work through."

"Tell me," coaxed Greer. "Why did the abbot hustle you off so quickly? What did you do?"

Greer believed he saw Roland smile. "I told him that if he didn't accept me I'd pick up where the accident left off twenty years ago. Douse myself in gasoline and set myself on fire. Like the Buddhist monks did in Vietnam. As an act of protest."

"And he believed you? He didn't know it was a joke?" said Greer.

Roland held out his empty glass to Greer. Jack filled it, topped up his own. He found Roland's reluctance to answer disconcerting. "It was a joke, wasn't it?" he demanded.

"Oh yes, a joke," said Roland. "For the time being at least. But it's always wise to reserve the right to the last laugh, isn't it?"

The waiter arrived with their lunch, plate after plate of dumplings, Cantonese chow mein, Kung Po chicken, Szechwan shrimp, curried beef, ribs with black bean sauce. Both men welcomed this interruption of what had been verging on an uncomfortable conversation and dug into the food, exclaiming over the dishes, heaping their plates, pretending to argue over the division of the shrimp. Roland was even making a gallant attempt to manipulate the chopsticks in his claw. Finally, he tossed them aside, picked up a rib, and began to gnaw it. "It's like the beer commercial. It doesn't get any better than this, does it, Jackie?" he asked, mumbling around the bone.

"A subtle reminder," said Greer, signalling the waiter to bring another pitcher. He had already exceeded his daily quota of booze, but this was different. This was his friend's going-away party. Greer was beginning to feel better than he had in weeks, exhilarated like a kid on holiday. Today he need feel no guilt for not writing, need not ask himself why he failed whenever he tried. For the first time he realized how the dreariness, the sameness, the regimentation of life in the monastery had been weighing on him. He was becoming a little giddy. So was Roland.

Green asked, "Did you hear the one about the absent-minded priest who put his hand in his pocket and said, 'Plums, plums? When did I buy plums?' "

Roland began to giggle. He picked up his chopsticks, held them to his forehead, and waggled them like antennas. "Worker ant. Clerical division. Library," he said.

Greer collapsed with laughter. Roland winked at him, cocked his head in the direction of the other table. Greer glanced over his shoulder. One of the daiquiri-drinkers was staring at them with an indignant, offended expression. She leaned over to her neighbour and said something. The other woman primly nodded her agreement.

The second pitcher had emptied in no time at all. Madox ordered more. "This one's on me," he said. "I ought to contribute something to the party. Besides my charming self."

After the third pitcher arrived they went quiet, sat looking at their glasses. Suddenly Roland asked, "And you, Jack, what does the future hold for you?"

"More of the same, I suppose," he replied evasively.

"You mean writing," Roland prodded.

Greer shrugged.

"So what do you want to write next?"

Greer shifted on his chair. This talk of writing was turning his mood self-abusive and self-accusing, qualities which Miriam had deplored in him and which had never failed to infuriate and upset her. "I'll tell you what I want to write," said Greer with a bitter smile. "A Chekhov story. He left an outline for one he never got around to writing himself. It's a natural for a guy like me. The story concerns a brown-noser, the son of a serf or small shopkeeper raised to respect rank, kiss priests' hands, worship others' ideas, play the hypocrite before God and his betters because he cannot forget his own insignificance. Anyway, that's roughly the way Chekhov describes his character." Greer paused. "Change a few details – the son of the serf business, kissing the priests' hands – and Chekhov is describing Jack Greer. Except for one other difference. In Chekhov's story the young man presses the bad blood out of himself one drop at a time until one morning he wakes up with human blood running in his veins. That's the one essential difference between me and Chekhov's character."

All the time he had been delivering this sardonic discourse, he had kept his eyes fixed on his glass of beer while he slowly rotated it, grinding it into the tabletop. It came as a complete surprise to him when he looked up and encountered a stony stare of unrelieved, naked animosity.

"Well," said Jack, "it's just a story I thought might be interesting to write. You don't have to agree with me."

Madox erupted. He shouted that he knew who Greer was really talking about. Who kissed priests' hands? Who was the hypocrite before God? Who was a slave? Who worshipped others' ideas? Fuck him. He was wrong. All Roland's convictions had been arrived at on his own. And he *had* convictions, which was more than Greer could say. Another thing. He was getting pretty damned pissed off with Greer and his snide remarks about his religion. His religion was nobody's business but his own.

The more Greer tried to assure him that he had not been talking about him at all, that it was a terrible misunderstanding, the more furious Madox became. At first Greer didn't realize what was wrong: the immobility of Roland's face helped hide the fact that he was drunk. It was the swearing that tipped him off – Roland was not a swearer – and the rage, the rage born of utter frustration, his voice booming out asshole, dicklicker, cunt, cocksucker throughout the dining room. "So fuck off and mind your own fucking business, why don't you?" he ended by shouting.

Greer felt a tap on his shoulder. A man from the table of

merry makers, silver-haired, distinguished, stood over him. His face was beet-coloured. "I don't know what your friend's problem is," he said in a tone that is acquired only after years of handing out orders to subordinates. "But if you're going to take him out in public he ought to control himself. His language and behaviour is offensive to the ladies. Please make him stop it." Before Greer could collect himself to reply, the executive turned briskly on his heel and marched smartly to his table, several of the women greeting their champion with approving looks.

Greer rose to his feet.

Roland had suddenly regained his composure. "Forget it, Jack," he said in a calm voice. "One way or the other, it's always the same. Sit down."

"No," said Greer. "I won't forget it." At the same time he wondered what had come over him. He hated scenes.

Some minor awkwardness with his chair alerted Greer that he too might be suffering the influence of alcohol. Concentrating on carrying himself in as dignified a manner as possible he approached the table. There was a stir. The gentleman in authority squared his shoulders in an expensive blue suit and ran a hand down the length of his tie, appeared to be readying himself to stand but, in the end, settled for defensively shoving his chair back from the table a few inches.

Greer halted directly in front of him. "Why don't you tell him yourself?" he said.

"What?" said the man sharply, taken aback.

"You want him to shut up, why're you talking to me? I'm not his babysitter. Come on back to the table and say what you have to say to him directly, man to man. He is a man, if you haven't noticed. Then he can tell you to go fuck yourself to your face."

"This is ridiculous," said the suit. The comment was meant for the table, not Greer.

"He's not an idiot," said Jack. "He can understand you perfectly well." Greer began to motion the man out of his chair. "Come on over to our table and give him a piece of your mind, such as it is."

"I don't know what's wrong with your friend," he said, "but you're drunk."

"Really," said Greer, "won't you speak to him? An old-fashioned Dutch Uncle talk would mean the world to him. To both of us actually." He leaned forward. "Just a few pointers on life and how the best people behave in Chinese restaurants."

Roland, following this performance eagerly, was excitedly trying to rise from his chair. "Come on over," he suddenly shouted, beckoning with a crutch. "I never had a conversation with a fucking doorknob before!"

"You see," said Greer, "he would love to chat. Won't you spare him a minute, up close and personal?"

"Hey, the red baboon's ass in the blue suit!"

All around the table there was general consternation, people were getting hurriedly to their feet, fishing for purses underneath chairs, exchanging whispers and agitated glances. One of the junior-looking executives from the far end of the table was squeezing his way past the ladies, hurrying to reinforce senior management. In the high polish of a nearby gong Greer caught a glimpse of himself, his cropped head sinister, a model for the escaped convict, galley slave, Magwitch, Jean Valjean. Little wonder respectability was beating a retreat.

"Anything I can do, Mr. Tyler?" asked the young man, eager to ingratiate.

He was ignored. "I'd watch my step if I were you," said Mr. Tyler to Greer. "If you two insist on making public nuisances of yourselves you'll get mixed up with the police. That's just a friendly warning."

Roland was standing now, swaying as he tried to disentagle one of his crutches from chair legs. "Hey, Jack," he bellowed. "Need any help with those two?"

To Mr. Tyler, Jack said quietly, "I think you've confused public nuisances and misfits. The two of us are misfits. Get it right, why don't you?" From behind, he felt the hands of white-jacketed Chinese waiters closing on his arms.

Public disgrace, getting tossed out of a restaurant, had them howling all the way to the airport, laughing school boys recounting and reliving a stupid prank. Self-appointed rogues and rascals, they swaggered through the terminal. The shared adventure heightened the emotion of the leavetaking, Greer impulsively throwing his arms around Roland's neck at the gate, Roland letting one of his crutches fall to the floor so he could thump his friend's back. "Have a good flight," said Greer, his voice tight. "Wherever it takes you."

"You too, Jack," said Roland.

Only after Roland passed through security did Greer remember that he had meant to ask his friend whether it was really true that he could ride a bicycle.

Out in the parking lot Greer stood under the hot glare of the afternoon sun listening to the jets take off. He had felt nothing like this in years, was still keyed-up, wildly elated. A plane soared into the summer sky, its engines whining. Greer checked his watch. Five-thirty. That would be Roland on his way. Jack closed his eyes. He realized he would never see his friend again but he knew how he wished to hold Roland Madox in his mind. Forever like this, in reckless pursuit of his destiny. The bicycle, swift ghost in the gloom of an October evening, rubber tires whirring madly on the pavement, the roar of a jet under a cloudless blue canopy. The same headlong rush against the odds.

Mad, whirling monk, thought Greer. And then it was he remembered that Chekhov had had his monk too. Greer had never been able to make head nor tail of the story "The Black Monk" because this fantastic, dream-like fable was like nothing else Chekhov had ever written. As unlike his other stories as the monastery in which Greer had spent the past month was unlike the outside world.

In Chekhov's story, a brilliant young man by the name of Kovrin becomes obsessed with the legend of a black-robed monk who, a thousand years ago, wandered the wildernesses of Syria and Arabia. The mirage of this black monk was projected onto a lake many miles distant and this mirage produced a second mirage which produced a third, and so on, until the image of the monk had flown all about the world, to Africa, to Spain, to India, to the Far North, perhaps even beyond, to Mars, to the constellation of the Southern Cross. But the legend held that after a thousand years the mirage would return to earth and make itself known to men. Which it did to Kovrin, in the form of a cyclone whirling across the Russian landscape, a cyclone which transformed itself before his eyes into a monk who addressed Kovrin – something that optical illusions are not supposed to do. The message which it whispered to him was that he was a genius.

Exalted by this news, in the months that follow, Kovrin discovers the sweetness of life. He falls in love, enjoys his wine and cigars as never before, works on his philosophical investigations with unremitting energy and purpose, is filled with inexpressible joy. But one night his new wife awakes to find him sitting in their bedroom talking to an empty chair. Only Kovrin sees the black monk seated there.

He is handed over to doctors to be cured of his delusion. After treatment, the black monk ceases to appear to him. Kovrin is a changed man, but scarcely for the better. Where once he was interesting and original, now he is cruel and listless, a mediocrity. He quarrels with his wife and insults his father-in-law. The marriage falls apart, Kovrin and his wife separate.

Then one night in a resort hotel, Kovrin hears a song which reminds him of the black monk's first visit to him. Filled with the rapture of anticipation he sees a black waterspout forming across the bay. The waterspout sweeps down upon him and the monk materializes. He chides Kovrin for passing his last two years so sadly and barrenly, all because he refused to believe the monk's message. Kovrin, in ecstasy, cries out for his wife, cries out for the work he gave his youth to, cries out for the beautiful garden which had been his dead father-in-law's single passion and, in crying out, his tuberculosis-ridden lungs begin to haemorrhage. In the morning he is found dead.

Yes, said Greer to himself, slowly walking up and down the parking lot. Yes, yes, yes. Things as they are. But did things outside a man or woman simply mirror things *inside*? On the drive back to the abbey he, like Kovrin, began to recall the past. A gentle rain in Amsterdam. The harsher rain of last month, a muddy dog, a dead child in a church, the ringing of bells, Roland groaning down a corridor to kneel before something Jack could not imagine.

Two months later, Greer was present to watch the monks harvest their crops. What had been green was now yellow, the roads were dust, the pines soared even darker against the hot blue sky of August. It was good to walk among the heaped and bristling swaths like Chekhov in his beloved Melikhov, to have begun a nineteenth-century kind of story.